THE KING OF THE TREES

For Karen— "May your leaves never wither." (Ps. 1:3)

God Bless you

Bill Burt

9/23/02

THE KING OF THE TREES

WILLIAM D. BURT

WINEPRESS WP PUBLISHING

Packaged by WinePress Publishing, PO Box 1406, Mukilteo, WA 98275. The views expressed or implied in this work do not necessarily reflect those of WinePress Publishing. Ultimate design, content, and editorial accuracy of this work is the responsibility of the author(s).

Illustrated by Terri L. Lahr and Rebecca J. Burt
Cover by Terri L. Lahr

Library of Congress Catalog Card Number: 97-62570
ISBN 1-57921-090-2

And he showed me a river of the water of life, clear as crystal, coming from the throne of God and of the Lamb, in the middle of its street. And on either side of the river was the Tree of Life, bearing twelve kinds of fruit, yielding its fruit every month; and the leaves of the Tree were for the healing of the nations.

(Revelation 22:1–2, NAS)

CONTENTS

CHAPTER 1

MARKET DAY

"Witch boy, witch boy, hair-as-red-as-pitch boy! Bee in his bonnet, bee in his bonnet, bees in the hive and Rolin's sat on it!"

Rolin jerked awake, tore off his quilts and rushed to the window. He saw no one outside, except a few blue jays warming up for the day's chatter. An early morning mist still swirled among the firs and pines in the foothills of the rugged Tartellan mountains, where Rolin's father, Gannon, had built their cozy cabin.

Rolin groaned and flopped back on the bed. His nightmares were always the worst before market days, practically the only times he and his father went down to bustling Beechtown. Was it his fault he'd been born with red hair (though it was really chestnut) or that his father was a beekeeper? As if that weren't enough, the "Crazy Toadstool Woman" had been his grandmother.

Had been. Rolin screwed his eyes shut, squeezing out the tears. Several years earlier, first his grandmother, Adelka, then his mother, Janna, had died under mysterious circumstances, leaving Rolin and his father to mourn their losses in lonely bewilderment.

"Ho! Rolin! Sun's up and it's market day," boomed a voice into the log-walled bedroom. Rolin yawned and stretched, then hopped out of bed. Market day! Already he could see the crowds of traders and travelers, vendors hawking wooden trinkets, and the food stalls set up in the square, with their mounds of candied fruits, toasted beechnuts, smoked fish, and box upon box of luscious winter pears. And he could hear the children's cruel taunts.

"Up with you now, sleepy head," Gannon called again from the next room, interrupting Rolin's daydream. "It's oatcakes if you come now and nothing if you don't! We must leave soon or we'll miss the best of the market." Rolin knew his father's blackberry-blossom honey would command the highest prices in the morning, when buyers were wanting their breakfasts.

That did it. "Coming, Father!" After hurriedly dressing, Rolin pushed open the kitchen door. There stood his father, a tall, red-bearded man with a jaunty wool cap, stirring a crock full of oatcake batter with a wooden spoon. Beside him, a griddle smoked on the roaring wood stove. Rolin's mouth watered at the delicious wood-smoke-and-hot-griddle scent filling the room.

"So, you finally decided to get up after all," Gannon observed. "Your hair looks a fright, you know."

Rolin grinned at the good-natured gibe. His unruly hair always seemed to stick out every which way, especially in the morning. "So's your beard," he shot back.

Gannon self-consciously combed batter-caked fingers through his tangled beard. "Don't just stand there; the first batch is on the table." Gannon waved the spoon as he spoke, flinging bits of batter onto the floor and walls.

Rolin pulled up a chair and poured golden honey over a heaping plateful of oatcakes. "Do you think we'll do well at market today?" he asked his father between mouthfuls.

"The best ever. With the heavy honey flow we've had this spring and last year's bumper potato crop, we should fare very nicely. After I've bought supplies, there might even be enough money left over for your gadget."

Rolin's eyes shone. "Oh, I hope so!" Market days always attracted clever peddlers and magicians with their intriguing tales, astonishing tricks and marvelous inventions. At the last fall market, a wizened little man had been selling the most extraordinary devices: long, wooden tubes with round pieces of glass set in their ends. "*Starglasses*," he'd called them. Rolin had peered through one of the tubes at a sparrow perched in a distant tree. To his delight, the bird appeared life-sized. The old peddler had told him the moon and stars themselves would leap down from the sky, so large would they loom through the eyepiece.

"Don't set your hopes too high," Rolin's father advised him as he spooned more batter onto the griddle. "You can't buy peddlers' wares with promises."

"I know," replied Rolin with a sly glance at his father. "You can't hawk honey with batter in your beard, either!" With that, he darted out the door, just before a spoonful of batter splattered on the door behind him.

Outside, Gannon's bees were flitting in and out of their conical clay hives, which were steaming in a warm spring sun. Rolin savored the rain-washed mountain air, spicy with the pungent scent of fir needles and cottonwood balm. Already, the sponge mushrooms would be sprouting among the poplars.

He scooped up an armload of firewood and brought it into the house, where another tall stack of oatcakes awaited him at the rough oak table. His father soon joined him with an even taller stack. Before you could say *oatcakes and honey*, they had gobbled up everything in sight. Rolin twirled his last bite of oatcake in some honey, popped it into his mouth and sighed.

"Fetch me the money box and some punkwood, will you, my boy?" Gannon asked, licking the honey from his plate. The money box, like oatcake breakfasts, was reserved for special occasions—chiefly the spring and fall market days. Rolin hopped down from his chair and threw back a tattered rug lying beside the table. Pulling up on a small handle recessed into the floor, he opened a trapdoor to a musty-smelling cellar.

Clambering down a flight of creaking stairs, Rolin felt his way in the darkness to a tall cupboard, its shelves sagging under the weight of potatoes, carrots, flour, honey and beans. As his eyes adjusted to the dim light, Rolin spotted a pile of the half-rotted, dried wood whose thick, sweet smoke had such a calming effect on angry bees. He stuffed a few pieces in his pocket, then searched for the money box. It was nowhere to be seen.

He groped about on the shelves, raising a cloud of dust. Still, no box. Standing tiptoe on a wooden crate, he peered over the top shelf, seeing only some broken tools and pottery, a few yellowed scraps of parchment—and a box. *What's it doing up here?* he wondered. He seized the box and jumped down, nearly tipping over the cupboard.

After blowing dust off the lid, Rolin realized he had the wrong box. This one was wooden, not metal, its lid adorned with intricate engravings of trees and mythical-looking creatures. Spidery lettering ran around the sides.

"Rolin!" Gannon's voice echoed into the cellar. "No need to look for the money box; it was here all along." Rolin scrambled back up the stairs with the punkwood and his new find, closing the door behind him. Gannon was at the table, holding a plain-looking box with rust around its edges.

"Father, look at this!" Rolin exclaimed. "What is it?"

"Why, it's your grandmother's old box. I'd forgotten all about it." Gannon's fingers caressed the carved lid. "It must be very old. You don't see such fine workmanship these days."

"Do you suppose there's anything inside?"

"I doubt it—at least nothing valuable, like gold or silver. Your grandmother might have kept some spices in it, but they've probably turned to dust by now. Heavy, though, isn't it. Let's see what's on the bottom." As Gannon turned the box over, a distinct rattle came from within.

"I knew it!" exclaimed Rolin. "There *is* something inside!"

"That's odd," Gannon remarked, feeling around the corners. "I can't find any hinge or latch." He put the box down, shaking his head. "We'd better be going now. I'll try to open this after we get back." Gannon tucked the money box under his arm and strode out the door. Rolin lingered, brushing his fingers across the carvings on the wooden box. As he touched the tree design in the center, *Pop!*—the top flew open. Inside lay a coin-shaped, silver pendant, cushioned on a bed of dried, faded flowers.

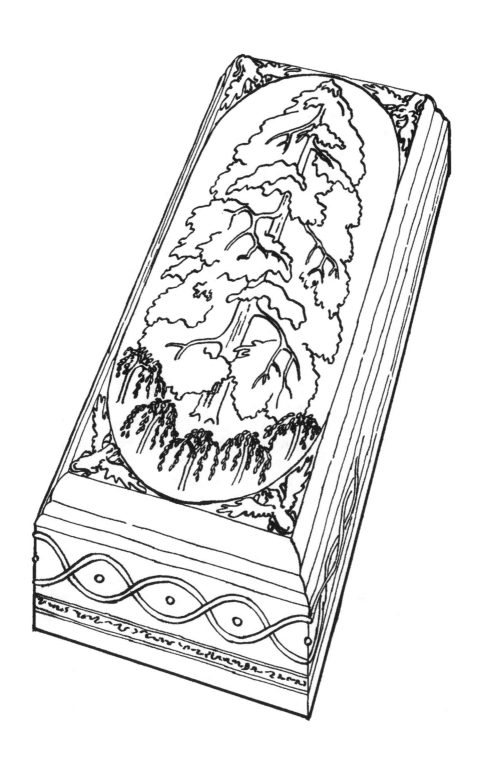

Rolin gasped. As he picked up the gleaming medallion by its chain, a ray of sunlight struck fire to a blood-red, faceted gem in its middle. The piece's rim bore markings like those on the box, except at the bottom, where the metal was melted.

"Boy, why are you still here? Didn't you hear me calling?" Gannon demanded, beckoning from the doorway. His face softened when he saw the pendant dangling from Rolin's fingers. "Ah, yes, your grandmother's necklace," he said, a faraway look in his blue eyes. "She used to wear it when she missed 'the old country,' as she put it."

The old country. Rolin remembered the same faraway look in his grandmother's eyes whenever she mentioned that place. Once, he had asked her to take him to visit the land of her childhood. "We can never go back there," the old woman had said with a bitter laugh. Rolin had never again dared ask Adelka about her birthplace.

Gannon fingered the pendant. "She never would take it out of the house. How did you get the box open, anyway?"

Rolin shrugged. "I just touched it."

Gannon nodded. "You always did have a knack for puzzles."

"Can you tell what the writing says?" At an early age, Rolin had taught himself to read from some moldy books he'd found in the cellar. The letters engraved on the box and pendant, however, were unlike any he'd seen in all his thirteen years.

Gannon shook his head. "Only your mother and grandmother could read those chicken scratches."

"Since I found the box, may I keep it?"

"I suppose so," Gannon sighed. "Now that I think of it, Adelka gave it to your mother years ago, and your mother wanted you to have it. You may as well keep the necklace, too. It can't be worth much with that damaged spot, though the stone might fetch a handsome price. Just don't lose it."

Rolin promised he wouldn't. He looped the chain around his neck, letting the pendant drop inside his shirt. After hiding the box under his bed, he clapped a cap on his head and took a seat on the wagon beside his father.

"Giddyap, Nan!" Gannon shouted to his flop-eared mule, and they clattered down the dirt lane leading to the river road below, the wagon groaning under its load of potatoes and honeycomb. A warm spring breeze frisked among the alders leaning over the narrow track, drying the muddy ruts.

Rolin chewed a piece of honeycomb while keeping an eye out for unwary sponge mushrooms poking through the weathered leaves beside the road. "How much farther?" he asked, already knowing the answer.

"Far enough that if you keep eating our honey, there won't be any left!" Gannon retorted. Rolin laughed, knowing that all of Beechtown couldn't eat so much rich honeycomb at one sitting. He rode in silence for a mile or two, recalling the years he'd made the same trip sitting on Janna's lap. "Father, please tell me again how you and Mother met."

The skin around Gannon's eyes tightened. Rolin hated upsetting his father, but he never tired of hearing the tale of his parents' unusual courtship.

"It was in a tree—a tree house, you might say," Gannon began and clucked his tongue at Nan. The mule quickened her pace.

"Rumor has it that when Beechtown was still just a sleepy village, your grandmother, great with child, appeared late one night on the doorstep of a local farmhouse. Though Adelka couldn't speak a word of our tongue, the farmer and his wife took her in and looked after her until she gave birth."

"To a daughter," Rolin murmured.

"Then Adelka retreated with her child into the depths of the woods," Gannon went on, "where she made her home in the hollow of a great beech tree. From the beginning, her queer ways aroused the suspicions of our superstitious townsfolk. The 'Toadstool Woman,' they called her, because she used to poke about under the trees with a basket full of mushrooms. After word of her healing powers got around, though, people started coming to her with their ailments. There wasn't any magic in her concoctions of herbs and ointments, but some still thought she was a witch." Gannon shot a sideways glance at his son. "She wasn't, of course."

Though Rolin already knew as much, it was a relief to hear his father say so. Gannon cleared his throat. "When I was about your age, I was a-hunting wild bees' nests up in these hills and got myself as lost as can be. I was hungry and scared—and fevered, too. After a couple of days, the 'Toadstool Woman' herself found me sleeping under a tree. She gave me a terrible fright, all dressed in green, with that deep look in her eyes. 'I heard you were lost,' she said and took me to her tree house. You know the rest."

Rolin did. While Adelka nursed young Gannon back to health, the beekeeper fell hopelessly in love with her daughter, green-eyed, willowy Janna. Rolin smiled, remembering how his mother had taught him the secrets of the forest: where the tastiest mushrooms hid and how to tell the delicious, golden Lisichki from the sickly green, deadly Poganka; how to prepare a soothing poultice from Sweet Amentine leaves, using plenty of honeycomb; and when to cut willow and elderberry stems for making flutes and whistles. Rolin had also enjoyed gathering mushrooms and herbs with Adelka, transforming the contents of their brimming baskets into savory soups. On one such foray, Rolin had plucked up the courage to ask his grandmother where she had learned her woodlore.

"From listening to the forest," she had wistfully replied. Ever after that, Rolin listened carefully whenever he was out in the woods but heard only the wind rustling in the tops of the trees and the scolding of squirrels.

Presently, Rolin and his father joined the jostling mass of other market-goers on the broad road running beside the river Foamwater. Droves of goats, sheep and cows plodded beside wagons and carts piled high with bacon and fat hams, cabbages and cauliflowers, skeins of wool, sacks of candles, and tools whose uses were a mystery to Rolin.

"Could you help a poor old woman with her baggage?" a shrill voice cut through the din of rumbling wheels and lowing cattle. Rolin glanced down at a swaying bundle of quilts bobbing alongside the wagon. The patchwork fabric parted, revealing a mop of hair as red as Gannon's beard and a pair of shrewd blue eyes set in a plump, seamed face.

"Hullo, Aunt Glenna," said Rolin with a polite nod, tossing the hitchhiker's quilts over Gannon's potatoes, then helping her clamber up beside his father.

"What, is my nephew the only one here with a tongue in his head?" Glenna demanded. "Or have you gone deaf and blind, Brother?" Gannon rolled his eyes. Rolin smirked. His father and outspoken aunt agreed on very little, particularly when it came to raising children.

"Good day to you, Sister," Gannon grunted, gritting his teeth and clenching the reins in a white-knuckled grip. "May you live to see your great-grandchildren, and may your eyes never grow dim!" Rolin stifled a snicker. His spinster aunt was childless, and her eyesight was poor from years of needlework.

"Hmph!" Glenna snorted. "You know very well I can't tell a horse from a haystack at fifty paces. As for great-grandchildren, if you want any of your own, you'd better buy a place in town. The boy needs a mother, and he'll soon need a wife, too. You won't find either one up in those hills."

Rolin bit his lip. He didn't want another mother. He'd been happy with the one he'd had and still didn't understand why she'd died. Three summers before, a fierce mountain storm had torn through the forest, toppling Adelka's ancient, hollow beech. Though the old woman no longer lived in the tree, she pined away before her family's horrified eyes. Within a week she was dead.

A month later, Rolin and his mother were listening to the woodcutters chopping their way up the mountainside through the ravaged timber. Janna flinched at the crash of each falling tree, as if feeling its final splintering agony. Then she had rushed into the woods. The next morning, Rolin and his father found her curled up beside a downed beech in Adelka's grove, as pale and cold as a frozen lily. She revived only long enough to tell Gannon, "Mind the box—and the birch!" With that she had breathed her last.

The birch. Hot tears stung Rolin's eyes at the memory of the seedling his mother had helped him plant in the bee yard on his fourth birthday. Ever since, Rolin had protected the skinny sapling from fire and drought. When a hungry beaver gnawed it down the spring after Janna's death, the bleeding stump mirrored Rolin's heart, cut afresh with the loss of his mother.

Gannon broke the strained silence. "We found Janna's box."

"That dusty old thing?" Glenna said. "I can't imagine why she wanted Rolin to have it. Still, plain or pretty, a keepsake's a keepsake, I always say. Goodness knows, the boy has little enough to remember his kinfolk by. Look how thin he's become, moping about in your woods. City life would do you both a passel of good."

"As I've said before, what would I do in town?" Gannon protested. "Where would I keep my bees? The townsfolk would throw my hives in the river and me with them. 'Beekeepers make fine friends but poor neighbors.'"

"Then find other work. They need more raftsmen nowadays."

Gannon's lips compressed. "You know I can't swim."

Glenna shrugged. "You can learn." Her voice dropped to a conspiratorial whisper. "Besides, it's not safe in the woods anymore, what with all the strange goings-on lately. Why, just yesterday, five of Farmer Stubblefield's sheep up and disappeared. Disappeared, I tell you! Mark my words, first it's sheep being carried off, then it'll be people. They say there are unholy noises in the night, too, such as human ear has never heard. Something evil's astir, and you'd be wise to move to the safety of town as quick as you can."

Rolin's ears perked up. Only the week before, a bloodcurdling night cry had set his hair on end. "What kind of noises?" he asked. His father shot him a warning glance.

"I think I saw some sponge mushrooms under those cottonwoods," Rolin said. "I'll catch up with you later." He kissed his aunt on the cheek.

"Don't be too long," Gannon told him. "You know how you lose track of time when you've found a mushroom patch!"

"And there's another thing," Glenna continued. "You've got to put a stop to this toadstool-picking nonsense. It's just not healthy. The boy's apt to poison himself and you, too. Then where will you be? He needs to learn a respectable trade and stop wasting his time on these foolish excursions. . . ."

Rolin hopped off the wagon, dodged a cart full of squawking chickens and dove into the woods, where he poked among the old, gray cottonwood leaves carpeting the riverbank. "Aha!" he cried, pouncing on a cluster of little tan humps peeping out from the leafy litter. After uncovering the pitted, egg-shaped mushrooms, he deposited them in his cap, already tasting their delicate richness in a plate of steaming scrambled eggs. Then he searched the forest floor around him, discovering more of the shy sponges. Minutes later, he emerged triumphantly from the woods with an overflowing cap.

Rolin caught up with his father and aunt on the Beechtown bridge. He hid his hat behind him and put on a long face.

"Has the mighty hunter found any trophies?" asked Gannon.

"From the look on his face, I'd say not," remarked Aunt Glenna. Then, with a flourish, Rolin produced his hat.

Gannon laughed. "I might have known," he said, looking over Rolin's finds. "You don't often return from your mushrooming expeditions with an empty hat." He doffed his own cap, holding it out like one of Beechtown's beggars. "I trust my son will share this bounty with his poor, starving father?"

"I suppose," said Rolin with a grin, hoping to sell some of the mushrooms to buy his starglass. Then he darted into the crowd.

"Beware of pickpockets," Glenna called after him, "and Green-cloaks!"

Rolin lost himself in the babble of voices: drivers shouting at their horses and mules; hawkers announcing goods for sale in sing-song chants; children crying for their mothers; and troubadours playing wooden flutes. Full-bearded fur trappers hailed one another from under bundles of shaggy pelts; shepherds herded their bleating sheep with crooked staffs; and boisterous river boatmen dressed in bright red blouses sang out their ballads.

Towering above them all were the Green-cloaks. Though Rolin couldn't bring himself to believe these quiet, courteous strangers were capable of kidnapping, as his aunt claimed, he still avoided anyone robed in a dark green cloak and tunic. On reaching the market, he searched out the starglass peddler among the colorful tents, booths and tables crowding the square.

"Come right up! See the moon and stars as never before! Most amazing invention in the world!"

Rolin heard the peddler pitching his wares before he spotted the wizened little man surrounded by curious spectators, some of whom were already squinting through the wooden tubes. Rolin squeezed through to the front of the crowd, where he found one of the devices lying on a flimsy table.

"That's right, boy, have a look-see. It won't hurt you!" With his furrowed face, hooked nose, and deep-set eyes, the old man resembled an owl. Rolin set his hat on the table and had just picked up the starglass, when—*kerplunk!*—the eyepiece dropped out.

As Rolin bent down to snatch the piece of glass out of the dirt, he bumped into someone beside him. "Oh, I'm sorry," he stammered, "I didn't mean to—"

"That's quite all right," replied the stranger, who was wearing a green tunic, brown leggings and an amused smile. "Let me help you with that." As he reached for the eyepiece, the man glanced at Rolin's chest and the smile faded from his face. Rolin looked down to see the pendant hanging outside his shirt, its stone glowing brilliantly in the sun. The thing must have slipped out while he was retrieving the eyepiece.

"Where did you get that?" the man demanded. He whistled shrilly, then grabbed at the pendant. Rolin tried to escape, but the crowd hemmed him in.

"No! You can't have it; it's mine!" he cried. He lunged across the table, falling at the feet of the startled vendor. Picking himself up, he raced across the square, Green-cloaks following close behind. He had to reach the bridge!

CHAPTER 2

THE TORSIL TREE

Rolin leaned against a rock, gasping for breath. Far below lay Beechtown's gleaming tile roofs, its marketplace hubbub rising faintly into the hills. Closer by came the telltale sounds of men creeping through the forest.

They'd nearly caught him when he'd run into one of the bonfires dotting the square. Grim-faced Green-cloaks were closing in around him. Pulling a handful of punkwood out of his pocket, he'd flung it on the fire to produce a dense cloud of gray smoke. In the ensuing confusion and uproar, he had fled across the bridge.

Rolin was hoping to lose his pursuers in the maze of deer paths crisscrossing the hillside above the town. Alas, the strangers seemed to know those paths better than Rolin himself. They were driving him deeper into the fir and maple forests, where the deer trails melted into the underbrush. For the first time in his life, Rolin was truly afraid.

The crackling and rustling in the bushes grew louder. His lungs burning from the long climb, Rolin loped farther into the woods, then stopped. Shouts rang out behind him, then ahead. On his left, the ground fell away into a ravine; on his right, an alder thicket blocked the way. He was trapped.

All at once, a tall figure appeared on the path before him. Rolin gasped and backed away from the stranger, who was clad in dazzling robes that shone with an unearthly radiance. His flowing hair and long beard were as white as snowberries. The man's gray eyes fixed Rolin with a penetrating yet gentle gaze. Raising one arm in a beckoning gesture, he stepped into the alder grove. Rolin stood rooted to the spot. Was he seeing a ghost? If not, was this a friend or an enemy? Sensing the stranger meant him no harm, Rolin followed, stepping onto a path he'd somehow overlooked.

As they passed through the alders, Rolin fancied the trees swayed and nodded in greeting. Then they reached a sloping ridge, where sun-dappled ferns and violets sprinkled the forest floor with yellow and gold. The old man mounted a small, wooded hill jutting from the ridge, Rolin at his heels.

Near the top of the hill stood a most unusual tree. With bark broken into tortoiseshell plates and whorls and thick, polished green leaves, it resembled a transplant from some southern land.

With surprising agility, Rolin's rescuer sprang into the tortoiseshell tree and scuttled up its trunk. Concluding that the spry stranger was spying out the valley, Rolin sat down to await his return.

A heavy silence draped itself over the forest. Rolin peered upward into the tree, seeing only a tracery of leaves and limbs. A queasy feeling wrenched his stomach. What could have happened to the nimble fellow? Surely there'd been time enough to scout out the terrain. Rolin had a sudden urge to leave the funny little hill with its funny little tree and return home. The Green-cloaks must have given up the chase by now. In the end, his curiosity got the best of him, and he began climbing.

On reaching the top, Rolin discovered he was alone. Had his companion changed himself into a bird or butterfly? The tree was solid enough, so Rolin knew he wasn't dreaming. Since the evening shadows were creeping up the trunk, he started down, hoping Green-cloaks weren't waiting at the bottom.

As he descended, Rolin felt a peculiar dizziness, then a tingling in his hands and feet that nearly made him lose his grip. Pausing to clear his head, he noticed the branches and leaves were wet, though it hadn't been raining. The sky was darker, too, as if a shroud had veiled the sun.

He slid down the last few feet and dropped to the ground. Crouching beside the tree, he heard only the plop-plop-plopping of water dripping from mossy-trunked firs that stood like silent, watchful sentinels cloaked in a thick gray mist. Rolin's skin prickled. Something was dreadfully amiss.

The tree he'd just climbed was still there, but gone were the hill, the ridge and the valleys it divided. The ground for many paces around was flat. How could the landscape have changed in less than an hour? Thinking he had come down on the wrong side of the tree, Rolin circled the trunk. On every hand, he saw only tall, solemn firs, the fog swirling among them.

Rolin was lost, an experience new to him. Aunt Glenna's cautions to the contrary, he often returned home after dark from his woodland jaunts. Even without the moon or stars, he could find his way by the lay of the land and the smell of the earth and forest. Now, he recognized only this odd, tortoiseshell tree. He gripped its rough trunk the way a drowning man clings to a waterlogged timber. Never had he felt such loneliness.

Then Rolin heard a trilling sound, like the warble of the Water Ouzel dipping its feathers in a clear, cold stream. Yet, this was not birdsong but flute music! Rolin pushed his way through thickets of evergreen Salal, stopping every now and again to listen.

At last, the music sounded so close that the trees rang with the high, sweet notes. Entranced, Rolin was stepping out from behind a hemlock when he tripped noisily over a fallen branch. The music ceased.

Now you've done it! Rolin said to himself. Every living thing in the woods must know he was there! He crouched behind the hemlock and waited. All was quiet, except for a woodpecker's erratic drumming.

"Here now, who are you?" a gravelly voice demanded. Rolin whirled around to find two men behind him, both wearing green jerkins and cloaks and carrying wooden staffs. The shorter of the pair also clutched a wooden flute. The Green-cloaks had caught him after all.

"So this is your gorkin warrior, Opio!" laughed the taller and leaner of the two. Rolin tried to bolt but a staff blocked his escape.

"Hold on, boy, we mean you no harm," said Opio gruffly, tapping his flute on an ample potbelly. "We just want to know what you're doing here alone. It's not safe outside after dark. That's when the yeggoroth come out, you know."

Before Rolin could ask what a "yeggoroth" was, the taller man broke in. "The boy looks famished, Opio. He probably just wandered off and got lost. Let's take him back to Bembor for a bite of bread and a bowl of soup. Surely there's no harm in that. If Bembor objects, let his staff be upon my head."

"You know the rules, Gemmio," the paunchy flute player retorted, his round face flushing. "No strangers inside the settlement. No exceptions!"

"I know, Brother, but we can't very well send the lad back into the woods, can we? Besides, if you hadn't been playing your flute, he wouldn't be here! You're lucky it's only a boy who found us and not one of Felgor's spies."

"I suppose you're right," Opio sighed, running his fingers through a thatch of sandy hair. "He looks harmless enough, though he's got more freckles than ten lads and lasses. Just remember, if there's any trouble, it wasn't my idea." The two brothers set off through the forest, Rolin in tow.

Traversing rivers, streams and rotten logs, Opio and Gemmio kept to the low ground, even mucking through a marsh reeking of skunk cabbage. Once, they skirted a burned-over area, where only a few leafless tree skeletons stood and a choking stench hung in the air.

Rolin marveled at how the two found their way through the thick woods on a moonless night. When the undergrowth thinned out, he saw the reason: Every few yards, a splotch of greenish yellow light marked the trail. Curious, he knelt to examine one of the glowing spots. It was cool to the touch, with the spongy feel of punkwood.

"Hurry, boy! This is no time for a rest!" Opio called back to him. Rolin thrust the trail marker into his pocket and scurried on. He didn't want to be stranded alone in this strange place!

All at once, a shrill shriek split the night air, followed by another. "Yegs!" Opio hissed, pulling Rolin to the ground and clamping a hand over his mouth. "Don't make a sound!"

By pale starlight, Rolin could make out Gemmio's form crouching nearby. The Green-cloak was gripping his staff in both fists, pointing it skyward.

A third savage screech came from right overhead. Then an enormous shape swooped down. *Poof!* went Gemmio's staff, cutting off the next scream. Something large and hairy crashed to the ground, where it growled and thrashed about, one great, black, bat's wing flapping weakly. Fearsome jaws with rows of wicked teeth gnashed the air. Rolin wanted to run away but couldn't take his eyes off the beast dragging itself toward him with the long, cruel claws on its wing joints. The creature's red eyes glared at him.

At the next *poof*, the tentlike wings trembled and collapsed; the hideous head drooped and the red fire in the eyes dimmed, then flickered out.

"It can't hurt you now; it's dead," Gemmio said. Rolin gingerly stroked a leathery wing, then touched the snout, now frozen in a menacing snarl.

"Now do you see why you shouldn't roam around after dark?" grunted Opio.

"What is it, and how did you kill it?"

"It's a yeg, of course. Haven't you ever seen one?" asked Gemmio in surprise. He plucked a tufted dart from the creature's body, holding it up for Rolin to see. "Our staffs are hollow, to use as blowpipes," he said. "These darts are tipped with a deadly venom."

"But what is a yeg?"

"A yeg is a batwolf," Gemmio explained, "a wolf with a bat's wings and head or a bat with a wolf's body, depending upon how you look at it. Their eyes are weak, but they can hear a mouse in the dark at a thousand paces—with those." He pointed his blowpipe at the beast's shell-shaped ears. "The yeggoroth are Felgor's pets, may his staff wither!"

"There's no time for talk now," said Opio, shouldering his own staff. "We'd better be moving along. The yeggoroth hunt in packs. Where there's one, others are likely around."

Rolin was still recovering from the shock of the yeg attack when he saw Opio and Gemmio walk right past a second batwolf crouching beside the path. A warning cry rose in his throat before he realized the yeg wasn't moving. It was made of solid stone. But what was a yeg statue doing in the woods?

Presently, the Green-cloaks came to a gnarled tree growing on the brow of a cliff. Shinnying up the trunk, Opio called down to Rolin, "Please hurry! You don't want another yeg to come calling, do you?" Rolin gulped and climbed to the top, only to find the brothers had vanished.

"Just like the old man!" Rolin said crossly. He hunkered low on his perch, expecting a yeg to dive on him at any moment. However, no sinister shapes obscured the stars, glittering in their myriad unfamiliar constellations.

"Nothing to do but go down again," he muttered. Once more, he felt lightheaded but shook off the feeling before reaching the ground. He noted with little surprise that the cliff had disappeared.

"There you are," Gemmio greeted him. "We thought you'd gone yeg riding!" He and Opio led Rolin to a large tulip tree. Opio rapped on the trunk three times with his staff, and a rope ladder dropped down from above.

"Up you go!" said Gemmio, giving Rolin a boost. Swinging and swaying, Rolin climbed up to the stout limb supporting the ladder. Strong arms reached out and pulled him through an opening in the trunk.

CHAPTER 3

A QUESTION OF ORIGINS

R olin blinked. Having climbed down a wooden ladder inside the tree, he found himself in a room with three green men. Their hair was green. Their faces were green. Even their teeth were green! Then he realized that the walls of the room shed the same yellowish green light he'd seen along the trail, tinting everything green—even his own fingers!

Behind him, Opio and Gemmio were climbing down the ladder. They grinned greenly at him.

"Welcome to the home of Bembor, Father of the Oak Clan!" said Gemmio, introducing Rolin to an old man seated on a stool.

"And who might this be?" asked Bembor, rising to his feet. "A poor lad, lost while mushroom picking?"

"We found him beyond the Misty River," Gemmio explained. "We don't know his name or where he's from. Judging by the way he's been acting, I'd say he must have hit his head. Since we didn't know what to do with him, we brought him to you."

"Falling afoul of a yeg on the way," added Opio ruefully.

"Quite a night for such a young fellow," observed Bembor, stroking his long beard. "You're fortunate my scouts found you when they did." He waved a hand at the other Green-cloaks in the room. "These are my clansmen: my son-in-law, Emmer son of Fandol, and Larkin son of Gaflin." The two nodded in Rolin's direction. "Tell us now: Who are you, what is your tree clan, and why were you in the woods so far from any settlement?"

Rolin drew himself up, took a deep breath and said, "I am Rolin son of Gannon, and I live near Beechtown. Green-cloaks chased me here. I want to know where I am, and I want to go home!"

Emmer and Larkin gasped. "You brought a Thalmosian here?" roared Larkin, pointing his finger at Gemmio and Opio. "Don't you know Lucambrian law forbids such a thing?"

"He's just a boy!" shot back Gemmio. "Anyway, what were we to do? Leave him as gork bait?"

"What did I tell you, Gemmio?" Opio groaned. "I knew this one was trouble the moment we caught him skulking in the woods."

"I was not skulking! I heard your music and was curious, so—"

"Pricked with your own blowpipe dart, eh, Opio?" Bembor said. "I've warned you before about playing your flute on guard duty!" Opio reddened.

"How many more of your kind are loose in our woods?" demanded Larkin.

"Hush!" said Bembor, holding up his hand. "Let the boy continue. Tell us, Rolin, why were the Green-cloaks chasing you?"

As Rolin described how the pendant had fallen out of his shirt at the peddler's stall, his listeners glanced at one another. "Do you still have the thing?" asked Bembor. Rolin was pulling it out when two more Green-cloaks appeared at the entrance and quickly climbed down the ladder.

"Hail, Sigarth and Skoglund," cried Emmer. "What tidings from Thalmos?" The newcomers stared at Rolin.

"It's him!" exclaimed Sigarth, the taller of the two, leveling his staff at Rolin. "This potato eater has a soros!"

"Grab him!" cried Skoglund, lunging toward Rolin.

Clutching the pendant through his shirt, Rolin backed away from his accusers. He snatched up Gemmio's staff and brandished it threateningly.

"Leave me alone!" he cried. "Don't come any closer or I'll—"
The Green-cloaks pulled up short, then burst into guffaws. Rolin
lowered the staff and demanded, "Why are you laughing?"

"Forgive us," Gemmio chuckled. "We don't often see boys with
sticks trying to fight grown scouts!"

Bembor waved his men off. "Now then, Rolin," he said, "may
we see what's under your tunic? I give you my word that no one
will attempt to take it from you by force." Reluctantly, Rolin drew
out the pendant by its chain. Even in the room's feeble green glow
the gem glittered brightly.

"What did I tell you?" exclaimed Sigarth. "It is a soros!"

"So it would appear," Bembor remarked, examining the pendant. "But it is not one of ours. See how the metal is deformed
here? None of the other sorosa are similarly damaged."

"Maybe he tried to melt it down after stealing it," Sigarth suggested.

"No Thalmosian fire could touch this medallion," replied
Bembor. "It must be the seventh soros, lost after the death of King
Elgathel. The writing around its rim says, Sorc Friend and Healer.
That is unusual. All our sorosa are inscribed only with the words,
Sorc Master."

"Then how did this potato-eating Thalmosian come by it?"
growled Sigarth.

"Yes, where did you get it?" Bembor asked.

"It was my mother's, before she . . . before she died." Rolin
thought it best not to mention the wooden box.

"I am sorry," said Bembor softly, laying a wrinkled hand on
Rolin's shoulder.

"And who was your mother?" Sigarth persisted.

"Janna," Rolin sullenly replied.

"Oho!" said Bembor. "A good Lucambrian name. Let's have a
closer look at you, lad." Rolin peered up into Bembor's craggy face.

"Aye, and he's got the green of Lucambra in his eyes, too,"
Bembor chortled. "I'd wager my own soros there's Lucambrian blood
in his veins."

"Then he's a renegade," Larkin said coldly. "A half-breed. I say we send him back where he came from first thing tomorrow morning. We can't allow the son of a deserter to live among us, much less wear the soros that rightfully belongs to my family!"

"Didn't a certain young woman, a relative of yours, marry a Thalmosian some years back?" asked Bembor. Larkin became absorbed in something under his fingernail.

"If you were to scratch any of us deeply enough, I daresay you'd draw a little Thalmosian blood," Bembor went on, "so let's have no more talk of half-breeds and deserters. The council will decide what to do with the boy and his soros. In the meantime, we must play proper hosts to this young fellow."

"Begging your pardon, Bembor," Emmer interrupted, "but I've another question for the lad."

"What's that?" Rolin asked.

"We'd like to know how you got here. Few Thalmosians have ever found the way into our land."

Rolin then told the men how he had eluded his pursuers in the town square by throwing punkwood on the fire. Everyone except Sigarth and Skoglund grinned at Rolin's ruse.

"A little smoke threw you off the track, eh, Sigarth?" snickered Opio.

"How was I to know what he would do?"

"A clever trick, that, for a Thalmosian," Larkin allowed.

"With or without smoke, it was impossible to see him in that crowd," put in Skoglund. "Besides, we were there to buy linen for bowstrings, not to chase Thalmosian pickpockets."

"I'm not a pickpocket!"

"Here now, let the boy finish his story," said Bembor.

". . . and when I climbed down from the tree, I couldn't find my way home again," Rolin concluded. He said nothing about the mysterious old man.

"So that's why we couldn't find him," Sigarth said ruefully.

"I told you we should have cut down the torsils around that outpost," Larkin scowled. "There's no telling how many of these Thalmosians have slipped through. The woods are probably full of them!"

"And if they're all as dangerous as this lad here, we'll have our hands full!" retorted Gemmio.

"I still don't understand why you chose that particular tree," said Emmer.

Rolin shrugged, then stuck out his chin defiantly. "I think I've answered enough of your questions. It's time you answered some of mine. Who are you? What is this place? Why is my necklace so important to you?"

Larkin glowered, but the others hid amused smiles. "You really don't know where you are, do you?" Bembor sighed. "Under the circumstances, we do owe you an explanation. This is Lucambra; 'Land of Light' in your tongue. The only way to get here is by climbing a *torsil tree*, a kind of gate between our two worlds. Since there are few torsils left and they are well hidden, we rarely have unexpected visitors from Thalmos—your world, that is."

"Especially one so woodwise," added Skoglund. "It's a clever Thalmosian who can throw a Lucambrian scout off the track."

"Then why were your scouts at the Beechtown market?" asked Rolin. "What if someone followed them back to a torsil tree?"

"They'd probably be mistaken for elves, as often happens," Bembor smiled. "Yes, there's always the risk of discovery whenever we visit Thalmos. We only go there when we must, to barter for metal tools and other necessities.

"As for your soros, it is one of seven fashioned long ago by Lucambra's last king, who held it until he fell in battle. The other six sorosa remain in our possession. See, here is mine." Bembor lifted a gold-colored chain from around his neck, drawing forth a silver pendant hidden beneath his cloak. It was identical to Rolin's, only with a blue stone, rather than red. "I don't believe your soros is stolen but that it belonged to one of the Lost People, who fled to Thalmos after the king's death."

Rolin yawned, exhausted from all his hiking and tree climbing, not to mention the narrow escape from the batwolf. To make matters worse, his stomach was protesting over its missed meals.

"Here we are, prattling on about Lucambrian history, while our poor visitor is perishing from hunger and weariness!" exclaimed

Bembor. "Emmer, will you see to our guest's needs?" Emmer disappeared down a trapdoor in the floor, reemerging with a steaming pot and several loaves of brown bread.

Before you could say *fiddles and spoons*, Rolin was lapping up bowlfuls of sweet chestnut soup, served with thick slices of a rich, torsil nut bread. Meanwhile, a boy and a girl had popped up through the floor, bearing heavy quilts and blankets.

"These are my son and daughter, Scanlon and Marlis," Emmer said proudly. "They're eleven and thirteen. This is Rolin son of Gannon, a . . . a Thalmosian." Speechless, the wide-eyed children solemnly bowed.

"They've never met a Thalmosian before," Emmer explained.

Dark-haired Scanlon was shorter than Rolin, with big ears and mischievous green eyes. With her fine features, long lashes and winsome smile, Marlis stopped Rolin's soupspoon halfway to his mouth. She gracefully moved about the room laying out the blankets and quilts, exchanging shy glances with the beekeeper's son.

"'Marlis' means 'trillium flower' in our language," Emmer said, gazing fondly on his blond, lithesome daughter. Feeling a little less homesick, Rolin thought the whitest trillium would pale beside Marlis's fairness.

After supper, Emmer bundled his children off to bed, while Bembor sent the other scouts back to their posts. The Green-cloaks thanked Bembor for his hospitality, departing with, "May your sythan-ar ever flourish!"

"And yours also," replied Bembor politely. Rolin wondered what a sythan-ar was, and what would happen if it didn't flourish!

After the last scout had left, Bembor sat down beside Rolin. "You must forgive my clansmen their rudeness," he said with a kindly smile. "They mean no harm. Like most Lucambrians, they mistrust strangers. We fear that if the secret of the torsil trees should get out, Thalmosians would plunder our rich forests the way they have their own." Bembor paused, keenly regarding Rolin from beneath his bushy eyebrows. "That is why I must have the truth about your visit here. You didn't climb that torsil by accident, did you?"

Rolin shook his head sheepishly, then told Bembor of the silent stranger who had led him to the torsil tree. "Was he one of your scouts?" he asked.

Bembor paced back and forth, his forehead furrowed. "It's been many years since anyone has seen Him," he said finally.

"Seen who?"

"Gaelathane. The Father of all Lucambrians." Bembor seemed dazed. "But why a boy and a Thalmosian at that? Why not one of us, a staff-bearer, a clan leader? Could he really be the one? If only I knew for certain . . ."

"Knew what for certain?"

"Whether Gaelathane sent you here to fulfill the Prophecy!"

"What Prophecy?" Rolin was bewildered.

"I have said too much already," replied Bembor gravely. "I risk losing my position in the council and banishment from Lucambra for even mentioning these things to you. But if I am right, my boy, you are the one of whom the Prophecy speaks, he who will save us from our enemies!"

Bembor drew himself up as straight and tall as a young ash. Gazing at some luminescent words on the wall, he chanted in a deep, resonant voice:

> When darkness stalks across the land
> And evil lurks on every hand;
> When withered are the amenthils,
> From every stream and every hill;
> When fire devours both fern and flower,
> Then look for help in your final hour!
>
> From ancient root shall spring a shoot,
> Of field and forest, fairest fruit;
> A torsil tree of tender years,
> On him shall rest all hopes and fears;
> His stock shall be of Elgathel;
> His sythan-ar, an amenthil.
>
> For he shall seek the silver tree,
> The sentinel beside the sea . . .

Rolin was even more befuddled. "It sounds like poetry, but what does it all mean?"

"It is a poem, of sorts—the first part of the Prophecy Gaelathane entrusted to us long ago. Its words appear on the walls of every loyal Lucambrian's home. We have lost the rest. No one knows its true interpretation, for Gaelathane told us the meaning would become clear only in its fulfillment."

"If you don't know what the Prophecy means, how can you tell whether I am part of it?"

"It is true I cannot say for certain the Prophecy refers to you. However, I now believe that the eighth and ninth verses represent the same thing: someone in whose veins flows the blood of both Thalmos and Lucambra. 'Of tender years' points to the youth of this deliverer."

"But I've never been to Lucambra before! How could your Prophecy have anything to do with me?"

"Weren't you listening when I spoke of the Lost People? You needn't have set foot in Lucambra to be descended from Lucambrians."

"My father always said that his people have been beekeepers in Beechtown 'since bees had wings and frogs had toes.' That sounds like a long time."

"It does," Bembor agreed. "What of your mother's family?"

"I don't know much about them," Rolin admitted. "Father thinks my grandmother came from somewhere over the sea."

Bembor frowned. "That may be. In any event, I shall try not to ask you any more questions until I have answered some of your own! Before I do, you must solemnly swear not to reveal what I am about to tell you to another living being, Thalmosian or Lucambrian. Agreed?"

Rolin quickly nodded, his heart racing.

"Very good. Now then, let me begin with the Tree."

CHAPTER 4

THE ISLE OF LURALIN

B efore men walked in Thalmos or Lucambra, there was Gaelathane, the King of the Trees and Lord of all torsil worlds. In Lucambra, He first created the Isle of Light; 'Luralin' in the ancient tongue."

"Why did they call it that?" Rolin asked.

"I will explain everything if you will let me finish!" growled Bembor. "When all was yet cold and lifeless, Gaelathane formed the first living seed from a drop of His own blood, planting it at the center of the island, where it grew into a shining, red-barked evergreen, the largest and oldest of all the tree folk. He named it Waganupa—Tree of Life; for from its leaves He created us, the People of the Tree. Waganupa's radiance lit the sea for miles around, giving the island its name."

"How big was the Tree?" asked Rolin.

Bembor's eyes shone. "So thick that a hundred men with arms outstretched could not encircle its trunk, and so tall it pierced the clouds. Yet, for all its size, the Tree was not difficult to climb, for its lower limbs hung down to the ground, and its feathery foliage cushioned the fall of unwary climbers."

"Did anyone ever go to the very top?"

"I don't know," replied Bembor, scratching his beard. "Some say that if one climbed high enough into the Tree, he might glimpse a land even more fair than the Isle of Luralin. *Gaelessa*, we called it—Gaelathane's Country."

A land beyond the clouds! Rolin had often wondered what marvels lay in the lofty regions where only the birds were privileged to play. "Didn't everyone want to visit Gaelathane's Country?" he asked.

Bembor smiled. "Yes, but the King had already provided for our every need. Food was abundant on the island and in the sea, and there were plenty of torsils leading to different parts of Luralin, so that our people could get about in the blink of an eye without the bother of walking. Best of all, the flower scent of the *amenthils*, trees growing along the river Glymmerin, opened our ears to understand the speech of all living things."

"Do you mean trees and animals really can talk?" In his woodland ramblings, Rolin often fancied the wild creatures were calling to him in elusive words, like steam sprites dancing on a damp, sun-warmed roof.

"Yes, but not as we do. Trees, for instance, speak in the rustling of leaves, in the creak and groan of branches and in the silent burrowing of roots."

"I would like to learn the language of the trees!"

"Alas, that gift only the amenthils can confer. Since none now grow here, or in any other torsil world, we have become deaf to forest speech."

"So you cannot talk with the trees at all," said Rolin, feeling as if he had just found and lost a great treasure.

"Not as we did before, but we have learned at least to discern their hearts in the patterns of their bark. Would that I could touch the Tree's bark and read the history of the world written in its furrows! Would that we lived on Luralin once more, where death never darkened our days, and Waganupa's leaves healed all pains and illnesses!"

"May we go to Luralin, to see the Tree?"

"Alas, we cannot go back, though many have tried," Bembor replied. "Luralin lies a great distance from our shores, in the midst of the Sea of El-marin, where fierce storms can sink even the stoutest ships. No one setting sail upon its waters to seek the island has ever returned."

"Then how did your people ever get off Luralin in the first place?"

Bembor looked away. "We were tricked into leaving. You see, Gaelathane told us we were free to go wherever we wished upon the island or in the waters around it, and to do whatever we pleased, with one exception: We were never to plant a foreign tree on Luralin's soil, on pain of banishment."

"But what harm could there be in planting a tree?"

"A great deal of harm, as it turned out. On Luralin there once lived a lad by the name of Finegold. The son of a fisherman, he scorned the ways of his father and his people. His restless spirit fretted at the island's confinement, and he yearned to sail across the sea. In time he grew into a bitter young man, hating the island and all that lived upon it.

"One day, staring across the El-marin's green waves in hopes of glimpsing a ship from some distant land, he noticed a small nut bobbing in the water. Out of curiosity he retrieved the seed, secretly planted it, then forgot about it.

"Some years later, he came upon a sapling weeping for its planter. Until that day, sorrow had never visited Luralin. As clever as he was proud, Finegold realized the tree must have sprung from the nut he had found. The seedling called itself a Tree of Passage."

"A torsil!" exclaimed Rolin.

"Yes, but unlike Luralin's other torsils, this one led away from the island, to a vast, uninhabited country dark with fir and cedar, which Finegold named *Fineland*—after himself, of course.

"In Fineland, he found torsils opening to yet other undiscovered worlds: wide, treeless deserts; mountains locked in ice and snow; steaming jungles teeming with strange creatures. After entering any new land, he usually destroyed all its torsils, save one— his own private gateway to the place.

"Finally, at the very boundary of the lands of the living, he came upon *Gundul*, a realm of utter darkness and despair." Bembor shuddered, his face paling. "In Gundul, he found the *ashtags*, hideous perversions of Gaelathane's green and pleasant creation. Breeding them with the torsils of our world, he brought them up into the light of day, where they have taken hold and spread. Leafless, they grow by sapping the life out of everything they touch. As torsils, all ashtags lead only to Gundul, whence Felgor also brought forth the black serpent Gorgorunth to terrorize our people."

"What about the yegs?" Rolin asked. "Are they from Gundul, too?"

Bembor nodded grimly. "They serve as his spies and messengers and as winged mounts for the *gorku*, the Warriors of the Pit. May they all perish in the unquenchable fires of that foul place!"

"Did the people on Luralin know about Gundul?"

"Not at first. Finegold took great pains to conceal his comings and goings. When the time was ripe, however, he revealed the existence of Fineland, as if he had stumbled upon it while tree climbing. Enticed with promises of gold and rich gems, the people joined him in his explorations of that land.

"Then came the day, black in our memory, when Finegold held a feast in his own honor on Fineland's shores. All were invited and all attended. Men, women and children gladly lined up to climb Finegold's torsil, departing Luralin for a week of festivities. On the last day of the celebration, Finegold placed a jet-black crown of polished ashtag wood upon his head, proclaiming himself 'Felgor, Lord of Gundul, King of Fineland and of all the Vacant Lands.'

"At this, our people fled the feast in confusion, only to discover that Felgor had cut down his own torsil, destroying the sole tree leading to Luralin. They were trapped, exiled from their island home, just as Gaelathane had warned them would happen. The Ballad of Luralin recalls their anguish and speaks of ours today." Bembor cleared his throat and recited:

Luralin, O Luralin,
Isle of Everlasting Light,
Amid the night, your Tree shines bright,
Across the Sea of El-marin.

Our fathers walked beneath the Tree,
Which towered taller than the sun;
Its leaves were of the starlight spun;
Its shadow fell beyond the sea.

The voice of Gaelathane they spurned,
The Ageless One who never dies,
Whose counsel made our fathers wise;
To lies and greed their hearts had turned.

They wearied of the water's roar,
And longed for wider lands to win;
They left the Isle of Luralin
To weep beside a foreign shore.

Without the Tree, the people pined,
And walked the wooded hills, bereft
Of all the glory they had left
And ever after sought to find.

Though many a sturdy ship set sail,
With many a seaman, true and brave;
They foundered on the fathomless wave,
And none returned to tell the tale.

Yet Luralin appeared at night,
A faithful star still shining free,
Beckoning across the sea,
But bitterly they bore the sight.

Luralin, O Luralin,
The home of trees that never die,
Across the sea, beyond the sky,
In dreams, I'll walk your woods again.

Bembor wiped his eyes. "So ended the Age of the Three Trees, when our people lived on Luralin among the amenthils, the torsils and the Tree of Life."

CHAPTER 5

TORSILS, TUNNELS, AND TRILLIUM FLOWERS

Rolin awoke stiff and sore, with a gnawing pain in the pit of his stomach. He must have fallen asleep while Bembor was talking. Throwing back his blankets, he sat up. The tulip tree's trunk swayed gently beneath him, like a proud sailing ship at anchor. Sunshine was pouring through a rough, round window opening, dappling a low table beside him with the shifting shadows of leaves and illuminating a mural on the wall across the room. A great, red-trunked tree in the center of the scene glowed with life, while the smaller trees encircling it seemed to wave and bow in worship. At the bottom, winged, lionlike creatures pranced in a row.

"So you're finally awake!"

Rolin turned to find Marlis seated cross-legged on the floor behind him. "You slept through yesterday and all last night, too. Scanlon wanted to wake you, but I wouldn't let him. Grandfather said you weren't to be disturbed."

"Grandfather?"

"Yes, Bembor; he's my grandfather. Don't you remember?"

Rolin groggily shook his head.

"Anyway, I've fixed you some moonbonnet soup. I thought you'd be hungry." Marlis pushed a wooden bowl of yellowish liquid across the table toward him. Rolin mumbled his thanks and tasted a spoonful. It was warm and thick, with a pleasant, earthy flavor.

Spending most of his time tending bees up in the mountains meant Rolin rarely saw girls his own age. The Beechtown lasses were pretty enough, but looked down their noses at boys dressed in a hill dweller's rough garb. To Rolin's surprise, Marlis seemed not to notice his worn, travel-stained jerkin. She propped her elbows on the table and rested her chin on cupped hands.

"I've never been to Thalmos before," she said wistfully. "My father says it's too dangerous, and 'no place for a girl my age.'" She cocked her head to one side, eyeing Rolin like a robin about to pounce on a worm. "You don't look very dangerous to me!"

Rolin blushed and stared at his bowl.

"Is it true what they say about your people?" Marlis continued, gazing coyly at him. Her deep green eyes were flecked with gold, like maple leaves coloring in October's first frosts.

"Wh-what do they say?" he spluttered, his mouth full of soup.

"That Thalmosians eat bird eggs with their potatoes for breakfast."

Rolin choked. "Bird eggs!" he exclaimed. "You mean chicken eggs? Well, yes, some people do." Seeing Marlis's look of disgust, he added, "They're really not bad, and we don't eat them often. Father says they spoil too quickly."

Marlis nodded, then asked, "Do you have a sythan-ar?"

There was that word again. "A what?"

She gestured impatiently. "You know, a life tree."

Rolin shook his head. What was she talking about?

The Lucambrian girl stared at him warily. "You're not sick, are you?"

"I don't think so. Why?"

"Don't Thalmosians get the *sickness*?"

"Everybody gets sick some time. Don't you?"

Marlis's eyes grew round and solemn. "If you have the sickness, you die."

Just then, Scanlon popped out of the trapdoor in the floor. "Hallo!" he said, pulling himself up into the room. "Is Grandfather here yet?"

"No, he's still sleeping. The council meeting went on until late last night," answered Marlis, refilling Rolin's nearly-empty dish. As her hand brushed his, a shiver of excitement tingled up Rolin's spine.

"I'll bet all they talked about was their silly old rules," said Scanlon, helping himself to a bowlful of soup. "I just hope they don't banish Rolin."

"Banish me? What do you mean by that?"

"They send you up a torsil into some other world—usually a rather nasty one—then cut down the tree so you can't get back."

"Don't talk so!" Marlis scolded her brother. "You know the council only banishes the worst sorts. I think they should make him stay here."

"We'd have a lot of fun together then," agreed Scanlon, slurping his soup.

"Why wouldn't your council just let me go home?" asked Rolin.

Marlis and Scanlon exchanged glances. "Because you know," said Scanlon.

"Know what?"

"About the torsils, silly."

Rolin's face flushed. He felt like a caged animal, with rude Lucambrian children teasing him through the bars. "What does it matter if I know about your precious torsils?"

"Plenty," Scanlon said. "Once other-worlders get into Lucambra, we usually keep them here for good."

"Whatever for?" Rolin wasn't sure he wanted to hear the answer.

Marlis made a wry face. "So they don't go back and tell others about the torsils. Lucambra's supposed to be a secret."

"But I wouldn't tell anyone, not even my father!"

Scanlon shrugged. "There's nothing you can do about it now. The council's already met."

Rolin slumped against the table. How would his father and aunt manage without him? They'd send out search parties, but after a few weeks . . . He pictured his father sitting alone in the little log house, staring out the window, wondering what had become of his son. The two would never again walk the woods together or capture the thick swarms of wild honeybees. No more hot oatcakes smothered with butter and honey, no more trips to the Beechtown market. A tear squeezed out of one eye and slid down his cheek.

"I'm sure Grandfather wouldn't let them force you to stay," added Marlis. "He's an important member of the council, you know."

"Grandfather's the one who found Liriassa," Scanlon said proudly.

"Liriassa?"

"That's what we call our home," Marlis explained. "It means 'Valley of the Tulip Trees.'"

"We're safe here, because it's too steep for gorks to get in," said Scanlon.

"Then how do you get in and out?" Rolin demanded, hoping the brash boy couldn't give him an answer. Scanlon glanced at his sister, who nodded slightly as she poured Rolin more soup.

"We use *tara-torsils*," he whispered. "That's how you came here."

"Tara-torsils? What are those?"

"Grandfather Bembor invented them. They're just like other torsils, only they take you to a different place in the same world."

"Like Luralin's torsils, you mean?" asked Rolin.

"Yes, but ours don't start out that way. You have to—" Scanlon fished about in his pocket, producing a nut resembling a large, cream-colored acorn. "You split a torsil nut like this exactly in half, then plant the two halves in different spots, so that a tree grows from each one. When both torsils get big enough, you can travel between them just by climbing one or the other."

"How clever!" Rolin said. Years ago, Bembor must have planted one half of a torsil nut on the edge of the cliff overlooking Liriassa and the other in the valley below. When Opio and Gemmio had sent Rolin up the top tree, it had taken him to its twin at the bottom, saving the trouble of traversing a dangerous trail in the dark or climbing a rope. With a pair of tara-torsils, he realized, a person could cross mountain ranges and oceans in an instant!

Something thumped beneath the floor. "Shhh!" hissed Marlis. "Grandfather's coming!" Scanlon jumped up and busied himself straightening Rolin's makeshift bed just as the trapdoor opened and Bembor's head emerged, his beard all awry.

"Any soup left for me?" he called cheerfully, crawling through the opening.

"Of course, Grandfather," said Marlis, setting another bowl on the table and ladling it full. "You like my moonbonnet soup better than anyone's, don't you?"

"That I do, my trillium flower!" Bembor smiled broadly at his granddaughter and settled into a chair. "I see our guest has already had a bite of Lucambra's best," he said, winking at Rolin. "What do you think of it?"

"It's very good," said Rolin. "But what are moonbonnets?"

"Why, mushrooms, of course," Bembor replied. "My pardon— I'd forgotten this variety doesn't grow in Thalmos."

"They taste like lisichkis," remarked Rolin.

Bembor dropped his spoon. "Lisichkis! Where did you hear that name?"

"From my mother. She taught me to pick them."

"As any good mother would," said Bembor with a thoughtful expression. "Perhaps some day you can tell me more about her. I'd give my beard to know how she came by that soros."

Rolin remembered the wooden box with a pang of guilt. He would have to bring up that matter with Bembor later.

"Then Rolin can stay here with us, Grandfather?" Scanlon asked eagerly.

Bembor sighed, rubbing his eyes. "I fear not," he replied. "Despite all my efforts, Chief Councilor Grimmon used the occasion of Rolin's 'visit' to whip up hatred for the potato eaters. He accused Rolin of being a spy and all but branded me a traitor for defending him." Bembor shook his head. "Can't Grimmon see that our real enemy is Felgor and not the Thalmosians? Now Delwyn and his young hotheads won't rest until they've drawn some Thalmosian blood. If their voices prevail, the people of Beechtown will have much more to fear than flooding on the Foamwater."

"But what will happen to Rolin?" chorused Marlis and Scanlon.

"I persuaded the council to allow him to return to Thalmos."

"Thank you!" Rolin shouted. "When may I go home?"

Bembor hesitated. "No victory is without its price, of course."

"What does that mean?" asked Rolin suspiciously.

Bembor stared at the floor. "Rolin, you may never again return to Lucambra, or your life may be forfeit. Also, you must leave your soros with me, as a pledge not to reveal what you have seen and heard here. I'm sorry, lad; it's the best I could do."

Stunned, Rolin blinked back hot tears. He could never return to this wondrous place? Never hear Bembor's marvelous tales of Luralin again or see Scanlon or even Marlis? Never again sleep in the hollow trunk of a living tree? And what of the wild Lucambrian woods, just waiting to be explored? Numbly, he reached up to remove the pendant and its chain. It was gone! He clapped his hand to his chest, frantically feeling about for the familiar outline. What could have happened to his most prized possession?

"Don't fret yourself," said Bembor calmly. "I have your soros." Horrified, Rolin looked up to see the pendant lying in Bembor's hand.

"But you said—"

"Yes, I know, boy. I promised that no one would take it from you by force, and in truth, no one has. After you fell asleep the other night, I borrowed it to use in convincing the other council members of your innocence. Here, you may hold it one last time."

Rolin took the soros, suspending it by the chain. The pendant twisted to and fro, its gem pulsing with red fire. Sadly, he laid it back in Bembor's hand, already missing the reassuring feel of the metal beneath his shirt.

"You are fortunate it is only your soros you have lost and not your freedom," observed Bembor, dropping the pendant into his cloak pocket.

While the old man finished his soup, the only sounds in the room were the whispering of leaves, the creaking of limbs and an occasional muffled sob from Marlis, who sat huddled on Rolin's mattress. The boys looked at her, then at each other and shrugged. Rolin could never understand why Thalmosian girls cried, much less Lucambrian ones. Bembor had just pushed aside his empty bowl with a contented sigh when Marlis raised her head.

"G-Grandfather, is Rolin going to die?" she sniffled.

Bembor blinked, then threw a puzzled look at his granddaughter. "I don't think so, little one. Why do you ask?"

Marlis's face screwed up, and a tear trickled down the side of her pert nose. "He doesn't have a sythan-ar."

Bembor chuckled. "Of course he doesn't; Thalmosians don't need them."

Rolin's pent-up frustrations boiled to the surface. "What is a sythan-ar?" he exploded.

Bembor gazed at his guest with amused eyes, his chin resting on steepled fingers. "I suppose it won't hurt to tell you. *Sythan-ar* means 'life tree' in our language. When we left Luralin, we not only lost our ancestral home but also cut ourselves off from the Tree's sustaining life, leaving an aching void in our hearts that brought on an incurable wasting disease. The *sickness*, as we call it, felled more of our people than did gorkin arrows."

"May I tell the next part, Grandfather?" begged Marlis, scooting next to Rolin. Bembor nodded and helped himself to more moonbonnet soup.

"Only five years after Lucambra became our home," she began, "grownups were dying all the time—and children, too. Nobody knew what to do. Then a young girl named Sonya uprooted a birch seedling in the forest and replanted it outside her family's cave. Every day she nursed the little thing. Sonya's mother and father got the sickness, but she never did."

Bembor took up the story again. "Soon, others noticed Sonya's health and planted their own trees. They found that adopting a sythan-ar not only prevented the sickness but even cured it."

"My sythan-ar is an oak," Scanlon boasted. "It won't burn up if the dragon breathes on it."

"So is mine," said Marlis.

"All members of the oak clan take oaks as sythan-ars," Bembor explained. "They're hardy trees and recover better from burns than firs or pines."

"But what happens if one of your oaks grows sick or dies?" Rolin asked.

"So too will its owner sicken or die," replied Bembor sadly, "as Felgor knows full well. By cutting down or burning the forests around our settlements, he's destroyed many a life tree and with it, a Lucambrian man or woman, boy or girl. Most of us would prefer a swift death by sword or dragon fire to the slow withering that follows the loss of a sythan-ar."

"Then why don't you plant several sythan-ars, so that if one dies, the others will keep you alive?" Rolin suggested.

"A fine idea," Bembor replied, ruffling Rolin's hair. "But we plant only one, just as we take but one mate in marriage."

Rolin's face fell. Of the thousands of trees he'd planted, each was special. When summer's sweltering days scorched the cut-over hillsides above Beechtown, Rolin would appear with a watering bucket to nurse his parched beech seedlings through the dry spell. He'd also planted cottonwood cuttings along the creeks and rivers. Which of them all would suit him as a sythan-ar? But then, he was a Thalmosian, and Thalmosians didn't need sythan-ars.

"Do you have a life tree, Bembor?" Rolin asked.

"You are inside it, my boy! I planted this tulip tree many years ago. Now it serves me both as a sythan-ar and as a snug, dry home, though it is growing old, as I am. The trunk is still sound, thanks be to Gaelathane," he added, knocking on the curving inner wall.

"What about Felgor? Does he have a life tree, too?"

"He must, for he is still one of us, though the knowledge galls him."

"Then why don't you just cut it down?"

Bembor laughed bitterly. "His life tree is the ashtag Hrothmog, the Tree of Death, that grows at the very roots of Mt. Golgunthor.

Even if one could reach that tree, ashtag wood is proof against the sharpest blade ever forged in Lucambra or Thalmos. But let's not spoil your parting with such talk." Bembor clapped Rolin on the shoulder. "Thalmos awaits us! If we hurry, you may arrive home in time for breakfast."

Breakfast? Rolin glanced at the brightness outside the window. "No, Father and I always eat at daybreak, just before we work the bees."

Bembor stared at him quizzically. "Lucambra's sun rises hours before the Thalmosian dawn. Your father is still in bed." Then Rolin recalled how quickly the sky had darkened when he had descended the tortoiseshell torsil tree. What an odd world this was!

"We'll take the shortcut today," Bembor said, nodding at Scanlon, who pulled back the trapdoor in the floor.

"We're going down there?" Rolin asked, pointing to the opening.

"There's more than one way from my world into yours," said Bembor, a smile crinkling at the corners of his eyes and mouth. "If you're ready, I'll go first and you follow." Bembor squeezed through the hole and disappeared.

After bidding Marlis and Scanlon a hasty farewell, Rolin swung his legs into the hole and grasped the rope hanging under the edge. It felt none too stout. Taking a deep breath, he put his full weight on the rope.

"Come on, Rolin! It's quite safe!" Bembor's voice echoed up to him. Rolin lowered himself a few feet, trying not to make the rope sway. To his surprise, he was suspended in another room. With a neat little bed on one side and a short bow and quiver of arrows on the other, it was evidently Scanlon's. Sliding down the rope, Rolin discovered still other chambers: bedrooms, storerooms, even a tidy little kitchen and pantry, each room wider than the last and all lit with the same soft, yellow-green light.

The farther Rolin descended, the brighter grew the light, which not only radiated from the tree's inner walls but also filtered up from below. Then he dropped into a large, open space, where the cool luminescence burst upon him with all the brilliance of a hundred moons.

Rolin blinked in the dazzling, golden-green glow. As his eyes adjusted, he saw he was dangling in the midst of an enormous mushroom garden. Yellow-capped mushrooms by the thousands lined the inside of the tree trunk, each shining with a ghostly, yellow-green light. Rolin swung over and plucked one. The whole fungus was luminescent, from the slender stem and smooth cap to the delicate, thin-bladed gills, with a pleasant, musty-sweet odor.

Here and there among the mushrooms were dark patches where clusters had been broken off, but as Rolin looked down, those small imperfections melted into a shimmering pool of living light. What lay at the bottom, he could not tell. Continuing his descent, Rolin landed on a soft bed of moldering wood that had accumulated inside the base of the trunk. Several paces away, dirt was heaped around a large, burrowlike hole in the ground.

"Here you are!" said Bembor, catching hold of the rope and jerking it three times. "There—now they'll know we made it safely down. Goodness gracious, boy, I thought you'd stopped upstairs to take a nap!"

Rolin grinned and shook his head. "It's just that I've never seen such mushrooms before or so many of them! What kind are they?"

"Luniceps; 'moonbonnets' in your language," replied Bembor with a chuckle. "You ate them in your soup. Long ago, our people discovered the secret of growing these mushrooms in living trees. After the mushrooms have softened the heartwood of their host, we hollow out the tree to make it into comfortable living quarters, as you have seen. Since the luniceps will grow inside the trunk for many years, we can pick fresh mushrooms in any season without going into the woods to find them. Now, let's be off."

Rolin followed Bembor into the burrow, which became a slanting tunnel, weaving its way down among the tree roots. Eerily luminescent flecks and splotches lit the walls and ceiling with a soft, moonbonnet-like light.

Curious, Rolin removed one of the glowing patches from the wall. It crumbled in his fingers, scattering shining fragments everywhere, like sizzling embers popping from a burning log.

"I'm sorry," Rolin said. "I didn't mean to break it. I just wanted to find out what it was."

"No harm done," Bembor reassured him. "It's only a piece of 'moonwood,' as we call it. You see, once the luniceps have lived on a tree for a few years, the wood softens with decay and easily breaks apart. It won't grow any more mushrooms then but still glows in the dark, just as the luniceps do. We always carry a supply of moonwood with us when we travel, dropping pieces of it along the trail to help us find our way back in the dark. It also comes in handy for lighting up the insides of tunnels and caves."

"Where does this tunnel lead?" Rolin asked.

"Why, to Thalmos, of course!" replied Bembor with a knowing wink.

"But how—?"

"Roots and shoots, my boy, roots and shoots!" Bembor's hearty voice echoed down the clammy corridor. "The only way you'll ever go anywhere in a torsil is by passing beneath its roots or climbing to its very top."

"Do you mean your tunnel starts in Lucambra and ends in Thalmos?"

"Quite right. This way, I can be certain no one will follow us."

"Who would want to do that?"

"Grimmon, among others. He'd give his staff to know where you got that soros. Worse yet, Felgor may have learned by now that an other-worlder has stumbled into Lucambra. We dare not enter Thalmos the way you came, lest his spies discover your torsil. He's always on the lookout for new lands to plunder. Now, we'd better move along, or Scanlon and Marlis will wonder what's become of me!"

After that, only the shuffling of footsteps and the plip-plop of water dripping on the stone floor broke the suffocating stillness. Rolin was glad of the moonwood markers and their cheery light. "If only these fungus lamps would give off a little heat, too!" he muttered, shivering in the dank, chill air.

Just when Rolin thought the tunnel would go on forever, it abruptly ended in a blank stone wall. Without breaking stride,

Bembor stepped into the rock face and vanished! Rolin gaped, then squared his shoulders and also marched forward—straight into a small cave.

"Here we are!" said Bembor, peering through some brambly brush covering the cave's mouth. "Now, you mustn't tell anyone where you've been."

"What will I say to my father?"

"I'm sure you'll think of something," Bembor smiled.

Rolin fought back tears. "Will I ever see you again?"

"That I can't say for sure. The council has forbidden you from ever setting foot in Lucambra again, but nothing was said about my visiting Thalmos. So, if a certain boy were to leave a light burning in the west window of a certain cabin, when he was alone, surely no one would object?"

"I suppose not," Rolin shrugged.

"And if a certain weary traveler happened by, in need of rest and a bite of supper, he'd find a warm welcome, would he not?"

Rolin nodded, a grin spreading across his face. "You mean you could—?"

"Hush, boy." Bembor pressed something round and heavy into Rolin's palm.

"What's this?"

"A spasel—a ball of hardened torsil sap. Just warm it in your hands, and maybe you won't miss Lucambra quite so much. And don't forget: 'The greatest help oft comes in harm's disguise, to those with trusting hearts and open eyes.' Oh, yes—*lisichki* is an old Lucambrian word meaning 'little yellow goblet.' May your sythan-ar ever flourish!"

Before Rolin could thank him, Bembor strode to the back of the cave and disappeared. "And yours also," whispered Rolin. Then he ducked out of the cave and into the morning mists of his own world.

CHAPTER 6

THE EYES IN THE POOL

When Rolin opened the cabin door, his father and aunt jumped up, looking as if they'd seen a ghost. "Don't you know how worried we were?" Glenna fussed, smothering Rolin with hugs and kisses. "After Gannon found your cap full of mushrooms in the square, we all feared foul play." Then, planting Rolin on her ample lap, she poured out the saga of the search.

"They rang all the bells in Beechtown for you," she began. "The mayor even gave a little speech about what a fine boy you were." She dabbed her eyes. "The raftsmen dragged the river for your body but found nothing. I knew you were still alive, and I told them so, too."

"That you did, Sister," sighed Gannon, stoking the wood stove.

"Gannon went to all the neighbors up and down the mountain asking about you. Everyone tried to help. People can say what they like about these hill folk, but any one of them would have given his last gilder to find you."

"She's right," said Gannon as he prepared breakfast.

"After the other searchers had quit for the night," Glenna continued, "your father combed the woods along the river road with a beeswax torch."

"Got wax in my beard, too," Gannon grumped. "I wasn't about to give up, especially after the miller said you'd 'prob'ly got et by a bear.'"

"I didn't get chased by any bears," laughed Rolin.

"Then what did happen to you?" Glenna demanded.

"Peace, Sister, let the poor boy eat!" Gannon scolded her, setting bowls of steaming oatmeal, yellow cream and scrumptious honeycomb on the table.

"Bembor was right!" exclaimed Rolin. He was in time for breakfast.

"What's that?" asked his father. But Rolin's mouth was too full to answer.

Rolin knew he couldn't claim to have lost his way in the woods. Nor would it do to say he'd been mushroom picking, since he hadn't brought any home with him. In the end, he told as much of the truth as he dared.

"It was the Green-cloaks," he said, scraping the last of the oatmeal from his bowl. Then he explained how several of the mysterious strangers had chased and kidnapped him, mistaking his pendant for one of their own. Realizing their mistake, the men had let him go, but he had lost the pendant on his way home. "I'm sorry about your necklace, Father," he concluded glumly.

"Necklace?!" snorted Glenna with a theatrical toss of her head. "Better to lose a necklace than your neck! I always knew those Green-cloaks were up to no good. A pack o' baby-robbing gremlins they are, appearin' and disappearin' like a will-o'-the-wisp. I tell you, Brother, you'd be much better off living in town, where you could keep an eye on this boy."

Scowling, Gannon took down a stout wooden cudgel from a hook on the wall and made for the door. The last time Rolin had seen that club put to use, a bear had broken into one of the beehives. The bear's head now hung over the chimney, and its skin lay on the floor as a rug. Only Rolin's repeated assurances that his captors had treated him kindly prevented his father from storming off in search of Green-cloaks to trounce.

After breakfast, Rolin flopped down on his bed. His flimsy story had apparently satisfied both his father and his aunt and wasn't far from the truth, either. But what would Glenna say if she knew he'd befriended the very "gremlins" whose knack for flitting through the forest or vanishing into torsils had given rise to the old tales of elves, fairies and other forest folk?

Rolin rolled over to remove the spasel from his pocket. It wasn't much to look at, just a lump of clear, slightly sticky sap. He turned it over in his hands, wondering if it were like those hollow glass globes filled with water and white sand that made miniature snow-storms when shaken. To his disappointment, the ball appeared solid. He was about to shove it back in his pocket when he noticed a murkiness gathering at its center. The cloudiness grew until it had filled the spasel, then melted away to reveal a colorful scene that Rolin recognized as the valley of Liriassa.

"How wonderful!" he gasped. But what artistry could create such lifelike images of birds flying and trees swaying in the wind? This was no clever plaything but a living torsil window into Lucambra!

When Rolin laid the sap ball on his bed, the colors faded. Wrapping his hands around it made the scene return. So it was warmth that brought the spasel to life! After gazing into it most of the day, he placed the ball in his box among the dried flowers where the soros had lain, thinking he'd made a good trade. Even if he never returned to Lucambra, at least he had a bird's-eye view of it.

The next morning, Rolin found his father washing clothes in the pool behind the beaver dam on Cottonwood Creek. "I see you survived the night without being kidnapped by Green-cloaks again!" Gannon said in greeting, throwing a wet shirt at him. Laughing, Rolin caught the shirt and threw it back, nearly knocking his father into the water.

"Yes, but only after I promised them an oatcakes-and-honey breakfast!"

Chuckling, Gannon gathered up the wet clothes and went back to the cabin. Rolin sat down beside the placid pool, watching water skippers skimming across its surface. Then he softly sang the Song of Cottonwood Creek:

Bounding down hillside from bubbling fountain,
Burbling, gurgling as I flow;
Under the moonlight, under the mountain,
Ever the downward path I go!

Joyously singing, my waters are bringing
Blessings to fields and forests below;
Laughing, I set my river rocks ringing,
Rumbling, tumbling as I go!

Where am I bound for, where am I going?
When will my waters finally find rest?
From over the mountains, the west wind blowing
Brings me the answer I love best!

Under the cottonwoods, under the fir trees,
Down to the valley you shall fare;
Joining the river to find the sea breeze,
Always delighting your bounty to share!

Long boats and barges of men will you carry,
Slipping so slowly through flatlands low;
Green fields and forests will beg you to tarry,
But ever and onward you must flow!

Meander through meadows, follow the sea foam,
Spun from the shores where salt water meets sweet;
Turn to the sunset, seek your sea home,
Ever awaiting your waters to greet!

Many were the marvelous stories Rolin had heard of the Green
Sea, but never had he journeyed west of the Tartellan mountains
to glimpse its waves. Only during blustery winter weather, storm-
tossed seagulls rode the salt-scented seawinds into the valley of
the Foamwater.

But now it was spring, and the song sparrows were trilling
merrily among the cottonwoods and alders, whose gray trunks
were mirrored in the pool. Then Rolin noticed another reflection—
eyes! Quickly looking up, he saw the bushes swaying on the oppo-

site bank. Someone—or something—had been watching him. He told himself it was just an otter or a muskrat, but several days later, he glimpsed a furtive form slinking upright through the trees.

Soon, a wet and windy spring gave way to a balmy summer, and with it, a brisk bee season. Between building new hives, repairing old ones and capturing bee swarms, Rolin nearly forgot about the elusive shadow. One morning, however, he found an old log lying beside the creek where he could observe the trail without being seen. There he sat whittling on a stick, all the while watching and listening.

Around noon, he heard soft footfalls. Quick as a breath, he hid behind the log, then peered over the top—and right into a pair of startled green eyes.

Rolin jumped up with a yell, as did the stranger. It was Scanlon, wearing the green hood and cloak of a Lucambrian scout and carrying a staff.

"Scanlon! What are you doing here?"

"Looking for you—and please lower your voice! Grandfather sent me to tell you not to talk with any scouts, except me or my father. He's also wondering if you remember the all-clear signal."

"Signal?" Rolin frowned. "Oh, yes—a light in the west window."

"Good." Scanlon's face relaxed.

"When does Bembor plan to visit me?"

"He can't come now, because Grimmon's men are watching his tree day and night and your cabin, too. That's why I came instead." So that explained the mysterious reflection in the pool!

"But what should I do?"

"Just keep your eyes and ears open. If anything unusual happens around here, leave a note for us in the torsil cave." Scanlon turned to leave.

"That's all? What about—I mean, isn't there a message from—?"

Scanlon scuffed the dirt, then mumbled, "My sister Marlis wishes you well."

Rolin's heart leapt. "Tell her that . . . I also wish her well." There was an awkward silence, neither boy looking at the other.

"I must be going now," Scanlon said at last. "Grandfather will be waiting for me. May your sythan-ar ever flourish!" With that, the young Lucambrian disappeared into the forest.

Every evening thereafter, Rolin found excuses to stay home alone when Gannon went out walking, hunting or visiting his sister. As soon as his father left, Rolin would light the smoky oil lamp and set it in his bedroom window. Then he would await a knock at the door. Gannon always returned before the knock came. On such nights, Rolin would turn down the light and take out his spasel, warming it with his bitter tears until Liriassa appeared. However long he looked into it, he never saw Bembor—or Marlis.

BEE TREES AND TOWERS

F ather, when are we going bee hunting?" Rolin asked. It was
late June, when he knew hollow trees and logs would be dripping with the rich, dark honey that fetched such fine prices at the
fall market. Wild honey tasted so good that Rolin didn't mind the
few stings it took to get it.

"Not this month, Son," Gannon said. "I'm too busy tending our
own hives. You're old enough now to raid bees' nests without me.
Take a smoker and some sacks, and you can go out by yourself."

Rolin could hardly believe his good fortune. That night, he
packed his food, clothing and tools and set off early the next morning to seek out a bee tree.

Rolin whistled as he hiked along Cottonwood Creek, reflecting
that it was just the sort of warm, dry summer day that bees like.
Presently, he turned aside onto a trail that led up a narrow canyon.
After a mile or so, the canyon opened onto a broad meadow sprinkled
with fragrant wildflowers—the perfect place for bee tracking.

He sat down on a flat rock and unpacked his lunch, along with
a bag of honey and a little pot of red paint. Taking a stick, he smeared
some of the honey on a piece of bark, which he laid on the rock.
While he ate, he watched and waited.

It wasn't long before a bee alit on the bark and stuffed itself with honey. Soon, other hungry bees joined in. Just before the first bee flew off, Rolin dabbed it with paint. Then he observed the path of the bee's flight until the insect vanished from sight.

A few minutes later, the painted bee returned for more honey, then left again. This time, Rolin picked up the piece of bark and made his way across the meadow to the place where he'd last seen the bee. Once more, he laid his honey lure on a rock and waited. Much sooner, the painted bee was back.

Rolin tracked the little creature until he came to the edge of a steep cliff. Where had the bee gone? Straining his eyes, he spotted a swarm of dark specks darting in and out of a hole high in the gnarled trunk of an oak tree near the cliff.

After an hour's worth of slipping, sliding and scrabbling, a hot and grimy Rolin stood at the foot of the oak, surrounded by the thrumming of wings. Putting his ear to the trunk, he could even hear the bees droning deep inside. His father had told him of trees filled from top to bottom with honeycomb, but Rolin had never believed it possible. If this oak were only half-full of comb, there would be enough honey to supply all of Beechtown for a year!

He hurled a coil of rope over a stout limb near the bee hole, then tied one end of it to his rucksack. Next, he climbed the doubled-over rope and settled on the branch. He had just hauled up the knapsack when he heard a snorting sound. A big black bear was snuffling about beneath the tree.

Rolin froze. He wasn't surprised to see the bear, since bears and beekeepers, both being fond of honey, have a way of bumping into one another—usually without harm to either party. Still, he tied the other end of his rope to the limb. If the bear came up after him, that rope would be his only means of escape.

"Shoo, bear, go away!" he shouted. But the bear only shambled around the tree, grunted and flopped down beside it. Then the beast started snoring.

"Isn't this a pretty pickle," Rolin muttered. "Bees on top and a bear at the bottom!" Ordinarily suspicious of large, furry intruders near their nests, the bees seemed content to let the bear lie. Likewise, they ignored the boy sitting on the branch next to their front door. It was not the way bees and bears were supposed to behave!

Gone from Rolin's mind were all thoughts of harvesting his honey trove. He watched helplessly as the sun sank behind the fir-clad mountain peaks, while shadows cloaked the sleeping bear. A cool wind sprang up, pulling a white sheet of clouds across the sky. There would be little light from stars or moon that night. Soon, the bees would retreat to the warmth and security of their nest, leaving Rolin outside in the dark with the bear.

Rolin's eyelids were growing heavy when the bear awoke, shook itself and lumbered off into the woods. Waiting a few minutes to be sure the animal was really gone, Rolin slid down the rope, forgetting to untie the end and loop it over the limb first. After shouldering his pack, he decided against scaling the cliff ropeless in the dark and settled for a detour around it instead.

As he hiked down the mountain, stones and fallen limbs tripped him up, and branches slapped and poked him in the face. Worse yet, every dark and sinister shadow took on the outlines of a bear ready to make a meal of him.

Presently, Rolin noticed a light shining through the forest. Hunger and thirst overcoming caution, he crept toward it. If this were a hunter's campfire or a lamp burning in a trapper's cozy cabin, he might enjoy a bowl of venison stew for supper.

The light was neither. Instead, a small tree seemed to have caught fire. Coming closer, he saw no smoke or flames but only a soft, white light bathing the tree's crooked branches and oddly-shaped leaves. "Why, it's a torsil!" he exclaimed, running his fingers over the rough, tortoiseshell bark. To what land might it take him? Even if the tree led to Lucambra, it would be a simple matter to pop back into Thalmos without anyone being the wiser.

Carefully, he climbed to the top of the torsil. As he descended, a bright light shone upon him, and he heard a low, roaring noise, louder now, then softer. A pungent, fish-stall odor filled the air.

He was in a dark wood of leafless trees that marched down to the brink of high bluffs. Below them, white-capped, rolling waves rhythmically thundered on a deserted beach. Overhead, a full moon silvered the landscape, casting spidery shadows among the dismal trees and illumining the torsil.

On a broad knoll before him stood a tall, tapering tower. Rolin followed the remnants of a winding cobblestone path up to the fortress, which stabbed the night sky like a black, accusing finger. The dark trees crowded around its base, as if trying to break in.

Circling the tower, Rolin found a stone slab that apparently served as a door. It was perfectly smooth, save for a small, shallow depression in the center. Rolin pushed on the slab, but it didn't budge. "Hallo! Is anybody there?" he called out. His voice echoed harshly back from the cold stones.

Sensing a brooding malice about the place, he retreated along the path and shinnied up the torsil. On reaching the top, he took a last look around. All was dark and still as before—or were the tree shadows moving? With a shiver, he climbed down again.

Once back in Thalmos, Rolin draped a honey bag over one of the moonlit torsil's limbs, in case he should ever wish to find the tree in the daylight. Then he made straight for home. It was raining by the time he wearily stumbled through the cabin door to find his father waiting for him. His description of the bee tree brought a gleam of excitement to Gannon's eyes.

"With that much wild honey, I could buy a new ax, perhaps even another wagon," he mused. "But once we got the comb out of the oak, how would we bring it all back? Those mountain paths are too rugged for our old cart." Noting Rolin's downcast face, Gannon added, "Maybe you could coax your furry honey bandit into hauling it for us in a wheelbarrow!" Rolin grinned. His father always knew how to tease him out of a glum mood.

After a cold supper of beans and bread, Rolin fell into bed. Questions whirled in his mind like midges over water on a summer's eve. What land had he discovered? Who had built the tower, and why wouldn't its door open? Did anyone still live there? Then a deep sleep overcame him.

CHAPTER 8

VISITORS FROM LUCAMBRA

G ive me the pan, will you?" said Gannon. Rolin handed his father the heavy iron skillet, then went back outside to cut up more mushrooms for their supper. After the bee-tree episode, a drenching summer thundershower had swept through the mountains. Now, the crusty, brown caps of the delicious Scaly Stalk mushroom were popping up in every birch grove. Rolin had found enough for dinner, with plenty left to dry on strings for the winter.

It was a sultry evening, a fitful breeze stirring in the tops of the firs, which scented the air with their tangy incense. Swallows swooped above the forest, chasing mosquitoes in the waning light, while a few early bats flitted about in search of moths. Crickets *chirk-chirked* in the grass. Dusk settled comfortably around the cabin like a quilt over an old woman's shoulders.

Rolin and his father were just sitting down to their meal of venison and mushrooms when a *thump! thump!* rattled the door. Rolin looked up, surprised. He and his father rarely had callers, except for Aunt Glenna, who never knocked. The thumping became an insistent pounding.

Gannon hurried to the door. As soon as he opened it, a grizzled old man clutching a club pushed his way inside. Rolin recognized the man as a sheep rancher named Greyson, who lived down the mountain. From the wild look in his eyes, Rolin gathered something was wrong.

Gannon talked briefly with the visitor, then went to the tall kitchen cupboard and brought out his hunting bow, quiver of arrows, and a lantern. Rolin looked questioningly at his father.

"Something's attacking Greyson's flocks," Gannon said tersely.

"Like great eagles they are, but black as death!" the farmer put in. "You've got to help me. They're carrying off my sheep!"

Rolin glanced from his father to Farmer Greyson. Normally, Gannon had little to do with sheepmen, whose free-ranging flocks grazed the mountain grasses, herbs and tree seedlings right down to their roots. That meant no flowers or trees—and no forage for bees. Rolin also knew that when a man's livelihood was at stake, a neighbor always lent a hand. He hurried out the door after his father, grabbing his mushroom-digging stick from the porch.

"You're not coming," Gannon said flatly, tossing his bow and arrows into Greyson's horse-drawn wagon. Rolin ignored the order and climbed onto the wagon with the two men. He hated disobeying his father, but he had a feeling he might be needed. Gannon stared at him. "Rolin," he said, "you've got to stay home. There's no telling what we're up against, and you might get hurt."

"I'm not afraid," declared Rolin. "Besides, who will watch the horses while you're protecting the sheep? I'm old enough to help." Gannon frowned but made no reply.

"Giddyup!" cried the sheepman, and the horses galloped down the road. As the wagon clattered along, Rolin lashed his knife to the digging stick with a bit of twine, Farmer Greyson's words echoing in his mind: *Like great eagles . . . but black as death!* If batwolves were on the loose, he'd need a weapon.

"What's that you're making?" Gannon asked, holding the lantern up to Rolin's handiwork.

"Just a spear," replied Rolin casually.

A grudging respect grew in Gannon's eyes. "You've changed since we went to market last May," he said. "You're becoming more of a man." Rolin sat up straighter and smiled. Little did his father know what had made the difference in him!

After a breakneck, bone-jarring ride, the sheepman pulled his wagon off the road and into a rocky field. "Whoa!" he shouted, then threw the reins at Rolin. "Make sure they don't bolt," he ordered. Then he and Gannon leapt off the wagon and disappeared into the night, taking the lantern with them.

From out in the fields came the bleating of frightened sheep and a dog's frantic barking. There were other sounds, too: a growling and a hissing, as of an animal at bay or defending its prey. Then a dreadful chorus of howls and screeches broke out. As Rolin had feared, batwolves were on the rampage, and they had caught the scent of blood.

Screams and curses mingled with the yegs' guttural cries. "A fire! Light a fire!" someone shouted. Flames spurted up in the distance, silhouetting several dark shapes wheeling and diving above the panicked sheep. Bowstrings twanged and arrows whistled.

Suddenly, the horses whinnied in terror. A yeg had swooped over the wagon, vanishing into the blackness. "Don't you come near me again, batwolf!" Rolin yelled, shaking his spear. Then he remembered Opio's words: *Their eyes are weak, but they can hear a mouse in the dark at a thousand paces.* He crouched down, hardly breathing. Would the yeg return?

There—something had blotted out the stars for an instant. Then the creature was upon him, its jaws yawning wide. With no time to think, Rolin thrust the spear upward. A heavy blow tore it from his fingers, knocking him out of the wagon. He lay on the ground, too stunned to move or cry out. Then strong hands lifted him to his feet, and Gannon's face peered into his.

"Are you hurt, boy?"

"I don't think so," replied Rolin shakily. "Where's my stick?" The two searched the area around the wagon. Then Gannon gave a shout, holding the lantern over a black heap lying in the field. It was a yeg, quite dead, Rolin's makeshift spear protruding from its throat. In the lantern light, it looked rather like a large dog covered with a broken black umbrella.

"I killed a batwolf!" Rolin exclaimed, then covered his mouth.

"A batwolf?" said Gannon, scratching his head. "Why, it does look like a wolf with bat's wings, all right. So this is what's been terrorizing Greyson's sheep! I've never seen the like of it before. How did you know what it was?"

"I don't know—I mean, I didn't know what else to call it."

"Well, it's a good name for a foul creature," said Gannon, giving Rolin a curious stare. "I hope the rest of its kind go back to wherever they came from and leave us be."

Rolin and Gannon spent the remainder of that night with the sheepman and his five sons. At morning's first light, they all trooped out to view the field of battle, where they found five batwolves pierced with arrows. Gannon hacked off the head of the sixth yeg Rolin had slain with his valiant spear thrust. Then Farmer Greyson piled the carcasses in a heap, together with the three sheep he'd lost in the skirmish and set them all afire.

Later that day, Rolin helped his father nail the yeg's head to Nan's hitching post as a warning to other would-be rustlers. In the following weeks, townsfolk by the dozens straggled up to the cabin to see the grisly trophy. "My boy stuck his stick clean through its neck!" Gannon would boast, while Rolin squirmed and the visitors goggled at the gruesome head.

Not to be outdone, Farmer Greyson posted a sign outside his field reading: DRAGON SKELETON. For a few gilders, sightseers could gawk at the pile of burnt bones lying in a blackened circle of earth. Chills ran up Rolin's spine whenever he went near the place.

When there were no further sightings or attacks, the stream of idle gossips trekking to the cabin slowed to a trickle. Rolin welcomed this turn of events. He'd chafed under the constant attention and the awkward necessity of explaining his apt name for the half-wolf, half-bat beasts. Moreover, the many visitors rarely afforded him an evening alone in the cabin to signal Bembor. If only he could get word to his Lucambrian friends, perhaps they could destroy the yegs' torsil gate into Thalmos.

Several weeks later, Rolin awoke to find a dusting of frost on the grass. With its clear days and cool nights, autumn was splashing the cottonwoods, aspens and birches with gold. In Rolin's spasel,

Liriassa's tulip trees were turning a buttery yellow. Gannon stuffed fresh cattail fluff in the cracks and chinks between the cabin's logs, to keep out the winter winds.

One crisp fall morning found Rolin in a bronze-leafed beech grove. As he filled a honey sack with brown, three-cornered beech-nuts, he could hear the music and laughter of Beechtown's Nut-ting Festival drifting up from the village square. Rolin's parents used to take him to the festival every year, where they enjoyed fiddle music, dancing, roasted beechnuts and mugs of foaming hot apple cider. Rolin often took a turn at grinding the sweet, oily beechnuts into a rich butter.

None of the nuts he was gathering that day would end up in a crock of beechnut butter. Instead, he would lovingly plant each seed in the black earth among the crumbling stumps of its ancestors. Though he would never live to see his trees reach maturity, it was just possible that his children or grandchildren might.

Arriving home, Rolin pondered where to store the nuts. Not in the cellar; the mice would eat them. Not outside; the squirrels would find them. The kitchen? Too hot. Then he remembered the wooden box. Dragging it from under his bed, he set it on the kitchen table. With a touch of his fingers, the top sprang open.

After removing the spasel, he was about to dump out the musty, dried flowers underneath when something brown and shiny nesting among them caught his eye. It was a seed, similar to a beech's in color and shape but longer and flatter. He decided it must be a Lucambrian beechnut.

Rolin dropped the spasel back in the box and shoved it under his bed. Then he hurried outside to plant the beechnut. Up the trail beside the creek he hiked, the crisp, yellowed cottonwood leaves crackling underfoot. But where would a Lucambrian beech like to grow? He saw places that were too dry or too wet or over-grown with brambles or too close to other trees.

Then he came upon a grassy opening on the creek bank. In the sheltering shade of some old alders, it was the perfect place for a beech tree to begin life. Rolin poked the nut into the soft earth, marking the spot with a circle of smooth river rocks. Then he returned home to count his other beechnuts.

Later that afternoon, Gannon went into town to buy a new wagon wheel and supplies for the winter. "I'll be home late," he told Rolin as he hitched Nan to the wagon. "I promised Glenna I'd stop by on my way back."

"Watch out for batwolves!" Rolin called as the wagon jolted down the narrow, rutted road. He couldn't help worrying about his father traveling after dark, with hungry yegs possibly on the prowl. There was no telling what old Nan might do at the sight of one of the creatures. Not that there'd been any trouble with batwolves of late; perhaps the bloody losses they'd suffered in Farmer Greyson's field really had frightened them away for good.

At eventide, Rolin enjoyed a quiet supper by the kitchen window. Outside, squirrels and chipmunks scampered from tree to tree in the early autumn twilight, filling their cheeks with nuts for their winter larders. With every leap, the little animals shook loose showers of red and yellow leaves.

Leaves! Rolin lit the oil lamp and set it in his bedroom window before pulling out the old box and removing the spasel. If the leaves were falling in Liriassa, the sap ball might give him a glimpse of his friends walking about beneath the trees.

After warming the ball, Rolin realized he'd forgotten the time difference between the two worlds. Night had already fallen in Lucambra. Disappointed, he laid the spasel on his bed, closed the box, then settled down for a nap. Soon, he dozed off.

He awoke with a start. He'd heard a sound, a soft scratching at the door. The hairs prickled on the back of his neck. Rolin crept into the kitchen and was taking down his father's cudgel, when—*boom!*—the door flew open. A tall, bearded figure stood in the doorway, leaning on a staff.

"Well, aren't you going to invite me in?"

It was Bembor.

CHAPTER 9

THE QUEEN'S MESSAGE

Quite by accident, Rolin had signaled Bembor by setting the lamp in the window. Wide awake now, he scurried around the cabin, fetching his guest tea with buttered bread and honeycomb. While Bembor ate, Rolin told him about the batwolf raid on Farmer Greyson's sheep.

"This is grave news, indeed," remarked Bembor, brushing crumbs from his beard. "I had hoped Felgor would overlook your world a while longer."

"But we haven't seen a batwolf since!"

"That was just a sortie, not an actual invasion. Felgor's not forgotten you, nor will killing a few of his yeggorin scouts discourage him. Once Thalmos lowers its defenses, he'll fall upon your peaceful towns like a whirlwind."

"As for you," Bembor continued, gazing solemnly at Rolin, "beware the batwolves! They never forget a yeg slayer and will not rest until they have avenged themselves. Henceforth, avoid the meads and meadows, for if the beasts find you beneath the open sky, you will not escape their wrath!"

"Can't you stop them from coming back?" Rolin squeaked, wishing his father had burned or buried the yeg's head, instead of nailing it to a post.

"Stop them?" Bembor snorted. "We've tried for years. The cursed things breed like flies. Destroy a hundred or a thousand today and tomorrow they'll still blacken the skies."

"Why can't we cut down their torsil and burn the stump, so it won't resprout?" Rolin asked. "That would keep them out, wouldn't it?"

Bembor shook his head. "Even if we found the right one, the moment we put an ax to it, the yegs would swarm into Thalmos like red ants."

"What about your blowpipe? You could kill a lot of them with that."

With a quizzical look, Bembor gestured at his staff. "Go ahead, pick it up."

Rolin lifted the rod, which felt too heavy to be hollow. The ends were solid. "This isn't a blowpipe," he said. "What's it for?"

Bembor chuckled. "Not just for me to lean on! A Rowonah staff will turn any yeg or gork it touches to stone." Rolin dropped it. So the yeg statue he'd seen in the forest wasn't a statue after all. It had once been a real, live yeg!

"Oh, it won't hurt you," Bembor reassured him, picking up the stick.

"Where did you get it?" Rolin asked.

"This staff was my father's and his father's before him. Generations of staff-bearers have wielded it in battle. It first belonged to King Elgathel, who was once seeking a passage through the Mountains of the Moon when he was startled by a white-robed old man standing beside a quiet, green pool."

"Gaelathane!" Rolin exclaimed.

"The same. The stranger held seven stout staves in one hand and a birch-bark scroll in the other. 'These staffs are from the Tree of Life,' He said. 'They are for your protection and will never wither, so long as the Tree lives. One is for you. Entrust the others to faithful men whose hearts are pure. On this scroll are written the eternal words of My Prophecy; heed them well!'"

"Where are Elgathel's other staves?" Rolin asked.

Bembor leaned his staff against Rolin's bedroom door. "Only six remain, including my own, each belonging to a different clan leader. The seventh was lost when—"

A crash from Rolin's room interrupted Bembor, who leapt up from the table and seized his staff. Rolin snatched his father's club from the wall. Hearing no further sounds, the two burst through the door. The bedroom was empty.

Then Rolin noticed something was out of place. "That's odd; I left this on the bed," he said, picking up his box from the floor. "I hope it's not broken!"

Bembor gripped his arm. "Where did you get that?"

Red faced, Rolin explained how he had found the box in the cellar, with the pendant hidden inside. "I'm sorry I didn't tell you about it before. At first, I didn't think to mention it, and later, I was afraid your scouts would accuse me of stealing it. I didn't want to lose the pendant and the box, too."

Bembor examined the box. "This is of Lucambrian make," he said, "and very old. Our people have not crafted such works in many a year. See the large tree in the center? That's Waganupa, and the smaller ones surrounding it are amenthils. This box may even be carved from the wood of the Tree itself."

"How can you tell?"

Without answering, Bembor brought the box into the kitchen and placed it on the table. "Here, point this at it," he said, handing Rolin his staff. To Rolin's astonishment, the box inched toward him. He dropped the staff again.

"What made it move?" he asked, warily eyeing the box.

Bembor sat down at the table, cradling Rolin's box in his hands. "The Tree attracts to itself all things Gaelathane has created, especially its own wood. Your box fell off the bed and moved across the table, because—like my staff—it's made of Waganupa's wood. As Gaelathane's creations, we Lucambrians also yearn to return to Luralin to be reunited with the Tree."

"Does that mean my box can turn yegs to stone?"

Bembor frowned. "If I were you, I wouldn't go out of my way to find out! Now then, let's have a look inside this box of yours."

"There's nothing left but—" Rolin began, when he saw Bembor's determined look. He pressed the catch and the lid flew open. "You see? Just some old, dried-up flowers. I was going to throw them out."

"Throw them out!" cried Bembor, jumping to his feet. "Glory be to Gaelathane you didn't! These are dried amenthil blooms—*mellathel*, we call them—or I'm not a staff-bearer."

"But what use are they now? They've no color or scent."

Bembor sifted through the dried blossoms. "True, but these may well be *fallinga* mellathel—'message flowers.'"

"Message flowers? I didn't find any messages, just the flowers."

"That's because the flowers are the message," Bembor explained. "In long-ago Lucambra, if I wanted to send you a word in private, I'd hold a handful of freshly-picked amenthil blossoms to my forehead, then say what I wished you to hear. After breathing on the flowers, I'd then seal them in a box or pouch."

"How would I read the message?"

"I'll show you," replied Bembor. "Bring me a bowl of water, if you please—and hurry! Your father mustn't find me here."

Rolin ran outside with a bowl and dipped it in the stream. When he returned, Bembor instructed him to set it on the table.

"Now we shall see whether any virtue remains in these mellathel," muttered the Lucambrian. "Pour them into the water." With a puzzled glance at his friend, Rolin shook the flowers into the bowl, where they spread out, floating lightly on the water's surface. Then they gradually revived, their shriveled petals uncurling and flushing a deep pink. A sweet, refreshing fragrance filled the room, like mingled basswood blooms and hyacinths.

"Quickly now, breathe deeply of their scent!" Bembor urged him. Rolin leaned over the bowl, his nose right among the flowers and inhaled.

With the first breath, a sharp pain pierced his forehead. With the second, a gray mist swirled before his eyes, and with the third, Bembor, the bowl and the table disappeared. Instead, Rolin was looking into a spacious room with curving walls hung with colorful tapestries. From an arched window, a shaft of sunlight fell upon

a woman clad in a shimmering green gown, a circlet of white flowers on her head. She was weeping, one hand clutched at her brow. On the floor beside her lay a box much like Rolin's.

"Hail, heir of Elgathel!" her clear voice rang out. "I am Winona, Queen of Lucambra and bride of Elgathel. The king lies dead beside me, slain in battle." She motioned to a low stone platform whereon lay the body of a man, a shield across his chest.

"I have mourned him many days alone, for the People of the Tree are scattered, and the amenthils are burned. Only these few flowers of the king's life tree have survived, through which I now speak to you. Even the winged lions are gone. Having deserted Elgathel in the hour of his greatest need, those faithless creatures are sworn to return at the beckoning of the king's bell, to aid him who bears the tokens I place within this box.

"My lord the king knew it not, but I carry his child, whom I will take now to the land of the tree cutters. You who were born to fulfill the Prophecy, ring the bell and rid our land of the curse! May Gaelathane speed your journeys and bless your labors, and may your life tree ever thrive. Farewell, heir of Elgathel!" Winona bowed her head and faded into a sea of shadows.

"Rolin! Wake up!" Rolin opened his tear-blurred eyes. He was slumped face down on the table, and someone was shaking him. He took a couple of deep breaths to clear his head.

Bembor shook him again. "What happened? What did you see?"

"I saw the Queen, Winona," Rolin said, speaking with difficulty, "and the dead king beside her. She was tall, with eyes as green as the grass, and her hair fell across her shoulders." After relating the queen's message, Rolin was astounded to see tears streaming down Bembor's bearded cheeks.

"Thanks be to Gaelathane that I have lived to see your coming!" cried the old man, dropping to his knees. "Blessed are you, Rolin, heir of Elgathel, Scion of Tree Lords and King of Lucambra! Blessed be your hands, through which Gaelathane shall save us from our enemies, by the power of the One Tree!"

"Why are you kneeling before me like this?" Rolin protested. "I am a beekeeper and the son of a beekeeper, not a king!"

Smiling through his tears, Bembor shook his head. "You may not feel like a king, but king you are and king you shall be! Only Elgathel's heir could have seen and heard the queen. Had an impostor tried to revive these flowers, they would not have released their scent. See for yourself: Once the fallinga mellathel have served their purpose, they are spent." Sure enough, all that remained of the buoyant blossoms was a pink milkiness in the water.

"Then what are the *king's bell* and the *winged lions*?"

"Once, while Elgathel was exploring the coastline for a spot to build an outpost, he came upon three yegs attacking a creature with the legs, trunk and tail of a lion and the head and wings of an eagle. The beast was putting up a fierce fight, but the yegs had the advantage of numbers. With his bow and a handful of arrows, Elgathel shot all three yegs. Afterwards, he bound up the animal's wounds and gave it water to drink from his flask."

"What was it?"

"A *sorc*, or winged lion. Thalmosians would call it a *griffin*. They're pictured on your box."

Rolin stared at the box. "I didn't think such animals existed!"

"They do in our world, though in yours they may have died out. Anyway, Elgathel had saved Threeclaws, king of all the sorca. In gratitude, the griffin king swore lifelong allegiance to him."

"But how could Elgathel understand the sorc, without the amenthils?"

"I'll get to that later. This alliance with the sorca enabled Elgathel to drive Felgor's forces out of a broad swath of territory, ranging from the Willowahs in the south to the foothills of Mt. Golgunthor in the north, and west to the Sea of El-marin. Young scouts learned to ride griffinback and to engage the enemy in the air. They were known as sorc riders, or *sorcasorosa*."

"Sorosa!" exclaimed Rolin. "Isn't that what you call—?"

"The medallions? Aye. Using seven different gems, Elgathel fashioned a soros for himself and six of his bravest griffin riders, whom he titled *sorc masters*. The fiercest yeg would flee before a sorc master and his mount.

"To commemorate his friendship with the sorca, Elgathel built the fortress Hallowfast on the spot where he had rescued Threeclaws. Later, the king hung a silver bell in the top, ringing it whenever he wished to call the griffins. From what the queen has told you, Elgathel's heir must return to the Hallowfast to summon the sorca once more, though to what end I cannot tell."

"How did Elgathel die? The queen said it was in battle."

"It was—a battle he needn't have lost. After the passage of years, Elgathel grew careless, neglecting to station sentinels in the Hallowfast. Then on a fateful May morning, a boiling black cloud formed over the dragon's mountain, growing until it nearly blotted out the sun's light. 'The yegs are coming! The yegs are coming!' went up the cry, but it was too late. The yeg horde descended on us like a swarm of locusts, overwhelming our defenses.

"Next, flames and smoke seared the sky as the dragon scorched everything in his path to cinders, scattering the sorc masters like autumn leaves on the wind. Many griffins and their valiant riders perished that day, though most of the sorca fled riderless before the serpent's wrath.

"Elgathel mustered a few men, but Gorgorunth drove them into the sea. Armed only with sword and staff, Elgathel attacked the beast alone. As he raised the staff, the dragon burned his right hand to ash. Wielding his sword with the left, Elgathel pressed on, sorely wounding the beast on its leg. For all his courage, he suffered the swift death of dragon fire. No man before or since has dared challenge the black serpent to single combat."

"So that's what melted my soros," said Rolin. "What happened to the griffins?"

"Those that survived the battle returned to their homes in the snowy peaks of the Willowah mountains. We've never seen them since. It's probably just as well; lacking the amenthils, we cannot talk with the beasts."

"But Winona said the king's sythan-ar was an amenthil."

"So it was. One day, as the king stood by the shore, an albatross dropped a seed at his feet, which he planted beside the Hallowfast. It grew into a graceful amenthil, singing so sweetly that Elgathel made it his sythan-ar. Other trees sprang from its seeds, restoring our long-lost ability to converse with other living things. Yet, all Lucambra mourned, for the king had neither wife nor heir. He loved his life tree above all else, save Gaelathane Himself.

"Then on a summer's eve, a woman of extraordinary beauty appeared outside the Hallowfast. Her voice was like that of Elgathel's sythan-ar, and she sang of her love for the king. The two were wed soon after. Whether she was the spirit of the amenthil none could say, but the tree never sang afterwards."

"And that is the woman who spoke to me?" asked Rolin.

"The same. From your description, Winona must have been staying in the tower, preparing to take refuge in Thalmos, the land of the tree cutters. Here she bore a child, probably your mother."

"But that would make the queen my grandmother! How can that be, if all this took place so long ago?"

Bembor smiled. "Our people often live to a great age. Your mother was likely much older than your father."

"My grandmother's name was Adelka, not Winona," Rolin argued. "I think you've mistaken me for someone else."

Bembor's smile broadened. "In your tongue, Adelka means 'lonely flower,' while in the language of Lucambra, Winona means 'flower-which-is-alone.'"

Rolin's mouth dropped open. Through the message flowers, he'd just seen his grandmother and heard her voice before his mother's birth!

"If King Elgathel and Queen Adelka, er, *Winona* were my grandparents, then I must be half-Lucambrian," he reasoned.

"Precisely. That also makes you the 'torsil tree of tender years,' one belonging to both our worlds, whose 'stock' is of Elgathel."

"It's all very well to say I'm Elgathel's heir, but who will believe you without more proof? A bowl of soggy flowers won't convince your council."

"True, but didn't the queen say something about 'tokens'?"

"She said the sorca are supposed to 'aid him who bears the tokens I place within this box.' Did she mean the pendant?"

"Yes—that reminds me." Bembor lifted the soros on its silver chain from his neck and placed it around Rolin's. "This rightfully belongs to you, despite the council's decree. Guard it well!"

"Where are the other tokens?" Rolin asked, fingering the pendant's gem.

Bembor's beetling eyebrows rose. "Did you find anything else in the box?"

"No," Rolin replied, forgetting the odd-looking beechnut he had planted.

"Surely the queen was not referring to the message flowers, knowing they would perish in the using. Either someone has removed the other objects or they're still inside." Bembor hefted the box with one hand. "It does feel rather heavy, and this chamber doesn't take up the whole box."

Yet, after shaking, poking and prying, Rolin and Bembor couldn't find another compartment. Only when they upended the box did its weight shift slightly. Quite by accident, Rolin pressed down on two opposing corners of the lid at the same time, and a side panel popped open. Fine sand dribbled out.

"Why would anyone fill a box with sand?" he said.

"To keep something inside from rattling, I should think," replied Bembor, dumping the chamber's contents onto the table. Sifting through the sandpile, Rolin discovered a flat, shiny metal shard, pointed at one end.

"This looks like a knife blade with the handle broken off," he observed, holding it up to the lantern light.

"More likely a lance tip," said Bembor. "It's too heavy for a knife blade. What's this?" Pawing through the sand, Bembor had uncovered a tapering, silvery club, ball-shaped at the big end and pierced by a hole at the other.

"Now isn't this peculiar." Bembor turned the metal piece over in his gnarled hands. "A silver cudgel or a crude hammer?"

"Maybe it's a pestle for grinding flour," suggested Rolin, "and the hole's for hanging it on the wall." Even so, how would a broken spearhead and a pestle prove his lineage? Perhaps the queen had intended them for another purpose. He dropped the club back in the box and snapped the panel shut. The broken blade went into his pocket. It might come in handy for prying open beehives.

Bembor sighed. "This box has posed more mysteries than it has solved. I'd advise you to keep it well hidden. The day may come when you'll have need of it. In the meantime, I really must be leaving, before your father returns."

"Leave? Without me? Aren't we going to the Hallowfast?"

"We'd have to find it first," said Bembor wryly. "Nobody's been there in years, and it's surrounded now by ashtags. Blazing a trail through them would take axes forged of a stronger steel than any in your world or mine. Besides, it's autumn now, and you wouldn't want to spend all winter in Lucambra."

"All winter! What do you mean?"

"Why, the tree gates are closing, lad. Once they lose their leaves, the torsils sleep, shutting the passage between our worlds. 'When torsil limbs turn cold and bare, the trees won't take you anywhere,' as the rhyme goes. It's fortunate I came tonight; in a few days, I couldn't have entered Thalmos."

"Then you can't use the tara-torsils to get in and out of Liriassa, either."

"Tara-torsils! Who told you about them?"

"Why, I . . . that is, I mean—" Rolin stammered.

"So, my grandchildren have been telling tales again, have they? I must watch my words around those two. As for the tara-torsils, you are correct. After leaf fall, we cannot enter or leave the valley through them."

"Must I wait until spring to see you again?"

"So it would seem," said Bembor. "Of course, you should have no trouble from Felgor and his yegs until then, either. Just in case you do, I brought this for you." He took out a curved wooden horn and handed it to Rolin, who was putting its silver mouthpiece to his lips when Bembor snatched it away.

"Do not blow this horn unless your need is urgent!" he warned.

"Why? What does it do?"

"It's a torsil horn. Carved from torsil wood, it will sound in both our worlds. If you blow it, one of our clansmen will come to your aid, as long as a single green leaf trembles on a torsil's twig."

Rolin hung the leather strap around his neck and tucked the horn under his shirt with the pendant. "Thank you! I will carry this with me wherever I go."

Just then, Rolin heard the clatter of wagon wheels. "Father's home—you must leave quickly!" They rushed into Rolin's room and opened the window. "Some day, I hope you can meet my father," Rolin said wistfully.

"I'd be delighted," replied Bembor. "Just remember: 'When winter is long, your faith in spring must grow strong.' And get yourself a sythan-ar!" Then he pulled himself through the window and vanished soundlessly into the night.

Moments later, Rolin heard the creak of the door and his father's cheery voice. "I'm home, Rolin! What's all this sand on the table?"

CHAPTER 10

A LIFE TREE AT LAST

That winter was the longest in Rolin's memory. It was not that the snows piled high against the cabin walls and windows; heavy snowfalls were common in those parts. Rolin was chafing because torsil travel was impossible until the trees awoke from their winter's dormancy. Even his spasel grew sluggish, yielding murky images only after much hand warming. In the meantime, he could tell no one of his wonderful discoveries.

However, the cold weather could not dampen his determination to find a proper sythan-ar to replace the birch in the bee yard. Once a day, he trudged through the snow to the beaver dam, where he looked for pussy willows blooming at the water's edge. Finding none, he would repeat Bembor's words to himself, "When winter is long, your faith in spring must grow strong."

Long or short, all winters end at last. The icicles hanging from the cabin's eaves began dripping, finally dropping off with a tinkle and a crash. Hardy snowdrops burst through the thinning blanket of snow and ice, unfurling their delicate, ivory-white flowers. April gave way to May and May to June, with little more to mark the arrival of summer than a few bee swarmings.

One warm afternoon, Rolin could bear the boredom no longer. He'd had enough of scraping bee glue from beehives and knew the torsils must be in leaf. Surely it couldn't hurt to climb one or two! He packed a lunch of bread and honeycomb, then started up the path. Cottonwood catkins littered the rain-damp trail like fat, purple-and-yellow caterpillars, while the creek gurgled playfully beside him like a dog on a stroll with its master.

After a half-hour's hiking, he grew sleepy and turned aside to rest on some grass along the creek bank. Leaning against an alder's curving trunk, lulled by the soothing sound of splashing water, he fell fast asleep.

A sweet scent filled his nostrils. Then he was back in the cabin with Bembor, pouring message flowers into the bowl of water. His head throbbed as an ocean of voices swelled in a symphony of praise: "Blessed be the Tree and He who made all things and reigns as King of kings!"

He awoke with a start, his head spinning. A distant babbling still hummed in his ears, and his face was wet with tears. He had never seen the leaves such a lustrous, deep green or the sky such a brilliant blue. "How wonderful the life of a tree must be," he mused and sang:

If I were a tree, what would I be?

An oak, an ash or a cottonwood?
Or a fragrant cedar—if I could!
A birch or a beech or a tree-of-heaven?
Or maybe I'd try to be all seven!

Would I bear nuts or colorful berries?
Apples or acorns or sour cherries?
Would I have leaves that drop to the ground
Or needles of green that cling year-round?

Would I be stout, my limbs reaching out,
With mosses and ferns all covered about?
Or would I be slender and straight as a spear,
O'ertopping the other trees, both far and near?

And where would I stand—in some foreign land?

Or close to my home, in moist, earthy loam,
With plenty of room for roots to roam?
Or high on a hill, in fog all a-swirl,
Dripping and silent, surveying the world?

And what would I see, if I were a tree?

Green leaves around me (in summer, at least!)
And every imaginable bug, bird and beast;
Chickadees building their nests in my hair;
Squirrels playing "tag" with hardly a care;

Hillside or streamside, a breathtaking view;
Sunset and sunrise, of marvelous hue;
Sunlight and moonlight and star-sprinkled sky;
All of these wonders would greet my eye!
(But would I, as a tree, have eyes?)

And if I could hear . . .

Chirping of birds and humming of bees;
Patter of raindrops on whispering leaves;
Woodpeckers drumming and chipmunks chattering;
Wind-tossed limbs all set a-clattering;

Howl of the wolf and croak of the frog;
Cry of the marsh owl down in the bog;
Screech of the hawk and chirk of the cricket;
Growl of the grizzly deep in the thicket;

Squeak of the mouse and rustle of snake;
Quacking and splashing of ducks on the lake;
Crack of the lightning and grumble of thunder;
Rumble of rock that's split asunder.

But when summer had passed . . .

Autumn's crisp cold, with brushes so bold,
Would burnish my leaves yellow, brown, red and gold.

In these colors of fire, I would be attired,
Till in frost's frigid fingers their glory expired.

Then winter would strip my branches all bare,
Stalking the woods with fierce, biting air;
Flinging my leaves to the snow-slanting sky,
Exposing my secrets to passersby.

When twig-snapping chill creeps o'er every hill,
Silencing birdsong and trickling rill,
Then is the time when all trees cry:
'Spring! O spring! When will you arrive?'

So spring would creep in, with scarcely a sound,
Wakening willows, warming the ground,
Greening the poplars and flowering plums,
Till frogs in a chorus croak, 'Spring has come!'

Then I would awake with a terrible thirst,
Start drinking in sap, till every bud burst;
My flowers and leaves would unfurl bright and new,
Beginning their lives all spangled with dew . . .

Oh, what a wonderful life it would be,
Just to spend all my days—as a tree!

"Hmph! Just listen to how he prattles on!" a slow, deep voice boomed from behind Rolin. He whirled around. Had Bembor come at last?

"It's enough to make your roots turn up at the ends, isn't it?" chimed in another, higher voice. Rolin looked this way and that but saw no one in the surrounding woods. The cobbler's boys must be spying on him again. Stuffing some river rocks in his pockets, he vowed to teach them a lesson.

"'Oh, what a wonderful life it would be, just to spend all my days as a tree!'" mocked the first voice. "What rot! This runt of a two-legs doesn't know a twig about trees. If he traded places with us for awhile, I'll wager my cones he'd sing a different tune!"

"Aye," agreed the second voice. "He thinks it's a great lark climbing trees, bruising us with his heavy boots and lying in our shade for hours; but it's no picnic for us! Here we are, stuck in the same place, year after year, with the same scenery and no chance to see what's on the other side of the river."

"Now, if we were birds, wouldn't that be the life?" sighed the first voice. "We could fly wherever we wanted, whenever we wanted and never have to worry about a two-legs coming along to make kindling of us. When the weather turned cold, we'd just fly south for the winter."

Rolin stared up at the alder he'd been leaning against. "Why, you can talk!"

"Of course we can talk," rumbled the tree. "You're just the first two-legs to understand us. You are a two-legs, aren't you?"

"It must be," said the other alder. "It moves—has two legs— two branches—a big knothole in the front of its head—not enough hair for a bear—it's a two-legs, all right."

"Why don't you leave the poor thing alone?" said a third tree. "Can't you see it just woke up?" Rolin discovered the voice belonged to a shapely sapling growing along the creek. A circle of stones ringed its trunk, while delicate pink blossoms crowded its slender branches. So the beechnut he'd planted hadn't been a beechnut at all!

"I am Rosewand the amenthil," said the tree. "What is your name?"

"Rolin son of Gannon." Breathing in Rosewand's sweet perfume, he heard another chorus of voices sweep through the forest like a mighty wind:

"Praise to the Spirit, Who gives life to all creatures!" sang the birds.

"Praise to Him Who created all things!" sang the animals.

"Praise to the Tree that lives forever!" sang the trees. And the amenthil joined in, with a voice like the ringing of a crystal bell. Rolin wept for joy.

"How did I come to this place?" Rosewand asked.

"I planted you here," whispered Rolin.

"May the blessings of the One Tree be upon you and your sythan-ar."

Rolin hung his head. "I have no sythan-ar."

"Then I shall be yours."

"You? But how—?"

"Did you not place me here? Have you not encircled me with these stones? I am your life tree and always will be, so long as you shall live."

"Thank you, Rosewand," said Rolin, brushing his hand across the amenthil's bright leaves. At his touch, the tree's branches trembled.

"Are there others of my kind in this land?"

"You are the last," said Rolin sadly, "in this world or any other."

"How then may I favor others with my fragrance? Soon, my flowers will wither and fall and their scent will fade. I must gladden the hearts of all who love trees and the Tree Maker."

"And so you shall." Rolin put the torsil horn to his lips and blew on it three long, loud blasts.

CHAPTER 11

FIRE IN THE VALLEY

"Where could they be?" Rolin moaned. He was sitting on the stoop outside his home, head in hands, wondering what had become of Bembor and his clansmen. He'd waited for hours beside Rosewand, but no one had come at the summons of his horn. Now it was nightfall, and still there was no sign of green eyes, green cloaks or even the greenish-yellow glow of moonwood.

"Come eat your supper!" Gannon called out the door. Rolin reluctantly obeyed. He wasn't hungry; not even his father's savory mutton stew appealed to him. He listlessly picked at his food, then went to bed early.

After tossing and turning, Rolin got down on the floor and pulled out his box. Perhaps the sap ball held some clues as to Bembor's whereabouts. He wished he could place his lighted lamp in the window but feared the old Lucambrian would burst through the front door again without knocking.

Warming the spasel brought forth a bright glow that silently exploded into blossoming orange balls. A monstrous, black shadow wheeled in and out of the flames, spouting torrents of fire. Was this a trick of the spasel, or was Liriassa ablaze? Too troubled to look further into the sap ball, he slept.

Later that night, Rolin awoke to a tapping at his window. He snapped into wakefulness. Bembor! He flung open the window and someone crawled through, landing lightly inside the room. It was Scanlon, his face streaked with soot and sweat. The smell of smoke was on him.

"We heard your horn but couldn't come right away. There's been trouble."

"What kind of trouble?" Rolin asked. "What's happened to you?"

"Felgor and the dragon found our valley."

"How dreadful!" exclaimed Rolin. He should have known, from the fire he'd seen in his spasel. "What about your people? Did everyone get out safely?"

"I think so. Everyone who could climb a tara-torsil, anyway."

"Scanlon! Hurry up!" came a hoarse whisper through the window.

"Bembor and Father are here, with some other clansmen," Scanlon explained.

"Just let me get dressed, and I'll be ready," Rolin told him, throwing on his tunic and trousers. Then he followed Scanlon out the window.

He had no sooner dropped to the ground than something jabbed him in the side. "Hold on now; let's have a look at you," said an unfamiliar voice. Rolin slowly turned around, coming face to face with a stocky, silver-haired Lucambrian poking him with his staff. "So this is the lad all the fuss was about. He looks like any other Thalmosian urchin."

"He's neither an urchin nor a Thalmosian, Marlon. He's a *prince*." Bembor stepped out of the shadows, followed by Emmer, Opio, Gemmio, Sigarth and Skoglund, bows and blowpipes at the ready. Battle strain showed in every face.

"Hullo, Rolin," said Opio with a thin-lipped smile.

"You've grown since we last met," grinned Gemmio. "Lucambra must have agreed with you."

"Not the soros thief again!" groaned Sigarth. "I thought we were rid of him for good."

"Not by a bowshot, you aren't," Bembor retorted. "Why did you call us?" he asked Rolin.

"I . . . I can't explain," replied Rolin in a fluster, wishing he hadn't blown the horn. "I'll have to show you." Bembor's grim look frightened him.

"I hope it's not just a new mushroom patch. By the way, this is my brother, Marlon." Bembor nodded toward the silver-haired scout, who stiffly bowed.

"What are we waiting for?" Sigarth demanded. "If the boy's not in any danger, we'd best return to the ice caverns before we're missed."

"Ice caverns?" Rolin asked.

"Some caves and tunnels in the glaciers above Liriassa," Bembor said, waving behind him as if he were still in Lucambra. "Most of our people are hiding there. It's the one place where they'll be safe from the dragon."

Skoglund fidgeted. "Is the Thalmosian staying here or coming with us?"

"He's not coming with us," replied Bembor, giving Rolin an I-hope-you-know-what-you're-doing look. "We're going with him. Lead on, lad!"

Rolin took the scouts up the creek path, which he'd traveled so often in moonlight and starlight that his feet found their own way. "Oh, I hope she's still there!" he said aloud, sniffing the air.

"You hope who is where?" growled Marlon.

Rolin didn't answer. He was too busy imagining what might have befallen the amenthil. Had a hungry deer nibbled off its branches or a clumsy bear stepped on it? Then Rosewand spoke to him from afar.

"Is that you, Rolin son of Gannon?"

"Yes, and I've brought some friends with me."

"Who's he talking to?" asked Opio, staring about. "I don't see anyone."

"Here we are," Rolin announced, stopping beside the circle of stones.

"There's nothing here but trees," Gemmio grumbled.

"Not just trees—*the* tree," said Rolin, proudly pointing to the amenthil.

"He brought us all the way up here to show us this?" exclaimed Emmer.

"Can it be? Can it really be?" Bembor whispered, bending over the sapling. "Don't you see?" he said to the others. "Don't you remember the old paintings? Don't you—" He broke off mid-sentence as he caught the flower scent. Awe and wonderment on his face, he caressed the amenthil's leaves.

"What is your name, friend of Rolin?" asked Rosewand in her silvery voice.

"I am Bembor son of Brenthor son of Thannor."

"May you be blessed of the Tree. My name is Rosewand, Rolin's sythan-ar."

"We know who you are, Brother," Marlon said dryly. "Why are you talking to that tree?"

"It is an amenthil!" cried Bembor. "The tree that was lost is found! Glory to Gaelathane!"

Naturally, the other Lucambrians thought Bembor had taken leave of his senses. Then, as the amenthil's sweet fragrance wafted among them, they understood. Tears flowed freely as each man knelt in turn before Rosewand to touch her, to breathe deeply of her blossoms, to speak with her.

Next, the scouts all wanted to know how an amenthil had ended up on a Thalmosian creek bank. After Rolin's explanation, there was a stunned silence.

"Then the soros really was his after all," gulped Sigarth.

"So were the amenthil flowers that came with it," added Bembor.

"Were they *fallinga* mellathel flowers?" Marlon asked. Bembor nodded, then went on to relate Winona's message.

"Do you mean this potato eater is to be our king?" Sigarth gasped.

"Yes, this *Lucambrian* is to be king and more, if I read the Prophecy aright," Bembor replied. "Even now he is fulfilling it by taking this amenthil as his sythan-ar. And there's more." Then Bembor recounted Rolin's part in foiling the yeg attack.

"Now there's a true Lucambrian!" exclaimed Skoglund. The others grinned approvingly, slapping Rolin on the back and knocking the wind out him.

After that, the scouts asked to bring their friends and families to meet Rosewand. Bembor shook his head. "We can't risk leading the enemy to our torsils—or to the amenthil. In fact, we should post guards to protect Rolin's life tree." That task fell to the brothers Sigarth and Skoglund, who knew the woods above Beechtown better than the other Lucambrians and had even planted their sythan-ars there.

"Where will the rest of you go now?" asked Rolin.

Gemmio shrugged. "Back to the ice caves, I suppose."

"Then we'll do what we've always done," Opio said with a bleak look. "Since we can't live in Liriassa, we'll find another place to hide, until Felgor ferrets us out again and destroys our homes and life trees. We have a saying, 'Yegs today, gorku tomorrow; for those who stay, there shall be sorrow.'"

"Why don't you move to Thalmos?" Rolin suggested. "You'd be safe here."

Opio's lip curled. "We will never leave our homeland!"

"Besides," Bembor said, "Felgor would still smell us out, since he's already discovered a way into Thalmos."

Rolin wasn't ready to admit defeat. "Could the Prophecy help?"

"The Prophecy doesn't tell us where to live," said Bembor. "The last two verses say only that we're to 'seek the silver tree, the sentinel beside the sea.'"

"Do trees of silver really grow in Lucambra?" asked Rolin. How splendid that would be; a single silver leaf could buy his father a brand new wagon!

Scanlon and the scouts snickered. "No, lad," Bembor replied. "We've searched every inch of the shoreline. If such trees ever grew near the El-marin, the ashtags have no doubt smothered them."

"What if the tree were 'silver' only at night?" Rolin asked. Then he described the moonlit torsil and the dark tower he'd found on the other side.

"The Tower of the Tree!" Marlon exclaimed.

"Tower of the Tree?" repeated Rolin. "What's that?"

"Another name for the Hallowfast," Emmer explained.

"And the torsil you found may be the only way to get there!" said Bembor. "It's likely the very one the queen climbed when she left Lucambra. Evidently, your 'silver tree' shines in Thalmos with the light of Lucambra's moon. All this time, we were looking in the wrong world for the wrong sort of tree!"

"Can we leave for the Hallowfast tomorrow?" asked Rolin eagerly.

An impish light shone in Bembor's green eyes. "Not tomorrow—tonight!"

"Tonight!?" chorused the dismayed scouts.

"And desert our families, just when they need us the most?" Marlon cried. "They'll starve in those rat holes, if they don't freeze to death first!"

"They won't starve or freeze," Bembor calmly replied. "We've laid away enough food and blankets in the caves to last at least a year." He chuckled softly. "Don't you see? Felgor will expect us to flee northward, farther from his mountain fortress. Instead, we'll go south to the Black Lands, where his rule is unchallenged. We shall come knocking on the door of the Hallowfast."

"Of course!" said Opio, gleefully smacking his palm. "While Felgor is busy burning Liriassa, we'll retake the Tower."

"Retake it?" cried Sigarth. "Whatever for? If Felgor destroys Rolin's torsil gate, you'd be trapped in the Hallowfast forever! Even if you could maintain a garrison there, what are a hundred Lucambrians against the sorcerer's legions? He'd pluck you from his side like a splinter and cast you into Gundul's fires. I beg of you, Bembor, do not set foot in that place!"

"Peace, Sigarth," snapped Bembor. "We're not occupying the Hallowfast."

"Then why go there at all?"

Bembor shot Sigarth a withering glance. "To obey the Prophecy—and the queen! Winona herself commanded Elgathel's heir to return to the Tower, so to the Tower he shall go." There was no further argument from the scouts.

Bembor removed his soros. "Marlon, as my brother, you will take my place as leader of the oak clan. You may keep this as a token of my authority."

Accepting the soros, Marlon asked, "What shall I tell the people? You don't want them thinking you've turned renegade."

"Say only that we've gone in search of Elgathel's sword. They'll chew on that twig for a while." Bembor nodded at Emmer, Gemmio and Opio. "You three will go with Rolin and me to the Hallowfast."

"What about me?" Scanlon demanded. "I want to go, too!" He stood with arms defiantly akimbo. Emmer and Bembor looked at him, then at each other.

"If we don't let him come, he'll try to tag along anyway," said Bembor. "That could be dangerous, for us and for him."

"He has a knack for turning up where he's not invited," Emmer admitted.

Rolin cast the deciding vote. "If Scanlon doesn't go, then I won't either."

"Very well," Bembor sighed. "Scanlon shall join us. Of course, you'll both have to do your share of the work! You can start by going back to the cabin to pack some provisions for the journey. Don't forget to bring the box and plenty of sacks, too. We'll wait for you here."

By then, it was nearly dawn. Rolin and Scanlon dashed down the trail, hoping to reach the cabin before Gannon awoke. An impudent jay flew along behind them, screeching, "What's the hurry? What's the hurry? Afraid of a jay? Afraid of a jay?" Rolin reflected that there were times when understanding forest speech might be more annoying than useful.

The boys wriggled through Rolin's window and crept into the cellar to stuff honey bags with oatcakes, dried apples, raisins, cheeses and walnuts. Afterwards, they dragged the filled bags into the bedroom, where Rolin passed them through the window to Scanlon.

Next, Rolin gingerly handed out his box. Then he spied his knapsack and tossed it out, too, hearing a muffled "Ow!"

Realizing he might never see his father again, Rolin tiptoed into the kitchen to scrawl a note on a scrap of birch bark. "Father, Gone to visit friends in town. Will be back in a few days. Love, Rolin." Though he had few friends in Beechtown and had never spent the night there, it was the best he could do in a pinch. Gannon was still snoring when Rolin rejoined Scanlon outside.

While Scanlon packed the rucksack with the bags of provender, Rolin stole into his father's toolshed, where he took a heavy coil of rope from a peg on the wall. *Can't be climbing trees and towers without a rope,* he told himself, looping the coil over his shoulder. As he and Scanlon staggered back up the trail with the overloaded pack and their other bundles, squirrels, chipmunks and birds rudely heckled them.

"That one looks like a camel!" chortled a chubby squirrel.

"The other waddles like a plump turkey!" chittered a chipmunk.

"They're both as slow as tortoises!" sniggered a magpie. Rolin thought of some fitting retorts but held his tongue. Instead, he vowed to put out a little less food for the animals next winter. They were becoming too fat and sassy.

The sun's first sliver was sliding above the horizon when Rolin and Scanlon reached Rosewand, where the scouts divided up the bags. Then the six bade Marlon, Sigarth and Skoglund farewell and set out to find the silver tree.

"May the Tree guide you until we meet again, Rolin son of Gannon!" called the amenthil. "Do not tarry, for sweet are the fruits I will bear you!"

"Goodbye, Rosewand," Rolin called back. "May your leaves never wither and your roots never thirst!"

Rolin soon realized that finding the torsil wouldn't be as easy as he'd expected. The trees and other landmarks appeared much different in the light of day than they had on that moonless night.

"We've passed that fir snag twice before," Opio pointed out. "How do we know you're not lost or just playing with us?"

"Shush!" said Bembor. "If Rolin says there's a torsil growing in these woods, then it's here, or I'm not a staff-bearer."

After searching the thick forest, Rolin finally spotted his tattered honey bag hanging on a branch. As he and the others gathered around the torsil, Bembor eyed its gnarled trunk and lichen-covered limbs. "This is an ancient tree," he observed. "It's a wonder it has withstood so many winter storms."

"Indeed it is," croaked a dry, creaky voice. Startled, the six stared about, seeing no one. "I've been standing here over four hundred years with nobody to talk to except cranky old firs on this side and those wretched snake trees on the other. My, you all act as if you'd never heard a tree speak before. You've not come to chop me down, have you? I wouldn't care for that at all."

"We have no intention of cutting you down," Bembor replied.

"Forgive me," said the torsil, "I am forgetting my manners. My name is Lightleaf. Who are you, and what brings you to my part of the woods?"

Bembor introduced the little group, adding, "Rolin's climbed you before."

"Ah, yes, I do remember the young two-legs now. Very light he was and careful, too. Never broke a branch or tore a leaf coming or going. He seemed in a great hurry on the way back."

"I wanted to escape that horrible place on the other side," Rolin said, shivering at the memory.

"It was not always so," said Lightleaf sadly. "In my youth, fair were the trees of that land, and we never lacked for light and laughter. So many lads and lasses climbed me in those days that they wore my limbs smooth on top. Then the serpent demolished everything, burning most of my friends, good trees all. After that, the visitors stopped coming."

Bembor laid his hand on the torsil. "Do you remember the king and queen?"

"Indeed I do. Fine folk they were, strong but kind and gentle. They often came to talk with me. After the disaster, I was delighted to hear the queen's voice again. 'Lightleaf, dear friend,' she said, 'I must go to Thalmos now. I don't know how long I shall be away. Do not forget me or our people.' Then she was gone. That was the last I ever heard of her. Later, these ghastly black trees moved in. They'd like to crowd me out, but I won't let them."

"It is well that you have survived," said Bembor, "for Rolin, the queen's grandson, has need of your help this day."

"You don't say!" Lightleaf exclaimed. "What does the young tree lord require of me? I will do anything within my power to grant his request."

"We must pass into the queen's realm," Rolin said.

The tree quivered, though there was no wind. "Much evil awaits beyond my brittle branches. You would be wise to enter the queen's land another way."

"We would if it were possible, O Lightleaf," said Bembor, "but you are the only living torsil within sight of the Hallowfast, the object of our quest."

"Ugh! Foul things once dwelt there and may still."

"Nonetheless, Gaelathane's Prophecy and the queen require it."

Lightleaf sighed. "If it must be so, may the King of the Trees go with you."

"Thank you, noble torsil," Bembor replied. "I hope some day we may reward your faithfulness to the queen and to her heir."

"Your safe return will be reward enough for me," said Lightleaf. "Beware the black sap that burns like fire!" The morning sun lit Lightleaf with gold when Rolin took a last look back at Thalmos before climbing into the torsil.

CHAPTER 12

THE TOWER OF THE TREE

Phew! What a horrid place!" exclaimed Rolin, wrinkling his face in disgust. Wherever he looked, grotesque trees lifted their leafless limbs toward the gray sky, like petrified nests of writhing serpents. Beneath their contorted, coal-black branches hung a thick gloom. He gagged. "What is that stench?"

"That's the ashtags' corrosive acid," Emmer explained. "See how their limbs glisten with the oily stuff? Only one drop will raise red welts on the skin. Even if you don't touch them, the trees can bombard you with sticky seeds that will burn just as badly."

"There's the tower," said Scanlon, pointing at the stone shell jutting above the ashtags. Around it stood the bleached snags of long-dead amenthils.

"Hush!" whispered Bembor. "We must make for the Hallowfast as quickly as we can. These trees are Felgor's eyes and ears." Rolin and his friends were in the thick of the wood when the ashtags found their hollow voices.

"Why do you disturb us?" they muttered. "None may enter the forests of Felgor without his leave."

"In the name of Gaelathane, let us pass," cried Bembor.

"He has no authority here," they hissed. "The Tree is dead, and its roots have rotted! Come, let us embrace you until your skin blackens and your eyes shrivel in their sockets! Then if you're still alive, we shall cast you into Gundul, where your flesh will burn and your bones turn to powder. Nothing that breathes may pass this way and live! Come to us! Come to us!"

"Do not listen to them!" warned Bembor. Stopping their ears with their fingers, Rolin and Scanlon ran the rest of the way to the Hallowfast.

"It is locked! It is locked!" the ashtags screeched. "You cannot enter the Tower of the Skull!" Even as they spoke, Rolin saw a skeleton lying by the door, its fixed finger bones futilely clawing the stones.

"You see? He could not open the door. You will die! You will die!"

"They're only trying to frighten us," Bembor said, striding up to the boys.

Rolin shuddered. "They may be right about one thing. When I was here the first time, the door wouldn't open."

Exchanging worried looks, all four men put their shoulders to the stone slab and pushed mightily. The door refused to budge.

"There's no keyhole," Bembor said, "only this hollow spot in the center."

"Maybe that's the keyhole," Emmer suggested.

"If so, what sort of key would fit it?" mused Bembor. He poked the hole with his staff, to no avail. Then the scouts took turns pressing and prodding the place, but the door remained shut fast.

All the while, the ashtags' sneering and jeering continued. At last, Bembor turned his back to the Hallowfast, facing the encircling trees.

"Hear me, spawn of Gundul," he cried, brandishing his staff. "I, Bembor son of Brenthor, command you to be still, or by the Tree whose staff I bear, Gaelathane shall send you back to the pit!"

A hush fell across the forest. Then another voice spoke, harsh and dry with hatred. "I am Mulgul; 'Blacksap' in your tongue," rumbled a large ashtag. "Hear me, old two-legs! I care not whom you serve, nor do I fear your rotten stick. You cannot harm us—we are stouter than steel, tougher than the rock beneath your feet.

Come closer and I'll snap your weak bones like dry twigs and feast on your flesh!" The ashtags grated their branches together, raising an unnerving racket like the gnashing of granite teeth. The black trees edged closer, their limbs reaching out.

"Then may you burn in Gundul's fires!" cried Bembor. He lunged forward with his staff, striking Mulgul on the trunk.

Crack! With a mighty convulsion, the ashtag split asunder. "So shall you all perish, if you bar the way of the king!" Bembor thundered. A wailing and moaning rippled through the forest, dying away into an uneasy stillness.

"I fear I have said too much," muttered Bembor, turning back to the door. Despite all his efforts, however, it still would not open.

"I'm hungry!" said Scanlon, rummaging through Rolin's pack for an oatcake.

"This is no time to eat, boy!" Emmer growled.

"There's something familiar about this dimple in the door," said Bembor. "If only I could make out the markings . . ." His eyes fell on Scanlon's oatcake. "Let me have that," he ordered.

Squashing the cake into a lump, Bembor mashed it into the hollow, then studied the raised design imprinted on the dough. "Of course!" he cried. "It is the mark of a soros!" He took off his medallion and pressed it into the depression. Nothing happened.

"Would you like to try mine instead?" Rolin asked, holding out his soros. Bembor fitted it into the hole, but the door still refused to open—and now the pendant was stuck fast, too. "Roots and rattlesnakes!" Bembor exclaimed. "Trapped between ashtags and a locked door, and the lock's jammed."

"The ashtag's resprouting!" cried Scanlon, pointing at a black tendril worming its way up through Mulgul's stony remains.

"Never mind that," said Bembor sharply. "Help me open this door!"

"Perhaps turning the 'key' will unlock it," suggested Gemmio. Bembor twisted the soros a half-turn, and a grinding noise came from deep inside the stone. A thin, dark line appeared around the door, widening as the slab ponderously swung inward. A draft of cold, stale air eddied out.

"It's opening!" Scanlon whooped.

"And none too soon," Gemmio said with a grim glance backward. The ashtags were crowding closer, and Mulgul's twisting tendril had grown higher than Rolin's head, groping about like a blind snake in search of prey.

"Inside, all of you!" commanded Bembor. Rolin and Scanlon rushed in, with Emmer, Opio and Gemmio close behind. Bembor paused to touch the soros, which dropped into his palm. Then he and Opio shoved the door shut. The latch clicked into place and all was silent. They were inside the Hallowfast.

"It's as dark as a bear's den in here!" Scanlon whispered. Then someone brought out a piece of moonwood. Its light glinted greenish black on the close-fitting stones of a narrow, steep stairway spiraling upward into the shadows. Shields, helmets and other pieces of armor littered the floor. Rolin found a longbow, its string so brittle with age that it shattered in his fingers.

"Elgathel's own picked men must have garrisoned this place," Bembor said, poking through the discarded gear. "These helmets all bear his crest. It looks as though their owners left in a great hurry."

"Here's one that didn't," said Emmer, standing beside a jumble of bones propped against the wall. A broken spear shaft protruded from a tattered green tunic covering the skeleton's rib cage.

"The poor fellow must have crawled in here to die," Gemmio murmured.

"If we don't wish to meet the same fate, we'd better follow these stairs," said Bembor. Fixing a piece of moonwood to his staff tip as a torch, he led the others up the winding staircase. Frightened bats squeaked and fluttered, while the wind moaned through cracks and crevices in the walls.

Rolin brushed some cobwebs from his face. "This place does seem deserted," he remarked.

"Unless yegs have started a colony here," Opio said. "They love caves and abandoned buildings, just as bats do."

Scritch-scritch. Rolin jumped. What was that? A yeg creeping up the stairs behind him? He glanced back but saw nothing. *It must have been a rat,* he told himself and hurried on.

After what seemed hours, the stairs ended in a wooden door, daylight streaming through a split in it. Scanlon pressed his eye to the crack.

"No yegs in there!" he reported. Cautiously, everyone entered.

An uncanny feeling came over Rolin as he took in the curving stone walls, the narrow window and the low stone table. Then he noticed a garland lying on the floor, just like the one Queen Winona had worn—in this very chamber! The tapestries had moldered away, and where the king's body had lain there was now a casket, but all else appeared unchanged. Rolin half expected Winona herself to greet him in her robes of green.

He picked up the circlet, whose sprightly, snow-white flowers were still spangled with dew. At his touch, the fragrant petals crumbled into dust and the stems twisted and cracked. Sadly, Rolin placed the faded relic on the casket. While the blossoms' soothing, sweet scent lingered in the room, he heard the faint echoes of Winona's final words: *Farewell, heir of Elgathel!*

"Do not mourn their beauty's passing," Bembor said, stroking the withered wreath. "She who gathered these hemmonsils left them for you as a reminder of her presence and her love."

"What are hemmonsils?"

"They were a kind of flower that grew beneath the Tree. I recognized them from old engravings. Your grandmother must have planted some around this tower. Legend has it that whatever green thing she touched would burst into bloom, and all dying things revive, at least for a season."

"All things except Elgathel himself," said Emmer sadly. "Here he lies, forever sleeping in his throne room."

"'Two thrones all kings will share,'" said Bembor, brushing off the casket.

"What did you say?" asked Rolin.

"I was just quoting an old Lucambrian proverb: 'Two crowns all kings will wear: the baby bonnet and the graying hair; Two thrones all kings will share: the cradle and the coffin spare.'"

Rolin was about to ask if Elgathel had worn a gold crown when Bembor gave a shout, unsheathing a broken-tipped sword that had lain on the casket cover. "The sword of Elgathel! May you smite your enemies, head and heel!"

Just then, a terrific crash boomed up from below. Everyone rushed to the door, weapons ready, but all had fallen quiet again.

"Mulgul and his friends," Bembor said grimly. "They've forced open the door. When aroused, ashtags can crush the hardest rock to powder. I should not have provoked them."

Rolin pictured the black trees tearing out the Hallowfast's foundations and felt like a nestling whose home was falling to a woodsman's ax.

"What will we do now?" Opio asked Bembor.

"If we cannot go down, we'll go up," he said, raising his eyes to the ceiling.

While the scouts scrounged through dust piles, turning up musty objects the Hallowfast's occupants had left behind, Bembor searched the ceiling with his moonwood-tipped staff. Rolin and Scanlon guarded the doorway.

Tip-tap, went Bembor's staff. *Tip-tap*, echoed an answer up the dark stairway. Rolin's heart skipped a beat. Yes, there it was again: *tip-tap, tip-tap*, reminding him of blind Bartholomew and his cane, tap-tapping through the streets of Beechtown. The sound grew louder.

Bembor closed and barred the door. "That won't keep them out for long, but it may gain us some time," he said, returning to his probing.

"Ashtags can't climb stairs," Opio snorted.

All at once, there was a loud, hollow *thump* and a cry of triumph. "I knew it had to be here somewhere!" Bembor exclaimed, pointing his staff at a half-open, false panel in the wooden ceiling.

"What we need now is a ladder," Opio said.

"Here's one," said his brother, pulling a bundle of ropes and rungs out of an alcove by the table. But when Gemmio began unraveling the tangle, the rungs fell off. "The ropes are rotten," he groaned.

"Let me try," said Scanlon. After climbing onto his father's shoulders, he reached up and pushed back the panel. Then he hoisted himself through. "It's simply grand up here," he called down. "I can see for miles around!"

"How will the rest of us climb up?" asked Gemmio.

"This might help," said Rolin, pulling his rope out of the rucksack. With a practiced swing of his left arm, he tossed the coil straight up through the opening and into Scanlon's waiting hands.

"Well done!" cried Bembor. The scouts applauded. Rolin blushed, thinking it was no great feat compared with pitching a rope over the limb of a bee tree.

Once Scanlon had secured his end of the rope, Rolin shinnied up. He found himself under a wooden canopy at the pinnacle of the Hallowfast. The wind whistled and howled around the tower in a banshee wail. To the west, the sun was sinking behind cloud kingdoms, tinting them a fiery crimson.

"Quite a sight, isn't it?" said Bembor, coming up behind him. "The griffin-masters once met their mounts here before flying into battle."

"There's the sea!" Emmer called, pointing at the white-flecked sheet of blue green. "If the sky clears tonight, we might even catch a glimpse of—"

"Of what, Emmer?" wheezed Opio, who was out of breath from climbing the rope. "Of Luralin? If that island ever existed, it has long since sunk into the sea. You know how fierce the El-marin's storms can be."

"It is still there calling to me, Opio," said Emmer quietly, not turning his head. Rolin also sensed the pull of something beyond the western horizon. Then another force drew his eyes eastward, where Mt. Golgunthor loomed, its rocky slopes tinged blood red in the setting sun.

"I have not been so near the dragon's mountain in years," said Bembor softly, following Rolin's gaze. "When I was a boy, it was the finest peak in all Lucambra, thick with fir and cedar. Felgor changed all that. He's defiled it—like everything else he touches."

"Won't he see us up here?" asked Rolin nervously.

"Only if we were foolish enough to light a fire or run up the flag of Elgathel. We're still many miles from the mountain. It's farther away than it looks."

Rolin turned away, still fearing that some sharp-eyed lookout might spot him. Then he noticed Emmer and his son staring at the mountain. The scout's face was lined and gray. "Don't worry, Father," Scanlon said, "we'll find her."

Emmer shook his head. "It's been too long, and Felgor does not treat his slaves kindly."

Bembor drew Rolin aside. "Leave them be," he whispered. "They grieve for the lost. Five years ago, while Emmer was hunting game in Thalmos, Scanlon, Marlis and their younger sister, Mycena, were gathering chestnuts with their mother Nelda. A pack of batwolves set upon them, killing Nelda and carrying off Mycena. Only Scanlon and Marlis escaped. Emmer scoured the woods for weeks but never found any trace of his daughter."

"How terrible!" said Rolin. "But what does Felgor want with slaves?"

"They toil in his mines, scratching out rubies, diamonds, silver and gold," Bembor explained. "Death is their only reward."

Later, Rolin watched from the fire-blackened ramparts as darkness slunk out of the ashtags and up the side of the Hallowfast. Then he joined the others, who were huddled around a small pile of moonwood, their faces lit greenish yellow.

"This stuff doesn't have any heat to it," grumbled Gemmio, "but since we can't risk a fire up here, it's better than nothing." His fellow scouts nodded.

"If only Rolin's rope were longer," Bembor said, "we could get down—hello, what's this?" Stirring the moonwood with his staff, he had uncovered a string of inlaid letters. Golden figures astride flying sorcs surrounded the symbols. Scraping centuries of dirt off

the stones, the boys brought to light more of the curious script.
Bembor squinted at the writing, his mouth moving soundlessly.

"It is the Prophecy—the entire Prophecy!" he gasped, spreading his hands across the lettering. "Thanks be to Gaelathane!"

"What do the words say?" everyone asked at once.

Then Bembor read:

When darkness stalks across the land
And evil lurks on every hand;
When withered are the amenthils,
From every stream and every hill;
When fire devours both fern and flower,
Then look for help in your final hour!

From ancient root shall spring a shoot,
Of field and forest, fairest fruit;
A torsil tree of tender years,
On him shall rest all hopes and fears;
His stock shall be of Elgathel;
His sythan-ar, an amenthil.

For he shall seek the silver tree,
The sentinel beside the sea;
Beyond, the tower and the tomb
Await amidst the gathered gloom.

Then toll the bell of Elgathel,
Atop the silent sorcathel,
And ride the winds of El-marin
To win the Isle of Luralin.

He'll bring a sword and a dreadful death,
Though not by burning dragon's breath;
Its life for theirs the Tree will trade,
That men and trees may be remade.

But three days hence new life will grow,
In place of water, blood will flow;

To heal all hurts from shore to shore,
And what was lost, with love restore.

The gates of Gundul shall not stand,
When He shall come to cleanse the land;
They'll face a foe they cannot fend;
In drunkenness shall doom descend.

With royal line restored to reign,
The amenthils will bloom again;
The Glymmerin will flow in peace,
Her waters nevermore to cease.

"What's a *sorcathel*, anyway?" Rolin asked.

"The ancient meeting place of men and griffins—and we are in it!" Bembor replied. "From this vantage point, the swift sorca and their riders enjoyed a commanding view. Nothing could approach unnoticed by air, sea or land. At the first hint of danger, sentries would ring the bell that hung in this tower."

"And it's still here!" Sitting on a beam, Scanlon grinned down from the belfry, where a large silver bell gleamed in the moonwood light.

"Look! It hasn't got a clapper!" cried Rolin.

"What good's a bell without a clapper?" Opio fumed. Emmer untied the frayed bell rope and tugged on it. The bell swung freely but silently.

"Why don't you strike it with your staff, Bembor?" Gemmio suggested.

Bembor shook his head. "Lucambrian silversmiths fashioned each bell with its own special clapper. Nothing else would ring it. I can't imagine why anyone would remove this bell's clapper. It's quite useless without one."

"Maybe the clapper's somewhere in the sorcathel," said Rolin. He and the scouts searched, but found nothing.

"Even if we could ring this bell, the sorcs must have all died out by now," Gemmio said.

"Then why would the Prophecy tell us to 'toll the bell'?" asked Rolin.

"There's some writing on the rim," Scanlon called down from the belfry.

"Can you make out the words?" Bembor asked, holding up his moonwood staff. By its light, Scanlon read the engraved inscription:

Who rings this bell when need is nigh,
Shall summon sorca from on high;
Upon their backs the brave may fly,
But none can tame them, though they try.

"That tells us nothing we don't already know," grunted Opio.

"True, but now we can be sure this is Elgathel's bell," Emmer said.

"And that no one can tame a sorc," added Scanlon.

"I wouldn't want to try," Rolin remarked. "They're awfully fierce looking."

"Sorcs can be terrifying when they're angry," Bembor agreed, "and they have very sharp beaks and claws. Few creatures will pick a fight with one."

"Then I'm glad they are our friends and not our enemies!" said Scanlon.

"Friend or foe, what does it matter when we can't call them?" demanded Opio. "I say we give up this whole foolish business and go back to that blasted torsil that brought us here in the first place."

"The ashtags may have already strangled poor Lightleaf," Bembor replied, "so there's no point in—" A splintering noise cut him off.

Rolin and the scouts raced to the hole in the throne room's ceiling and peered into it. Long tentacles glowing with a blue light were writhing through the split in the barred door. Two of them curled around the door, tore it off its hinges and smashed it against the wall. Rolin quickly pulled up his rope.

"So ashtags can climb stairs after all!" Opio remarked, sliding the ceiling panel back into place. More crashing sounds came from inside the room.

"Better that the yeggoroth should find us first than that thing down there," Gemmio said, wiping beads of sweat off his face.

Poof. With a shriek, a dark form skidded across the stones. Emmer's blowpipe spat again, driving a dart between another yeg's eyes. Unarmed, Rolin took cover behind a belfry post just as a yowling and yelling, yipping and yapping, screeching and scratching erupted around him. Any yegs that escaped Emmer's darts and Opio's and Gemmio's arrows met Bembor's whirling staff. From the belfry, Scanlon picked off others with his own blowpipe.

The batwolves broke off their assault, leaving behind some fifteen of their number shot through or petrified. Rolin warily eyed the lifelike yeg statues.

The defenders had suffered their own casualties. Emmer's arm and Gemmio's head were badly gashed. A stone yeg had crushed Opio's toes. Rolin was wrapping Gemmio's head wound with cloth strips he'd torn from a honey bag when Emmer cried, "They're regrouping! Rolin—look out!" A huge batwolf was flying at him, its fanged, ferocious jaws gaping. Having nothing else at hand, Rolin hurled his box into the creature's maw. *Crunch.* The yeg bit down on the box. *Thud.* Its petrified body smacked into Rolin's post. Box-splinters trickled through grinning teeth.

"It worked!" Rolin yelled. Then something else dropped from the yeg's half-open jaws and clattered to the stones. It was the silver club. As Rolin picked it up, the glint of moonlight on metal caught Bembor's eye.

"It's the clapper!" he cried, lifting Rolin into the air, clapper and all. "To me, clansmen, to me!" The scouts rallied around their leader in a circle, facing outward.

"Up on my shoulders, boy," growled Bembor. "Hang that clapper and be quick about it!" While Rolin balanced on Bembor's back, Scanlon steadied the bell from above, and the scouts fended off the batwolves' savage attacks.

After several attempts, Rolin felt the clapper slip over its hook. "Ring it! Ring the bell!" Bembor bellowed, and Emmer pulled on the rope with a will. The bell of Elgathel sang, its clear notes resounding through the tower and echoing across the dark land.

The yegs retreated in confusion. When no enemy reinforcements appeared, however, they returned with redoubled ferocity. Emmer stopped ringing the bell to help Opio and Gemmio, who had run out of arrows and were using their blowpipes instead. When one yeg fell, two more took its place.

Then there was a harsh cry, and the batwolves fell back again. All but one, that is: a battle-scarred, one-eyed monster perched on the parapet.

"Hear me, tree rats!" he growled in the guttural tongue of the yeggoroth. "I am Blackwing, chief of all the yeg scouts! You have slain many of us, but our numbers are far greater than the hairs on your puny heads. Surrender or we will devour your flesh and leave your bones for the birds to pick!"

"And if we do surrender?" Bembor shouted back defiantly.

"We will bind and deliver you to Gorgorunth, who will roast you slowly before swallowing you whole!" At this, the batwolves threw back their heads and shrieked and screeched with hideous yeggorin laughter.

"Hear *me*, foul servant of Felgor!" cried Bembor, pointing his staff at the yeg chieftain. "We will never surrender to you or your vile master. Flee back to your stinking lairs, lest the wrath of Elgathel fall upon you!"

Blackwing hissed and bared his teeth. "Do you 'look for help in your final hour'? Then look in vain, for none will come. *Gor* fried the last of those mangy feathered lions years ago. Now curse your dead Tree and die!" With that, he sprang toward Bembor, only to pitch forward with an arrow in his one good eye. Howling with rage, the yegs swarmed into the sorcathel like a cloud of angry hornets, recklessly hurling themselves at the scouts.

Then a rending sound rose above the racket. Pieces of the false panel flew into the air, and something dark slithered out. "It's Mulgul!" Bembor cried. The ashtag's thick, black tentacles encircled the bodies of dead and dying batwolves, tossing them aside as if they were floppy rag dolls. More branches spilled out, like snakes wriggling out of an overturned basket.

Recognizing the ashtag, the yegs' yelps of fear turned to howls of triumph, and they renewed their attack. Having used up their blowpipe darts, Emmer, Opio and Gemmio slashed at the enemy with their long knives, while Bembor's stout staff swung here and jabbed there. Still, the yegs' relentless onslaught was driving the defenders within reach of the black tree's cruel embrace.

All at once, the yegs pulled back. Vulture-like, they hunched on the sorcathel's battlements, waiting for Mulgul to finish off their enemies.

"Curse you, yegs!" shouted Opio, shaking his knife at them. "Come over here, and I'll slit your hairy throats!" Suddenly, a batwolf lurched forward. Rolin struck it with a petrified yeg leg, but the beast was already headless.

Yowling in dismay, the yegs scattered. One by one, other figures settled on the ramparts. Like great, tawny lions they were, but with the broad wings and sleek, snow-white heads of eagles. The sorca had come at last.

CHAPTER 13

IN THE GRIFFINS' LAIR

Hail, People of the Tree! We have come at the summons of the king's bell," purred the largest of the griffins. "You must leave with us at once. More yeg packs are on their way here, and we are too few to hold this place against so many."

Rolin needed no urging. He and Scanlon hopped on one sorc, while Bembor and the scouts mounted four others. With a *whoosh* of wings, the griffins swooped off into the night.

"Oooh," cried Rolin, gripping his mount's fur with both hands. The height made him dizzy, and his sorc was flying at a terrific pace, its golden wings flapping strongly and rhythmically. He tried not to look down.

"Why don't you move up toward my head?" suggested the sorc. "Then you can hang onto my neck instead of pulling out my hair." Rolin inched forward and grasped the griffin's neck, while Scanlon clung to his waist from behind.

"There, isn't that better?" the sorc said. "You needn't choke me—I won't let you fall! By the way, my name is Windsong and you, young two-legs, are—?"

"Rolin son of Gannon." How much could he safely tell a sorc? The bell's inscription said griffins couldn't be tamed. Perhaps they

couldn't be trusted, either. He relaxed his hold and asked, "Are any yegs still about?"

"Not a one," said Windsong shrilly. "They gave up the chase. Even the swiftest yeg scouts cannot catch us when we put on our best speed. Besides, they don't see or fly as well once the sun is up. The light blinds them."

Rolin looked eastward, where the sun was peeping above gray mountains. Its first rays gilded other griffins flying above, below and behind him. Some carried scouts, while others evidently were acting as escorts.

"Ashtag, bashtag, can't catch a rashtag!" Scanlon was chanting. Rolin glanced over his shoulder to see his friend staring back at the tower. Already, Mulgul had filled the sorcathel with his wiry limbs, searching in vain for his prey. Scanlon stuck out his tongue and made rude noises.

"Is the other two-legs all right?" asked Windsong.

Rolin laughed. "Scanlon? Don't worry about him. He's just happy we all escaped from the Hallowfast in one piece."

The sorc cocked his head to one side, birdlike. "Those are happy sounds?"

"For Scanlon they are!"

"I see. I shall remember that. This is how we sorcs express amusement." Windsong screeched and clacked his beak. Rolin gulped. If that was amusement, he didn't want to see a sorc in anger! And that reminded him: What did griffins eat? He didn't recall Bembor mentioning the subject. Maybe a boy or two would make a tasty sorc snack.

"Where are we going?" he asked, hoping to be let off at the nearest hill.

"To our dens in the Willowah mountains."

Dens. Rolin pictured smelly holes filled with half-gnawed bones, some belonging to prey of the two-legged kind. "Er, you're not hungry, are you?"

"Not at all, thank you. I feasted on some fat ground squirrels last night." Windsong twisted his head back to regard Rolin with one bright, kindly eye. "Even if I were starving, I still would not make a meal of a two-legs!"

"Look down now!" called Scanlon. Rolin forced himself to peep over the sorc's side. Far below, rivers wove their silver ribbons through the dark fabric of sleeping forests. Here and there, ugly black blotches marred the landscape where ashtag colonies had gained a foothold.

Despite the brisk, biting wind, Rolin was warming to the exhilarating sensation of flight. "I'm a bird!" he whooped, waving his arms. Windsong's head swiveled back again.

"I beg your pardon?" the griffin said, blinking his eyes.

Rolin grinned. "Just more happy sounds!"

Presently, craggy, snow-clad peaks loomed in the distance, their tops flushing pink with the sunrise. The air turned crisper. "We are approaching the Willowahs, ancestral home of all the sorca," explained Windsong. "You're the first of the tree people to visit us since the death of the griffin-friend, Elgathel, and you'll be received as honored guests. We've never forgotten your people's kindness to us."

"Nor shall we ever forget yours!" replied Rolin.

An hour later, Windsong and the other griffins banked toward a high cliff and dove into a cleverly-concealed tunnel in its smooth face. Rolin held his breath as the sorcs sped down the shaft single file, rapidly clicking their curved beaks. Flying in the opposite direction, other sorcs flashed by, also making click-clack noises. Rolin guessed the griffins used the echoing beak clicks to find their way in the dark and to warn others of their approach.

"How large is this tunnel?" he asked, ducking as a sorc whizzed overhead.

"Wide enough to permit four to fly abreast," Windsong replied between *clacks*, "but too narrow for Gorgorunth to get through! There are miles and miles of such shafts beneath these mountains."

"How did you dig them all?" asked Scanlon from over Rolin's shoulder.

"We didn't. These tunnels are the work of stoneworms."

"Stoneworms!" said Rolin. He couldn't imagine any worm large enough to bore such holes in solid rock. "Are they very . . . big?"

"Oh, yes. And terribly ugly, too. But they're quite harmless."

Presently, Rolin heard a low, steady hum. Then Windsong popped into a vast cavern ablaze with flaming torches. Griffins of every description flitted about, some bearing food and supplies in their paws or on their backs, others carrying babies. There were rolly-polly griffins and skinny griffins; pint-sized griffins and over-sized griffins; young griffins with brown-feathered heads and necks and white-feathered older ones. Most were tawny-colored, but some were black, tan or even orange. A few sported leopard's spots. The place was abuzz with their clicking and clacking, chittering and chattering.

Windsong spiraled down to the cavern floor, where he excused himself to bound off in search of bandages for the wounded scouts. Meanwhile, his companions properly introduced themselves to Rolin and his friends.

"I am Keeneye, the king's courier," said Opio's sorc, "and these are Snowfeather, Spearwind and Longfeather." The three other mounts lowered their heads in greeting and flicked their tails from side to side.

"It's been many years since we've had the privilege of bearing your people on our backs," said Spearwind. "Welcome to the kingdom of the sorca!"

"Thank you for rescuing us and for your hospitality," Bembor replied.

"I regret King Whitewing cannot be present to meet you personally," Keeneye continued, "but he is visiting a colony farther south. Since he won't be back for several days, you'll have plenty of time to rest before we take you to see him. Now, since you must be hungry and weary after your ordeal, Flamefeather, Farsight and Sharpclaw will see to your needs."

Keeneye chirk-chirked, and three more griffins trotted up to lead the six companions into another tunnel. Hundreds of sorcs stopped to gawk at them along the way. With their sleek, supple bodies and long, proud necks, all the griffins looked like kings to Rolin!

The sorcs led their guests to a chamber with a wide, airy window looking over a forested valley. On the walls were faded scenes of griffins and Lucambrians battling batwolves and dragons.

"We haven't used the riders' room in years," said Farsight, "but we thought you would like it. Our ancestors once entertained the griffin-friend here."

"It is an honor to renew our alliance in this hall!" said Bembor with a bow.

Relieved to see the sun again, Rolin gazed out the window until Windsong returned with dressings and ointments. Then the boys wrapped Gemmio's head and Emmer's arm. Only after sniffing suspiciously at the salves and muttering something about "beastly bandages" did Opio allow Scanlon to tie up his foot. Soon afterwards, Flamefeather and Sharpclaw arrived with platters of food on their backs. There were roasted quail and rabbits; poached duck eggs; hazelnuts; currants and huckleberries stewed in honey, and fresh thimbleberries. To Rolin's relief, there were no squirrels. After talking with the little creatures, he didn't want to eat one!

"I apologize for the poor fare," said Farsight, "but it's all we could find on such short notice."

"'Poor fare'!" exclaimed the scouts, looking at one another. "We haven't eaten this well in months!" No one mentioned that the other People of the Tree were freezing in the ice caves, eating dried fruit and stale nuts. Rolin noticed the sorcs touched none of the food they had brought their guests but instead picked at something he couldn't see and wasn't sure he wished to.

Afterwards, more griffins brought in rough straw mattresses and overstuffed goose-down pillows. With a groan of relief, Rolin flopped down on one of the mattresses and immediately fell into a deep sleep.

Over the next few days, while the scouts recovered from their injuries and Bembor conferred with the royal counselors, Scanlon and Rolin enjoyed long excursions on Windsong's back. They flew over sky-blue rivers, thundering waterfalls shrouded in mist and needle-sharp peaks streaked with snow.

"Why do you live underground, when it's such great fun up here?" the boys asked Windsong one day, as they swooped over a splendid mountain meadow. The sorc gazed back at them with an amused expression.

"We don't like being cooped up in those dismal tunnels any better than you do! If it weren't for Felgor and the serpent, we'd have left that lair long ago to build our aeries in the rocks. We love the sun on our backs, the wind under our wings and our bracing mountain air. That's why I enjoy flying lookout."

"How about entertaining guests?" Rolin teased.

The griffin clicked his beak. "That rare privilege I also find very pleasant, especially since you are my first two-legged passengers."

"What about four-legged guests?" asked Scanlon. "What would you do if Felgor sent yegs after us?"

"He wouldn't dare! His fiercest yeg warriors are no match for us. We'd cut them to shreds."

"But couldn't just a few yegs sneak into your tunnels?" Scanlon persisted.

"It is true that the wolves-with-wings are more at home under the earth than we are," said Windsong. "For that very reason, we've sealed up all but a few entrances to our stronghold and those we heavily guard. One or two of the yeggoroth might find their way in, but they would never get out again!"

"What about the dragon?" asked Rolin.

"Gorgorunth?" The sorc snorted. "He knows better than to fly this far south. We'd send him packing in short order. I wouldn't mind poking some holes in his scaly hide myself. Naturally, one must avoid the snout. Dragon fire can sear one's fur and feathers. Now, let us speak of more cheerful subjects. Have you ever heard the Ballad of Elgathel?"

Rolin groaned. The royal bard and chronicler of griffanic history never seemed to tire of spouting epic poems and historical narratives. Once, Rolin had fallen asleep listening to Windsong recite the endless lineages of the griffanic kings and had nearly toppled off the sorc's back.

Two days later, however, the boys found their friend slumped dejectedly in his den, his wings splayed out in a most undignified fashion. "The sorcathon is tomorrow," he croaked, when Rolin and Scanlon had coaxed him into talking.

"Sorcathon? What's that?" Rolin asked.

"It is our high assembly," explained Windsong, "consisting of the king and twenty-four elders. It meets every full moon or on very special occasions."

"That does sound boring," said Scanlon. "Must you attend?"

"I must, as I am the official scribe."

"Cheer up, then!" Rolin said, stroking the griffin's tawny fur. "When your council is over, we can spend more time together."

"I fear not," said the sorc, with a twitch of his drooping tail. "Once the sorcathon has adjourned, you will probably be leaving us, and I confess I've become rather fond of you both."

The following morning, Windsong and Keeneye escorted Rolin and his companions to the sorcathon. Opio still limped but no longer referred to sorcs as "those scruffy lion things." Rolin suspected the scout's opinion of griffins had improved on a steady diet of roast quail, grouse and goose!

Entering an echoing cave, the visitors took their seats on wooden benches their hosts had supplied. Before them stood an elaborate golden throne flanked by the twenty-four griffin elders, twelve on either side. Around each griffin's neck hung a golden chain. Some of the elders talked quietly with their neighbors, while others preened themselves or sharpened their claws on the stone floor. Windsong sat poised at a nearby table, gripping a quill pen in his beak. His solemn pose nearly sent Rolin and Scanlon into fits of laughter.

Presently, they heard a whistling sound, and a princely griffin with snow-white wings and a jeweled crown strutted into the room. The Lucambrians rose to their feet, while the elders bowed their long necks to the floor.

"Long live King Whitewing!" the sorcs chorused as their leader padded up to the throne and settled back on his haunches. Like the elders, Whitewing wore a gold chain on his neck, though of more ponderous proportions.

Then the king unfurled his great wings, raised his right paw and said, "In the name of the One Tree, and before the Maker of all things, the sorcathon is now convened. Let all that is said and done henceforth be to the honor and welfare of the King of the Trees, Lucambra and all sorca!"

"May the king and his realm prosper," intoned the elders.

Whitewing nodded for his audience to be seated, then turned his gaze upon Bembor, who had remained standing. "Bembor son of Brenthor, come ye here with these others as friends or foes?"

"As friends, O King of the Sorca," said Bembor.

"Then you and your companions are welcome in these halls."

"Thank you, King Whitewing," replied Bembor, bowing low. "We are most grateful to you for answering the summons of Elgathel's bell and for your generous hospitality."

"It is we who are indebted to you, Father of the Oak Clan," said the king. "In ringing the bell, you helped us fulfill our oath of fealty to the griffin-friend and his queen. We no longer need hang our heads in shame. Moreover, thanks to you, an amenthil lives again, in itself a cause for rejoicing! You may now give an account of yourself and of these your friends and fellow travelers."

Bembor's tale of Rolin's accidental journey into Lucambra and of the events following drew astonished exclamations from the assembled griffins. Otherwise, the only sound in the hushed chamber was the scritch-scritch of Windsong's pen furiously scratching out words on parchment.

"Excellent!" said Whitewing. "I am pleased to hear you've found the Prophecy's lost portion. We sorca also have long sought those missing verses. The two-legs named Rolin—is he here today?"

Rolin stood and Whitewing fixed him with a stern, unwavering stare. "How many summers have you seen, two-leggling?" asked the king.

"Fourteen, sire," answered Rolin, his heart thudding painfully.

Whitewing glared at Bembor. "How can one so young bring about the promised deliverance?"

"He is truly the 'torsil tree of tender years,'" Bembor replied. "May I remind Your Highness that the Prophecy's fulfillment depends not upon age or strength but on our obedience to Gaelathane's call."

"Well spoken," purred Whitewing. The griffin elders rumbled approvingly. "There remains one test which the boy Rolin must pass," the king went on. "The Prophecy states that 'His stock shall be of Elgathel.' Have you evidence that he belongs to the royal line of the griffin-friend?"

"We offer this token, King Whitewing," said Bembor. "Behold, the sword of Elgathel!" He drew the gleaming sword from beneath his cloak and held it aloft. The sorc elders lashed their tails and craned their necks to catch a glimpse of the legendary weapon. "Also, we could not have rung the king's bell without the clapper, which Rolin had in his possession."

"I doubt not your words," said the king, "but we must know whether this sword truly belonged to Elgathel. Call Meekheart!"

Minutes later, the doorkeepers entered with a decrepit-looking creature hobbling between them. The sorc was blind in one eye and had bald patches on his back and flanks. A cloth pouch hung from his scrawny neck. Yet, a gleam of pride shone in the old griffin's good eye as he bowed before the king.

"What does my lord wish of me?" he quavered.

"Meekheart," the king said gently, "the time has come."

At Whitewing's words, the sorc's shriveled legs straightened, and his neck snapped to attention. "I am Meekheart son of Trueheart son of Stoutheart," he cried in a voice clear and strong. "My grandfather was with the griffin-friend when Gorgorunth attacked. Stoutheart alone stood fast when the king defied the dragon on the seashore. After Elgathel fell in battle, my grandfather rescued his body and brought it to the queen, who made him take the oath. Stoutheart also found this, which he guarded with his life, and my father and I after him." Meekheart tossed the pouch over his head and deftly caught it in his beak. Then he presented it to the king.

In turn, Whitewing hooked the bag with one curving claw and shook it. Out rolled a round, bright object. The Lucambrians gasped. It was a colossal emerald, as brilliant and blue-green as glacier ice. The griffins seemed only mildly impressed.

"We have whole storerooms full of gems," the king yawned. "However, few are so large and perfectly formed as this one. Threeclaws once gave such an emerald to Elgathel in gratitude for saving him from the yegs. Your king later set the stone in his sword."

Bembor held the sword hiltfirst toward Whitewing, who dropped the emerald into an empty socket in the handle. It fit. The sorcs rapidly blinked their eyes, and a buzz of excitement filled the hall.

"I realize, O King," said Bembor, "that Elgathel's sword does not strengthen Rolin's claim to the throne, since we found it in the Hallowfast. However—"

Rolin stared at the sword. Something in the blade's shape and luster stirred a memory. He felt for the sharp steel in his pocket. Could it be—? He jumped up and ran to Bembor, who frowned and put a finger to his lips. Then he saw the tapered piece of metal lying in Rolin's palm.

Trembling, Bembor fitted the point on the sword. The broken edges matched perfectly. "This, King Whitewing, proves that Rolin son of Gannon is Elgathel's true heir. The sword tip belonged to his mother, Elgathel's daughter. There is more proof of his lineage. Rolin, your soros, please." Rolin handed the pendant to Bembor, who held it up before the griffin king. "He also received this rider's medallion from his mother. It is the seventh soros, long feared lost. See where the serpent melted it with his accursed fire?"

There was a breathless silence in the chamber as Whitewing examined the medallion. "It is Elgathel's soros!" he cried. "Hail Rolin, King of Lucambra!"

"Hail Rolin, King of Lucambra!" echoed the scouts, leaping to their feet.

"Long live Rolin, King of Lucambra!" joined in the sorc elders, beating their wings in a frenzy. The quill pen fell from Windsong's beak as he crowed, "May King Rolin live forever!"

Whitewing raised a paw to restore order. "Rolin grandson of Elgathel," he said, "we the members of the sorcathon, and all griffins of this realm, acclaim you as Lucambra's king. May your sythanar ever flourish! I must beg of you one favor, however."

"Anything, King Whitewing."

"As you can see, my elders and I wear chains of gold. The weight of the gold recalls our cowardice and faithlessness, while its glory reminds us of Elgathel's reign. On every anniversary of his passing, we have added one link to each chain. By decree, only death or the griffin-friend's heir may relieve us of our burdens. Rolin, blessed child of Thalmos and Lucambra, we have long awaited your coming. Will you take our fetters from us?"

"Gladly!" Rolin replied. One by one, he removed the chains from around the sorc elders' necks. However, the king's chain was too massive for him to manage alone. There was an awkward moment until Opio and Gemmio helped him lift the yellow coils over Whitewing's head.

"Thank you!" the sorcs chorused, stretching their necks.

"We shall melt down these chains to make a crown and scepter for the new king, when he takes his throne in the Hallowfast," said Whitewing.

Bembor cleared his throat. "I must remind your lordship that there is much to do before Rolin can claim his rightful title, since Felgor still sits on Lucambra's throne. The Prophecy has brought us this far. We have yet to 'ride the winds of El-marin to win the Isle of Luralin.' We must go west, to seek the Tree." At these words, a dismayed murmur rippled through the assembly.

"Luralin lies many leagues from here," Whitewing pointed out. "No ship setting out for that island has ever returned to these shores."

"I do not speak of a sea voyage," Bembor said. "The Prophecy states that we must *ride* the winds, not catch them in our frail sails."

The griffins looked at one another. "Surely you do not expect some of us to take you on such a perilous journey!" exclaimed Whitewing.

"Only because we have no wings of our own," Bembor said, smiling wryly.

"No sorc has ever flown to Luralin and back, though many have tried," growled the king. "A man's added weight would make the trip all the crueler. My subjects were hard-pressed flying you here from the Hallowfast as it is."

"Besides," one of the elders argued, "we don't know where the island lies or even if it still exists." The other griffins bobbed their heads in agreement.

"Luralin is still out there, and we will find it," replied Bembor. "The Prophecy is very clear about that. See here, is not my Rowonah staff as green as a willow wand in spring? The stone yegs lying in the sorcathel testify to its power. While this staff lives, the Tree must live also."

"While the Tree may live, would we live to see the Tree, if any of us attempted such an ill-fated expedition?" the king retorted.

"Ill-fated or not, to the Tree we must go," Bembor said, folding his arms.

"If you had but asked rubies and emeralds of us, we would have bestowed them in plenty," sighed Whitewing. "But this request I am loth to grant. What say you, my brothers? Will anyone among you undertake this venture?"

"Not carrying those sandbags on our backs!" muttered one member of the sorcathon. The others nodded and clicked their beaks. Rolin's shoulders sagged. Without the sorcs' help, there was no hope of reaching the island.

"I will go," said a quiet griffin voice. All eyes turned toward Windsong. "I have flown with both the young two-legs for days now. They are as light as autumn's first snowflakes and have even learned to hang on with their knees, instead of pulling out my hair and feathers."

"He's right," chimed in another sorc. "Though we couldn't make the journey with full-grown riders, it might be possible with these small ones."

Bembor stroked his beard. "Nothing in the Prophecy tells us who is to 'win the Isle of Luralin,'" he said, "and surely none of us is more worthy of that honor than Rolin. My lad, you know the risks; will you go?"

"Only if Scanlon comes, too!" Rolin quickly answered.

To ease the royal bard's burden, a sorc of legendary endurance named Ironwing agreed to bear Scanlon, leaving Rolin for Windsong to carry. The four would depart for Luralin the next night.

When the sorcathon had adjourned, Rolin waited for Windsong to pack up his parchments and sharpen his quill pen. Then the boy hopped on the sorc's back. "Thank you for offering to take me to Luralin, brave griffin!" he said, hugging Windsong's neck. "We'll have lots of fun there together."

"We must get there first!" said the sorc, nuzzling against him.

Seconds after Rolin rode Windsong out of the empty assembly hall, the last of the cavern's torches sputtered and died behind him, plunging the tunnel into darkness. Feeling a sudden downdraft, Rolin glanced up to catch the briefest flicker of black, featherless wings darting away. Whatever he'd seen, it was too small for a yeg but too large for a bat.

The next morning, Rolin and Scanlon were playing griffin chess with Windsong in the riders' room when Keeneye padded in. "King Whitewing requests the honor of Rolin's presence," the sorc announced. Rolin followed him through a winding, uphill passage until they reached the tunnel's mouth, where Keeneye politely lowered his head and departed. Rolin found Whitewing sitting outside on a broad, flat rock.

Bowing deeply, Rolin said, "You wished to see me, O king?"

"I did," purred Whitewing. He nodded southward, where the mountains sloped into rolling hills clothed with fir and pine. As the rising sun burned the morning mists off the waking earth, a golden sheen briefly shimmered over the landscape, then dissolved into the forest. Rolin caught his breath. "That was magnificent," he whispered.

"I am pleased that you enjoyed it," said Whitewing, staring at the sun with unblinking eyes. "I come here most mornings to speak with Gaelathane and to take in the *Slava*—the Willowan sun dance you just witnessed. But that is not the only reason I called you here." The sorc arched his back. "Climb on."

"I . . . I really couldn't," Rolin stammered. "You're the king, after all, and—"

"Never mind that," said Whitewing gruffly. "Just get on." Rolin obeyed.

The griffin leapt into the air and spread his white-feathered wings, arrowing nearly straight up for a dizzying half-mile. Rolin's stomach flip-flopped. It was his first experience with the raw power of a sorc in full flight.

At the top of his climb, Whitewing tipped over and dove toward the mountain. Rolin gasped as the jagged rocks loomed with terrifying swiftness.

At the last second, the sorc sideslipped, then gently settled to earth. After Rolin shakily dismounted, Whitewing trotted off a few yards and stopped beside a boulder with a dark hole underneath it. "I apologize for the abrupt ride," he said. "That is how I take my daily exercise. My subjects do not know the other purpose behind this morning ritual. Now, please follow me."

With that, the king squeezed through the opening beneath the boulder and disappeared. Diving in after him, Rolin found himself in a smooth, narrow passage delved into the solid rock. Down, down, the tunnel wound, until it opened into a small room lit by a single guttering torch. The chamber was empty, save for a cloth-covered basket resting on a stone pedestal.

Whitewing faced Rolin. "No two-legs has ever set foot in this hallowed place," he said softly. "Indeed, no two-legs has ever ridden me at all. Windsong was right; you are as light as a snowflake!"

With his beak, Whitewing pulled the cloth off the basket, exposing a pinkish ball. "Many years ago, my ancestors observed the first arrival of your kind on our shores," he said. "When the sorcerer cut down his own torsil, some sorcs formed a *wilith*—a spasel—out of the stump's oozing sap. Looking into it, they learned of Luralin's existence. Since that time, each griffin king has passed on the secret of this spasel room to his successor and to no other.

That is why I must ask you not to tell anyone what you have seen here."

Rolin nodded. "If it's so secret, why are you showing me?"

"Because you also are to be a king, and I wish you to see that the object of your journey is a very real place and not merely the stuff of legends." Whitewing gently warmed the wilith with his breath and a murkiness blossomed in the sap ball's center. When the cloudiness cleared, Rolin saw a sea of white flowers that glowed with an inner light.

"Behold Luralin," said the griffin king, "home of the Tree that never dies."

CHAPTER 14

ACROSS THE SEA
OF EL-MARIN

That evening, King Whitewing's servants escorted Rolin and his friends to the mouth of the main entrance, where Windsong and Ironwing were waiting, draped with sacks of provender. Ironwing was sulking, his black-tipped tail and dark brown neck feathers as droopy as wilted dandelions.

"What's the matter with him?" Rolin whispered to Bembor.

"I'm told he's always that way," Bembor said. "You won't find a more stalwart sorc in all of sorcdom, though." Then the old Lucambrian handed Rolin his rucksack, which felt much heavier. Scanlon was wearing Emmer's knapsack, which was also bulging.

Rolin opened his pack to find some of his honey bags filled with brown, pleasant-smelling loaves. He broke a piece off one loaf and nibbled on it, savoring the sweet, nutty flavor.

"Don't eat too much!" warned Bembor. "It's very filling, and you'll need all that's there for your journey."

"What is it?" Rolin asked, still chewing.

"The sorcs call it *dubaya*. It's made of dried fruit and nuts, with honey and other nourishing things thrown in for good measure.

Ironwing tells me he can fly all day on just a half-brick of it. There's enough in your packs to last two weeks, if you don't eat it all at once. The sacks may be useful after they're empty, too. You never know when you'll need an extra bag."

Rummaging around in the pack, Rolin discovered a flask among the sacks. "What's this?" he asked, holding it up.

"It's filled with *vilna*, fermented mulberry juice."

Rolin grimaced. He thought he'd rather drink seawater.

"You may also need these." Bembor handed him a long bundle of green fabric. "My cloak—and Elgathel's sword. The griffins repaired the tip. They're quite good at metalwork, you know."

"Thank you!" said Rolin, wrapping himself in the cloak and strapping on the sword. Just then, Keeneye trotted up.

"Whitewing is here," the sorc told Bembor. "He wishes to bless the young grifflings—er, two-legs, before they depart." Rolin and his companions lined up to receive the king, who stalked up to them with head held high.

"I give you all a new name," he announced. "Henceforth, you shall be known as the Servants of the Tree. I also bestow upon each the title of griffin-friend. You will always find a gracious welcome in our lair."

Everyone bowed and thanked the king. Then Whitewing reared up on his hind legs, placing one enormous paw on Rolin's shoulder and the other on Scanlon's. "Farewell, my young friends!" he said. "May the wind always be at your backs, and may Gaelathane go with you. I shall look forward to hearing of your adventures when you return."

"May your wings never falter!" they replied, as Bembor had taught them.

Then Rolin stepped forward. "This is for you, King Whitewing, by way of thanks for your kindness and hospitality." He removed the soros from around his neck and hung it over the griffin's head. The other sorcs clattered their beaks in astonishment.

"Such a gift only one king may bestow upon another," Whitewing purred. "I will treasure it above my crown!"

Bembor raised his staff. "Luralin awaits. Make way for the sorc masters!" Scouts and sorcs moved aside, allowing the boys to approach their mounts. After climbing on Windsong, Rolin asked Bembor, "How will we find Luralin?"

"Once you cross the mountains, just aim for the Tree's light."

"But what will we do once we get there?" Scanlon asked his father.

"Follow the Prophecy's words, of course!" Emmer replied, securing Ironwing's saddlebags.

"May Gaelathane guide and watch over you both," Bembor added hoarsely, his face a pasty gray. "Remember, 'Judge not by what you see but by the Prophecy.'" He brushed a shaking hand across moist eyes. "Now go!" he shouted, slapping Ironwing's flank. The griffins launched into the darkness.

Rolin's stomach lurched as Windsong dropped through the cool air, then caught the wind under his wings and leveled out. There was an eerie sensation of movement without motion under the emerging canopy of silent, changeless stars. Only the rushing wind betrayed the griffin's great speed.

Beyond the coastal mountains, darkness was swallowing up the tattered remnants of a crimson sunset. Glancing down, Rolin saw a small, leaflike shape flit up from the forest. When he rubbed his eyes and looked again, the thing was gone.

"Can you see the island yet?" he asked Windsong.

"Not from this distance," the sorc replied. "Just watch the horizon for the Tree's light." Rolin could make out only a few early stars. He gripped the griffin tighter with his knees, recalling his first terrifying night flight with batwolves breathing down his neck. Looking back, he saw no pursuers.

Between the silvery peaks they soared, the griffins' wings thrashing the thin air. Surging higher, the sorcs cleared a glittering ice field and began their gliding descent toward the coast.

Rolin caught the distant glint of starlight on white-capped waves. "The sea!" he cried weakly, out of breath from the height.

"Hush!" Ironwing hissed from nearby. "Your voice will echo for miles in these mountains."

All at once, Windsong's body quivered. "Look left!" he chittered.

"Where?" Rolin asked.

"There—between the stars and the sea."

Scanning the horizon, Rolin noticed one star that didn't flicker, its pure white light shining as brightly and steadily as the moon's. "It's the Tree!" he exclaimed, as the griffins veered toward the light. Miles of thick, dark forest slid silently beneath them until the El-marin's broad beaches came into view. Rolin gulped in the sharp-scented sea air while the sorcs flew over the foaming breakers and onward into the night, aiming for the faraway pinpoint of light. Lulled by the swishing of Windsong's wings, Rolin rested his head on the sorc's warm back and dozed.

At the breaking of the dawn he stretched and yawned. Below him rolled the El-marin's endless, blue-green waves, while a robin's-egg sky gazed serenely down at him. Blue above, blue beneath.

A seabird sailed by with a startled cry at the sight of sorcs so far from shore. Ironwing flew a few yards off, his wings beating in time with Windsong's. The griffins spoke little, saving their breath for flying. Rolin waved at Scanlon, relieved to find the other boy hadn't fallen off during the night. "Have you seen anything yet?" he called to his friend. Scanlon shook his head, then pointed forward, as if to say they were on the right course.

By noon, the sorcs' wing strokes were slowing, and their breathing becoming more ragged as they sank closer to the waves. "Gaelathane, please help us find the Tree!" Rolin prayed. That day, he took only a sip of vilna and a bite of dubaya, feeding most of his share to Windsong.

Toward evening, the sun's burning eye blazed orange-red through a bank of gathering gray clouds, then sank into the waiting sea, burnishing the water bronze. As a suffocating darkness rose out of the restless waves, a silvery ray broke through the blackness in the west.

The boys cheered, their voices carrying thinly through the air, while the griffins flew with renewed vigor. The breeze freshened, singing a song of hope: "The Tree is near! No need to fear! The Tree is near! No need to fear!"

Then the clouds settled over the sea, forming a dense fog that engulfed the griffin riders. Water drops quickly collected on Rolin's hair and eyebrows and dampened Windsong's fur. Yet, a halo of light still shone through the mist, leading the way to Luralin. Hour after hour, the foursome flew deeper into the fog, until they broke out in front of an immense column of light.

"It's Waganupa!" Scanlon shouted. Its top piercing the clouds, the gigantic tree radiated a soothing splendor that reminded Rolin of Lightleaf, bathed in the silver light of Lucambra's moon.

Suddenly, the wind changed course and whirled them around the Tree's massive trunk. "We're in a cyclone!" wailed Scanlon, but the wind gust merely deposited them on Luralin's sloping shore. Stiff from their long journey, the boys dropped from their mounts and lay groaning on the white sand. The sorcs likewise collapsed in a heap, panting heavily. Rolin tried to rise, but a dreamless sleep overtook him where he lay.

He awoke to find Scanlon, Windsong and Ironwing asleep beside him. For a moment he thought he was back in the griffins' lair. Then he remembered the harrowing flight across the sea. He was on Luralin! Sitting up, he saw a stately forest standing where the glistening beach ended.

Above the woods towered the Tree, its light barely subdued in the afternoon sun's cheery brightness. Rolin tilted his head back, following the outlines of the colossal, cinnamon-colored trunk. Never had he seen anything so large, yet so flawlessly formed.

"Splendid, absolutely splendid!" marveled Windsong, craning his neck at an impossible angle. "Ironwing, you really must see this!"

With a grunt and a groan, Ironwing struggled to his feet and tried to focus his eyes. Seeing the Tree, his beak dropped open and he fell over. Rolin laughed, awakening a rather grumpy Scanlon.

Fortunately, a hearty breakfast of vilna and chewy dubaya bread improved everyone's spirits. Afterwards, the four adventurers lounged comfortably on Luralin's warm sands, chatting in hushed tones.

"I say we collect a few Tree staffs and go home," said Ironwing, scratching his tan flank with one hind leg.

"No need to hurry," Windsong objected. "My wings are still too sore to fly. Besides, I want to record the account of our journey in my notebooks."

"You brought your notebooks?" exclaimed Ironwing. "It's a wonder that—"

"Come to Me."

"What did you say?" asked Rolin, turning to Windsong.

"I said I needed to record—"

"Come to Me!" the resounding voice repeated. Rolin glanced at Scanlon, who was looking about with a puzzled expression.

"Did you hear that?" Rolin asked his friend.

"Yes—who was it?"

"I don't know." Rolin stared fearfully at the waiting forest.

Windsong quizzically cocked his head at the boys. "What's the matter with you two?"

"I'm not sure," Rolin said. "We thought we heard—"

"*Come to Me!*"

"There it is again!" gasped Scanlon.

"There is what again?" Ironwing growled. "You're not playing a trick on us, are you? Griffins don't care for games."

"Speak for yourself," retorted Windsong.

"We just heard a . . . a voice," Rolin said.

"I didn't hear any voices," snapped Ironwing.

"But both Scanlon and I heard it!"

"What did it say?" asked Windsong.

"'Come to Me!' Isn't that right, Scanlon?"

Scanlon nodded. This touched off a heated discussion between the griffins.

"I say they've had too much vilna," argued Ironwing.

"And I say they've heard something," said Windsong. "What if someone really has spoken to them?"

"Then why can't we hear it?"

"*COME TO ME!*" the voice thundered. Both sorcs jumped, their hair standing on end. There was no further argument. Rolin and

Scanlon repacked the provisions, and everyone slogged through the soft sand toward the Tree.

Rolin stopped at the woods, fearful of trampling the delicate wildflowers carpeting the forest floor. At Windsong's gentle nudge, he plunged in, treading lightly on the fragile-looking blossoms. Looking behind, he saw the resilient plants had sprung back into place, leaving no trace of his steps.

In contrast to the dainty wildflowers, ancient oaks with trunks six feet through thrust out their thick limbs like long, sinewy arms, while tall, white-boled birches brushed the sky with slender fingers. The whole forest was bursting with health, but something was missing. . . .

"I have it!" he cried.

"You have *what*?" asked Ironwing peevishly.

Rolin gestured at the trees. "Don't you see? There's something different about these woods."

"I've noticed it, too," Scanlon said. "The place is too perfect, like a park."

"Exactly—we haven't seen any old bones, rotting limbs, or tree trunks on the ground. And just look at the size of these ferns! Do you know what I think? Nothing ever grows old or dies here; everything just gets bigger!"

"If that's true," said Windsong, "then what if we've brought death with us to this island? We could ruin everything!"

The woodland was certainly as still as death. No birds twittered; no frogs croaked; no squirrels chattered. Neither tree nor beast spoke in Rolin's hearing as he and his companions tramped deeper into the forest, with only the rustling of their footsteps to break the eerie silence. Rolin was reminded of the breathless calm that often precedes a sudden summer thunderstorm.

"Why don't they speak to us?" complained Scanlon. "Grandfather always said our people could talk with the trees and animals on Luralin. I haven't heard a sound—except for the Tree, of course."

"I don't think we're unwelcome here," Rolin said. "There's just a sort of sadness about the place."

Scanlon nodded. "As if something bad were going to happen."

"Let's not have any more such talk," said Ironwing gruffly. "Nothing will happen to us so far from yeg territory."

Presently, Rolin heard a low, rushing sound. Minutes later, he and his friends came to the wooded banks of a broad river.

"It's the Glymmerin!" Scanlon hooted. "If we follow it upstream, we should find Waganupa. Say, what are these?" he asked Rolin, pointing to some slender, pyramidal trees growing near the water. Most were loaded with golden, pear-shaped fruits, together with fragrant pink blossoms.

"I'm not sure, but—" Rolin bent down a branch to smell its flowers, and a sharp pain pierced his forehead. "It's an amenthil!" Plucking one of the fruits, he cautiously took a bite. While Scanlon and the sorcs anxiously looked on, he finished the first, then started into another.

"What's it taste like?" asked Scanlon, hungrily eyeing the fruit.

"Like pears and persimmons mixed together, only better," Rolin replied, smacking his lips and reaching for a third. "You should try one!"

Soon, everyone was gobbling down the luscious fruits, juice dribbling from the corners of mouths and beaks. Ironwing flew into the top of the tree, devouring all the fruits he could reach.

After eating their fill, the boys stuffed their pockets with more fruits. Then they all set off along the Glymmerin. An hour later, Rolin noticed the river was narrowing. "We must be getting close to the Tree," he told the others.

Sure enough, around the next river bend, the four companions came upon a broad, open space. In the center stood Waganupa, its fluted trunk shrouded in billowing foliage. The griffins made chirring sounds and twitched their tails.

"Truly, this is the Tree that never dies," Windsong murmured. "Never did I dream that one day I would see it with my own eyes."

"I only half believed such a thing could exist," admitted Ironwing. "Now I understand why Elgathel built the Hallowfast near the sea. To gaze upon such a sight, even at night and from afar, would be worth a king's ransom."

"How tall do you suppose it is?" Scanlon asked.

"Higher than the hills, taller than the sun!" Rolin replied in awe, shielding his eyes from the brightness of a white coverlet surrounding Waganupa.

"Look at all the snow!" Scanlon cried. He ran forward, then stopped. "It's hemmonsil flowers, not snow!"

Recognizing the scene from Whitewing's spasel, Rolin waded chest deep into the rippling sea of ivory, bell-shaped blossoms. Like the forest flowers, the trampled hemmonsils closed ranks behind him. Their sweet scent soothed away his weariness and worry, just as Winona's circlet had done.

Windsong and Ironwing rolled in the fragrant flowers like cats in a bed of catnip. The boys laughed at the sight of the great beasts frisking like playful kittens. Then they, too, romped through the flowers, shouting and chasing each another like a couple of schoolboys. It was evening when the four friends finally reached Waganupa's buttressed base, where they quenched their thirst in the Glymmerin's pure waters bubbling up from beneath the Tree.

Rolin dropped a twig into the spring, watching the water carry it away. To his amazement, the Glymmerin appeared to meander on forever through the meadow. Beyond, wooded hills nestled against rugged, snow-capped mountains. Where the land ended and the sea began, he could not tell.

"I feel more at home here than in Liriassa," Scanlon remarked, sitting down beside the stream. "I never want to leave this place."

The griffins nodded in agreement. "Although we sorcs live together in large prides, I could be content to stay here alone," said Windsong.

"And I, too," said Rolin. As he gazed upward into the Tree's long, limber branches, a deep serenity stole over his soul.

"Welcome to the Blessed Isle, Rolin, Scanlon, Windsong and Ironwing!"

"Who . . . who are You?" asked Scanlon.

"I am Waganupa, the Tree of Life, Whom you have come so far to seek. I have been expecting you!"

"How did You know our names and that we were coming?" Rolin asked.

"Long before creating this world, I had already planned My good purposes for your lives and even ordained the day and hour of your arrival on Luralin."

Rolin felt very uncomfortable. What else did this tree know about him?

"Oh, you needn't worry," the voice rumbled in gentle laughter. "I did not call you here to embarrass you or your friends."

"Call us here?" said Rolin. "We never heard Your voice until today!"

"Oh, but I did call you. I drew you to Me through the Prophecy, through the words of Bembor and Winona, and by speaking directly into your hearts."

"Then You must know why we are here," said Ironwing.

The Tree gave a long, deep sigh. "You have come seeking My gifts rather than Me. You wish to use My branches for smiting your enemies to stone. Yet, you cannot overcome evil without first receiving new hearts from Me."

"We need only a few staffs," Ironwing argued. "Five or ten will do."

"You need all of Me, not just a limb or two," the Tree replied. "You must allow Me to grow in your hearts."

"How can such things be?" asked Windsong. "Surely You aren't suggesting we become creatures of wood and sap as You are?"

"That which is born of flesh is flesh, and that which is born of wood is wood. Neither can help you, for both are destined to perish. Only My Spirit grants true freedom and the living waters welling up within to eternal life."

Rolin glanced at Scanlon. What were these "living waters"? Was Waganupa referring to the river Glymmerin? He scratched his head. It was all so perplexing. Without more staffs, how could they defeat Felgor?

Then he noticed clusters of green, egg-shaped cones dangling from the Tree's boughs. "May we gather some of Your seeds to plant?" he asked. "Then we could grow our own staffs."

"You may pick all the cones you wish, but they will yield you no seeds."

"Why not?"

"Only great heat can force open My cones. Since Luralin has never known fire, they have never opened. The time will come, though, when I shall release My seeds. Then you must gather and sow all you can."

"Until then, what must we do, O Tree?" Windsong asked.

"Trust in Me, not just in My power. I have much to teach you, but you are not yet ready to receive it. For now, let these words sink into your hearts: I shall soon suffer many things, as it is written in My Prophecy."

"*Your* Prophecy," Rolin repeated. "Isn't the Prophecy Gaelathane's?"

"Did you not know? Gaelathane and I are one."

"That's impossible!" Scanlon said. "You are a tree, and He is a—"

"A what? Scanlon son of Emmer, you do not yet know Me as you should. You must be remade and renewed, as the Prophecy teaches."

Scanlon frowned. "How do I do that?"

"Abide in Me and learn of Me, while there is yet daylight. The night is coming, when I will no longer be with you."

That evening, Rolin and his friends ate supper by the river. Scanlon picked listlessly at his dubaya bread, while Rolin toyed with the vilna flask.

"What do you suppose Waganupa meant by, 'The night is coming, when I will no longer be with you'?" asked Windsong.

"I don't know, but I didn't fly all this way for a 'new heart,'" Ironwing grumbled, lying dejectedly with his feathered head between his paws. "I'm perfectly happy with the one I've got."

"And I don't want to be 'remade and renewed,'" Scanlon said crossly.

"I know I do," yawned Rolin. "I need a good night's rest!" Curling up under Bembor's cloak, he wondered again why Waganupa had answered each of their questions with a riddle.

CHAPTER 15

GAELESSA

R olin stood before three tall, burning candles. Suddenly, a deep darkness fell upon Luralin, and a wind gust blew out the candles. Unable to relight them, Rolin wept. A violent storm followed, drenching the island with a lashing rain. Then the candles burst into flame again and rose high into the heavens, where they outshone the brightest stars.

"Rolin," a voice softly spoke. Rolin's eyes fluttered open, still moist with tears. The Tree was flooding the landscape with light, like the candle-stars in his dream. "Rolin," the voice repeated. Who could be calling him? Scanlon was snoring nearby, bundled in his cloak. Windsong and Ironwing were also curled up on the ground, heads tucked under wings. Rolin gasped. A tall figure was beckoning to him from the foot of the Tree. It was Gaelathane.

"You have followed Me before," the king said quietly. "Now you must trust Me again. Come up here, and I will show you marvels beyond mortal knowledge." With that, Gaelathane swiftly climbed into the Tree.

Rolin pulled himself onto one of Waganupa's sturdy, boy-sized branches. Following Gaelathane, he climbed higher and higher, until he was above the clouds, where the sea winds sighed through the Tree's graceful sprays of green. Once, he lost his hold on a slippery limb but fell only a few feet before another caught and held him in its springy embrace.

"Climb higher! Farther up!" urged the Tree. Faster he went, a rushing wind boosting him all the way to the Tree's pole-thin top, which rocked gently to and fro like a ship's mast.

Though it was night, he could see the Hallowfast, still locked in the ashtags' iron grip and Mt. Golgunthor, wrapped in a gathering gloom. Then something like a window opened, and he recognized his little log cabin, where his father sat slumped over the kitchen table. "Father, dear Father, I am up here!" Rolin called to him, but Gannon did not stir.

"You must climb down now."

Rolin looked up to see Gaelathane calmly sitting on a branch. His robes were a radiant white, far surpassing the purity and brightness of hemmonsil flowers. Supposing his journey had ended, Rolin obediently clambered down.

All at once, he felt strangely lightheaded, and a wave of whitest light washed over and through him. When his eyes cleared, Rolin was gazing across the threshold of a world more glorious than any he had ever seen or imagined.

"Where are we?" he asked.

"This is Gaelessa," said Gaelathane with a smile, "an eternal land where there is neither age nor death, pain nor illness, sorrow nor weeping. Take My hand, and I will show you My home." When Rolin's hand touched Gaelathane's, the two floated weightlessly into the clear, sweet air.

Below, stunning mountains, meadows and waterfalls basked in a warm light, though no sun hung in the azure sky. Delicious scents wafted up from flowers of dazzling hues. Rolin saw all sorts of trees, too—but no torsils.

"Waganupa is the only torsil to Gaelessa," Gaelathane said, "for no one may come here except through Me. Would you like to see more of My kingdom?"

"Very much!" said Rolin and instantly found himself in a rolling field of fragrant purple flowers. Gaelathane stood beside him.

"What flowers are these?" Rolin asked.

"We are the Flowers of Death and Life," they replied, "for we are the color of the death-that-brings-life." Rolin touched one of the violet-red blossoms.

"Please take me with you," begged the little flower. Rolin hesitated.

"You may pick it," smiled Gaelathane. "Here in Gaelessa, the fragrant self-sacrifice of love is our greatest delight."

As Rolin plucked the exquisite flower, he saw that his fingers glowed with their own light. Indeed, his whole body shone softly.

"Gaelessa's splendor is the expression of My love and goodness," Gaelathane explained. "In this land, there is no need of sun or moon. Even the Tree reflects the glory of this place." Then the purple flowers sang:

High praise to Him who made the Tree,
And all that lives and breathes;
Who was and is and is to come;
His blood will make men free!

"How can anyone's blood 'make men free'?" Rolin asked Gaelathane.

"Only the offering of a perfect life can cleanse and deliver My creation. As the Prophecy says, '. . . that men and trees may be remade.'"

"But why must we be remade?"

"Felgor's rebellion has incurably tainted all that lives beyond the Isle of Light," Gaelathane replied, tears filling His eyes.

"Even me?"

"Even you, My son. Will you let Me purify your heart, to do with as I wish?"

"Yes, but will it hurt?"

"Terribly. But you will find healing when the Glymmerin runs red."

In a twinkling, Rolin was back at the base of the Tree, still clinging to Gaelathane's hand. "Why did You bring me back to Luralin?" he cried. "I wanted to stay with You in Gaelessa forever."

"One day you will, My child," said Gaelathane tenderly. "In the meantime, you must serve Me here and in other torsil worlds. Tell no one where you have been until I have defeated death!" Then the King vanished.

Tears of joy and sorrow streamed down Rolin's face. How could he go back to his drab and dreary life after visiting such a wondrous place? Already Gaelessa's brilliant colors were fading from his mind. Had it all been a dream? Then he saw the wilted flower still clutched in his hand and felt himself floating again over the fragrant purple field.

"Goodbye, Gaelessa," he murmured, placing the fragile reminder of paradise in his pocket.

CHAPTER 16

NIGHTFALL

R olin was surprised to find his friends still sleeping and the moon and stars unchanged in their positions. Apparently, no time had passed during his absence. Too excited to sleep himself, he sat watching the Tree until the stars winked out and the sun's orange disc peeped over the horizon.

Scanlon stretched and groaned. "I dreamt that you climbed the Tree in the middle of the night and never returned," he yawned.

"Well, I'm here now," Rolin quipped, avoiding Scanlon's gaze. Recalling Gaelathane's warning, he said nothing about his visit to Gaelessa.

After the griffins awoke, they ambled off in search of fresh meat, while the boys foraged along the Glymmerin. Soon, they were all enjoying a scrumptious breakfast of apples, pecans and fish (which the sorcs ate raw).

They had just finished when Windsong sniffed the air, then fluttered above the treetops. "There's a storm brewing in the east," he said, blinking his eyes. As the four companions took cover under Waganupa, a hot breeze stirred heavily among the hemmonsils. Ironwing paced nervously.

"I don't think it's a storm," he growled. "My back hairs have been prickling. That means yegs are about—or worse."

"We're not in any danger here, are we?" Scanlon asked.

"Yowr!" Ironwing roared, prancing on his hind legs and batting the air with his paws. "No one will come to harm on Luralin while we sorcs are here!"

"And I've brought a weapon," said Rolin, drawing Elgathel's sword. "Anyway, Gaelathane wouldn't allow any evil on this island, would He?"

"Unless the Prophecy required it," spoke the Tree. "Do you not remember?

> He'll bring a sword and a dreadful death,
> Though not by burning dragon's breath;
> Its life for theirs the Tree will trade,
> That men and trees may be remade.

"If need be, I'll die in defense of Rolin and Scanlon," said Ironwing stoutly.

"No greater love has anyone than to lay down his life for his friends," said the Tree. "Your courage and devotion are admirable, Ironwing. However, you need not fear. The 'dreadful death' is to be Mine alone."

"That can't be!" Scanlon burst out. "Nothing can hurt the Tree of trees!"

"Sometimes, one must not resist evil, in order to achieve a greater good. If I remain here, I remain alone, but if I lay down My life, I will bear much fruit. Today you will have great sorrow, but in a short while you shall see Me again, and then your sorrow shall be turned to joy."

Rolin glanced at his friends, who looked as puzzled as he was. "I'll defend You to the death with my sword!" he declared.

"He who raises the sword must be prepared to die by the sword. No one can take My life from Me by force, but I lay it down of My own free will, that I may receive it back again."

The wind picked up, moaning through the Tree's branches. Rolin looked eastward, where a dark smudge was spreading across the sky.

"I may not have Keeneye's sight," said Ironwing, "but even I can spot a yeg swarm from afar."

"You allowed us to come here, knowing that the enemy would follow us?" Windsong asked the Tree in disbelief.

"I drew you here, just as I am drawing the sorcerer to Me."

"I knew I should have watched our backs more carefully," groaned Ironwing, gnashing his beak. "Now all the yegs in Gundul are after us!"

Windsong tried to console his friend. "You mustn't blame yourself. Who would have guessed Felgor could find us here?"

"I should have," said Rolin glumly. Then he told the others of seeing the mysterious, batlike creatures.

"Those were yeg scouts, all right," said Windsong. "I've never seen any that small before. I wish you'd told us about them earlier."

"I'm sorry," said Rolin, staring at the ground. He felt miserable.

"I'd like to drop that sorcerer off a high rock," muttered Ironwing. He raised his head to stare at the Tree. "Why are You letting him come here?"

"All must take place according to the Prophecy."

"Then we'd better leave before our 'guests' arrive," Ironwing snorted, jerking his neck toward the approaching cloud. "Those yegs will catch our sorc scent from miles away."

"Where would we go?" asked Windsong. "Our enemies have come between us and home. Even if we could evade them, our wings aren't ready yet for another long flight. We'd perish in the sea before making landfall."

"What shall we do? Oh, what shall we do?" Scanlon cried.

"You must not attempt to escape or leave the island, lest the darkness overtake you. Your only hope of refuge lies in Me. Oh, how I wish this day were already ended and my ordeal with it!"

While the Tree spoke, the blackness in the east continued to grow, threatening to blot out the sun. Lightning-like flashes lit up the clouds.

"The time of My departure is near. Now listen carefully, and do exactly as I tell you." Following the Tree's instructions, Rolin and his friends hurried into the forest to fill honey bags with all the amenthil fruits they could carry. Afterwards, they collected seaweed from the shore. Sopping wet and covered with slimy green strands, the boys wedged the bags of fruit and seaweed into cracks and hollows around Waganupa's trunk.

"I wish I knew why we were doing this," grumbled Scanlon. "I hope I never see another amenthil fruit again! And this seaweed smells terrible."

"The Tree must have a good reason," Rolin said. "And please hurry; I don't like the look of the sky."

"It's just a thunderstorm," said Scanlon, pointing at some dark streamers hanging beneath the swirling clouds. "See? It's already starting to rain."

Windsong peered upward. "That's not rain," he exclaimed. "It's yegs!" Sure enough, the black streaks were hundreds of exhausted batwolves and their gorkin riders tumbling through the air and splashing into the sea.

"They can't fly any more," crowed Scanlon. "They'll all drown!"

"Not all of them," said Windsong grimly. "The serpent is driving them on, the fiend!" Flames flared yellow in the black cloud looming over Luralin like a giant bat's wing. "More than death itself, yegs fear fire," the griffin added. "Their thin wing skin shrivels like a moth's at the slightest touch of it."

"It's fly or fry, eh?" grunted Ironwing humorlessly.

"Stay with Me!" wailed Waganupa. "My hour draws near."

From beside the Tree, Rolin and his companions watched in helpless horror as the barrage of batwolf bodies marched across the island in a hail of death. The screams of falling yegs and gorks mingled with the crashing of corpses through the treetops. Those sounds gave way to a deafening thunder of wings as the surviving batwolves descended on the hemmonsil meadow, completely surrounding the Tree.

Slaver dripping from their jaws, their red eyes glowing venomously, the yegs advanced. Many bore gorks, bulbous-headed creatures with large, luminous eyes and flesh the color of a frog's underbelly. Rolin's skin crawled.

"Look there!" one of the batwolves growled, glaring at Rolin. "That one has the smell of a yeg killer!"

"Grrr! Bird-lions!" snarled another. "They're yeg butchers, too!"

"Yeg butchers! Yeg butchers!" the yeg army took up the raucous chorus. Windsong and Ironwing hissed and snapped at their enemies, who hunkered just beyond reach of the sorcs' razor-sharp claws and beaks.

Rolin's hand found his sword hilt. "I'll make them wish they'd never come to Luralin!" he told Scanlon fiercely.

"Do not resist them."

Rolin shook his head in disgust. How could Waganupa expect him to surrender without a fight? Surely he and his friends would be torn to pieces!

"Do not resist them; you will only come to harm if you try."

"They won't take me alive!" growled Ironwing. Nevertheless, he and Windsong lowered their heads, their tails still lashing back and forth.

Suddenly, a hot, foul-smelling wind washed over them. The yegs pulled back in a panic, while the griffins flattened themselves against the ground, every hair standing stiffly erect.

With a hurricane roar, Gorgorunth swept down, scattering yegs and gorks like dry leaves. Belching smoke and reeking of sulfur, the enormous beast landed not twenty feet from the Tree. As the dragon gazed at him with malicious, mocking green eyes, Rolin's knees buckled and his mouth went dry. Then the massive jaws parted in a gruesome grin, showing rows of gleaming fangs. With each breath, smoke puffed out of the flaring nostrils.

Behind the scaly, hideous head hunched a black-cloaked figure. The rider stiffly dismounted and came forward, leaning on a staff. Felgor's bony face split in a death's-head grin. "So sorry to drop in unannounced," he chuckled.

"Do not answer him a word, unless I tell you what to say."

"Allow me to introduce myself," the sorcerer went on, bowing with mock courtesy. "I am Felgor, Lord of Lucambra. This is Gorgorunth, the Scourge of the Skies. Very impressive, is he not?"

When the boys kept silent, Felgor's features twisted in cold disdain. "I already know Scanlon son of Emmer, but who are you, tree urchin?"

Rolin drew himself up defiantly. "Rolin son of—oof!" he grunted, catching Scanlon's elbow jab in his ribs.

"You weren't supposed to answer him, remember?" Scanlon whispered.

"Rolin, is it?" The sorcerer's hooded eyes narrowed. "You must be that upstart Thalmosian I've been looking for, born and bred in that pigsty you call Beechtown." Rolin felt the blood drain from his face.

"I see I've hit the mark," Felgor sneered. "When I've finished with you and this troublesome Tree, I'll teach your river-rat friends not to interfere with me! The same goes for these mangy bird-lions. A little dragon fire will flush their relatives out of their stinking tunnels." The griffins growled.

"What did you meddling maggots hope to gain by coming here?" Felgor demanded. "A few more paltry sticks?" He brandished an ebony rod. "Behold the Black Staff! With it, I could send you all to Gundul in the snap of a bat's wing."

The sorcerer's features softened to a smirk. "But I am in your debt for leading me to Luralin. In return, you shall be my guests of honor." He nodded, and several gangly gorkin warriors rushed up wielding curved swords. They disarmed Rolin, then bound him and Scanlon with ropes. Those sent to subdue Windsong and Ironwing quickly retreated, however, clutching the bleeding stumps of missing noses and hands.

"I'd forgotten how stubborn sorcs can be," sighed the sorcerer. He snapped his fingers, and four scimitars whistled through the air. The griffins shrieked.

"What have you done to them?" cried Rolin, struggling with his bonds.

"I've merely disabled their wings," said Felgor lightly. "I can't have them flying about during the fireworks, or my pet might make a meal of them. I do hope you'll enjoy this spectacle, by the way. You'll have front-row seats!"

Two gorks threw the boys over their shoulders like sacks of potatoes, carried them some distance from the Tree and tossed them on the ground in a heap. Others dragged the wounded sorcs to the same spot.

"How badly are you hurt?" Rolin asked Ironwing.

"Badly enough," groaned the griffin, thrashing about in pain.

"The Tree was right. We shouldn't have fought back," moaned Windsong. "I'm afraid we've let you down. You can't get off this island now, unless you can convince a couple of yegs to carry you!"

"You haven't let us down," whispered Scanlon. "You were only trying to defend yourselves."

"That's right," Rolin said, inching closer to the sorcs. "Anyway, I don't think any of us will leave Luralin alive."

"Quiet!" barked the sorcerer, "or I shall have your tongues cut out!" He waved his staff toward the dragon. On leathery wings, the black serpent launched his sinewy, reptilian body into the air and circled the Tree several times. Then he opened his mouth and disgorged a great gout of flame. Even on the ground, Rolin could feel the blast-furnace heat. He held his breath, waiting for fire to break out among the branches. But when the smoke had cleared, the Tree was as green as ever. Time and again, the dragon belched rivers of white-hot flame, but Waganupa remained unscathed.

Roaring with fury, Gorgorunth repeatedly smashed his tail against the trunk, again without effect. Finally, he sank to earth, where he crouched glaring at the unbroken Tree. Rolin noticed only a single black claw remained on one foot, a memento of the beast's last battle with Elgathel.

"I expected as much," Felgor said calmly. "'He'll bring a sword and a dreadful death, though not by burning dragon's breath.'"

"You know the Prophecy?" gasped Rolin.

"Of course!" Felgor replied. "Better than any tree scum. How do you suppose I've foreseen your every move? You came here to find a way of destroying me. Instead, you've fallen into my trap!" The sorcerer wheezed with laughter. Rolin gulped, exchanging fearful glances with Scanlon.

Felgor snorted. "You can't hide anything from me! I already know Bembor is a descendant of that rebel Elgathel. He sent you brats because he's too old and feeble to come himself. After you'd done his bidding, he would have cast you aside to seize the kingdom, though doubtless he's promised one of you the throne."

Rolin's jaw dropped. Why hadn't Bembor mentioned his relation to Elgathel? Still, he knew the old staff-bearer had no intention of making himself king. Felgor was just trying to sow seeds of suspicion in their hearts.

The sorcerer poked his staff in Scanlon's face. "Lucambra has but one ruler—Felgor—and no tree toad can take that from me!" He spat, leering at his cowering captives. "Now I'm going to chop down your precious tree, and you're going to watch!" While his cruel words sank in, the sorcerer turned to his servants. "Let your axes bite deep. Death to the Staff Tree!"

"Death to the Staff Tree!" echoed thousands of yeggorin and gorkin voices. "Long live the Lord of Lucambra and his Tree of Death!" Then a howling mob of gorks descended on Waganupa. Armed with axes, swords and scimitars, they gleefully rained blows upon the silent, unresisting Tree.

"No! Stop them!" cried Rolin, knowing all the while there was nothing he could do. Then he felt a nudge at the back of his leg.

"Don't worry—they'll never cut it down at this rate," Scanlon whispered.

"That's right," said Windsong. "Unless my eyes deceive me, they haven't broken through the bark yet, it's so thick and spongy." The gorks redoubled their efforts, attacking the Tree with a mindless fury.

"Slash it! Kill it!" raved Felgor. The harried creatures whipped themselves into a frenzy of chopping, hacking and stabbing. Gnashing their teeth in rage and frustration, some even gashed themselves with their own weapons.

"What fools!" Felgor fumed. He hobbled toward Waganupa, where he struck every gork within reach of his rod. His unfortunate victims immediately shriveled into black ash. The remaining gorks hastily fell back to a safe distance from the ranting sorcerer.

"You haven't even made a dent in it!" cried Felgor, pointing at the Tree's trunk. "Have your axes gone dull—or is it your heads? I'll show you how the Lord of Lucambra deals with his enemies!" Muttering beneath his breath, Felgor struck the Tree three times with the Black Staff. The stick smoldered, then burst into flames. With a cry, Felgor dropped it, then limped back to Rolin and his companions.

"You're to blame for this!" he screeched, wagging a bony finger in their faces. With a strength belying his age, he dragged Scanlon before the serpent's horrible, scaly snout. "Tell me how to lift the spell that protects this accursed Tree," he grated, "or my pet will roast you alive, limb by limb!"

Scanlon blanched. "I don't know how," he squeaked. "But even if I did, I would never betray Waganupa!"

"Tell them to dip their weapons in the Glymmerin's waters."

"Brave words for one about to enter Gundul's gates!" snarled the sorcerer. "Prepare to die!" Flames licked out of the dragon's jaws. The yegs crept closer, poised to spring. "They're waiting for their share," Felgor cackled.

"Tell them!"

"I . . . I can't!" cried Rolin.

Felgor whirled to face him. "You can't what?"

"You must—there is no other way."

In an instant, the sorcerer had Rolin by the throat, his face contorted with anger. "You can't what? Tell me, or you'll be the first to taste dragon fire!"

"Don't tell him!" cried Scanlon.

"Don't tell me what?" Felgor's gaze flicked back and forth between them.

"*Tell him!*"

"They must dip their axes in the river," Rolin choked out, hanging his head.

Felgor screamed an order, and the whole company of gorkin warriors stampeded pell-mell down to the Glymmerin's banks, where they plunged their weapons into the water. At another command, they swarmed back to surround the Tree. Then a gigantic gork stepped forward, hefting his dripping, double-bitted ax. With a grunt, he swung it in a whistling arc.

The ax struck with a sickening thud, sending chunks and slivers of bark flying. A hundred other axes followed, biting into the now-defenseless Tree. Soon, the gorks had breached the bark, and red-stained wood chips began piling up around the trunk. An agonized groan rumbled through the earth.

"Your staffs saved others, but who will save You from us?" the gorks taunted. "If You really were the King of the Trees, You could turn us to stone. Now we shall hack You to pieces and burn Your stump with fire!"

The Servants of the Tree hid their faces. Rolin winced at the enemy's guttural jeers and at the rhythmic *thack-thack* of metal striking wood.

"Faster! Faster!" bellowed the sorcerer.

All at once, a deep gloom fell upon the island as black clouds boiled ominously overhead. Only Waganupa's waning light now lit the ghastly scene. Undaunted, the gorks continued their grisly task.

Without warning, the earth shook violently, throwing the tree cutters to the ground. Some fell shrieking into deep cracks that opened beneath them.

"Don't stop! Keep working!" Felgor shouted, shaking his fist. Picking up their weapons, the gorks dropped them again with howls of pain. Every sword, scimitar and ax head was glowing red hot. In seconds, the sizzling metal had melted into smoking globs. The gorks fled, splashing through puddles of wine-red sap still gushing from the gashed Tree. The enemy's derisive hoots died away.

"It is finished!" thundered Waganupa.

WHOOM! A searing lightning bolt sliced the sky, squarely striking the Tree. With a stupendous roar, it burst asunder, raining down blocks of wood as big as houses. Another massive earthquake ripped through the ground. Then there was silence.

CHAPTER 17

THE RING OF FIRE

Rolin opened his eyes to smoke and shadows. Had he been buried alive? Branches scratched his face as he thrust his head through tangled foliage. There—he could see again. Scanlon's bloodied head poked through another jumble of shredded bark and limbs, then Windsong's and Ironwing's badly-mussed head and neck feathers. Then Scanlon's face froze in a look of horror. Rolin followed his friend's gaze to see Waganupa's tall, jagged stump. He wept, and all Luralin wept with him.

Yegs and gorks wandered about in a daze. Rolin could hear the terrible screams and groans of others lying crushed beneath the steaming debris. Surveying the carnage, Felgor stood beside the dragon.

"The Tree is dead; long live Felgor, King of Lucambra!" he crowed. Then he swaggered over to deliver a vicious kick to Rolin's head. "Comfortable now, river trash?" he rasped. "I'd feed you to my pet, but you wouldn't make him a mouthful. It's a pity I can't take you back with me; I always need more slaves to work in my mines. Since I can't spare any yeg mounts, I'm afraid you'll all have to stay here."

Rolin blinked dirt and blood out of his eyes. Had he heard Felgor right? Though escape from the island would be impossible, at least they'd have plenty of food and water while awaiting rescue.

"I'm ridding this place of its vermin, once and for all," the sorcerer gloated. "Farewell, rats of Luralin!" With a mocking salute, the sorcerer climbed onto Gorgorunth and flew off with the remnant of his forces. Rolin and his friends watched the departing enemy host until it was only a blemish on the horizon.

"I don't like this," muttered Ironwing, licking his wounded wings.

"Nor do I," Windsong said. "Why threaten us, then spare our lives?"

"Perhaps he was just trying to scare us," suggested Scanlon.

"He seemed very serious to me," Rolin groaned, nursing his sore head.

"Before he comes back, let's get out of these blasted ropes!" Ironwing said. With their powerful beaks, the griffins clipped through Rolin's and Scanlon's cords as if they were straw. Once freed, the boys set to untying the sorcs' ropes. They had nearly finished when a puff of smoke and flame mushroomed on the island's edge. Other smoke plumes blossomed in a long line as dragon fire encircled Luralin with frightful speed.

"Hurry—get these ropes off!" cried Windsong. Rolin and Scanlon frantically tugged at the remaining knots. Even as the sorcs struggled out of the loosened ropes, smoke was billowing on all sides. A strong wind sprang up, whirling dust, leaves and branches high into the sky.

"It's a fire wind!" Rolin gasped. Only once before had he witnessed the awesome power of a forest fire as it sucked in air to feed its voracious appetite. Without shelter, he knew they had only minutes to live. But where could they go? Just then, a herd of panic-stricken deer rushed past.

"They're headed for the Glymmerin!" Scanlon shouted. He and Rolin helped the injured griffins down to the riverbank, where they found only a muddy ditch. Terrified animals wallowed in the mire, seeking relief from the heat. Dense smoke and glowing embers filled the air. Trees were exploding, scattering burning brands far and wide. The ring of fire was fast closing in.

"To the Tree!" Rolin cried, his face and arms blistering. When he and the others reached the stump, all were coughing and gasping for air.

"Yow! My fur's on fire!" Ironwing yelped. Scanlon slapped at a coal smoldering on the sorc's back. Soon, both boys were busy putting out sparks.

"Better to die here . . . than in Felgor's . . . dungeons," wheezed Windsong.

"Seaweed!" coughed Scanlon, swatting at the thick smoke. Searching the stump, he dragged out a dripping bag. He and Rolin slopped handfuls of the green, smelly weed over the sorcs, then over each other. Rolin plopped some right on his head, letting the cold salt water run down his face in rivulets.

"I smell fresh air in here!" said Ironwing, sniffing at a crevice in the bark.

"Maybe the trunk is hollow," Rolin panted. Hastily donning more seaweed against the heat, he felt his way around the stump, probing for openings as he went. Just before burning debris blocked his way, he felt cool air streaming from a cleft in the trunk and hurried back to report his discovery.

"Quick! Collect the other bags before the fire reaches them!" Ironwing ordered. Scanlon and Rolin gathered up all the soggy sacks they could find and shoved them inside the stump. Then everyone squeezed through the opening into a cool, shadowy cavern reaching high into the recesses of the hollow hulk. The stump's thick walls muted the fire's roar to a soft rumble. On the far side huddled a murmuring menagerie of squirrels, chipmunks, raccoons and other furry refugees.

Ironwing sniffed the air. "Smoke's coming in," he said. "We've got to plug that breach in the trunk! Use your seaweed bags; they won't burn."

As the boys hurriedly stuffed the wet sacks into the crack, the fire attacked their barricade with sizzling sounds. "Thank

Gaelathane for that seaweed," sighed Rolin, after the gap was plugged tight. "It saved our lives!"

"We should also thank the Tree for its thick bark," Windsong added. "Without it, we would surely burn to death in here."

In here. "Of course!" cried Rolin. "'Your only hope of refuge lies *in Me*.' The Tree was telling us we could escape the fire by hiding inside its trunk!" The four friends fell silent as the raging inferno hurled its waves of crackling flame against the stump. While the firelight played through holes between the seaweed bags, Scanlon petted a squirrel, the griffins paced, and Rolin sat hugging his knees to his chest, praying that Waganupa's roots would hold fast.

CHAPTER 18

NEW LIFE

R olin groaned and forced open his swollen eyes. Darkness surrounded him. His whole body felt afire, and his throat burned from smoke and thirst. "Water," he croaked.

He crawled toward a glimmer of light gleaming between the seaweed bags and peeked out. Charred, smoking wood, glowing coals and rippling heat waves greeted his eye. No water there.

Half delirious with thirst, he was dragging himself back across the tree cavern's floor when he bumped into some bags and caught the sweet odor of amenthil fruit. Pawing open a sack, he greedily devoured its contents. Next, he squeezed amenthil juice into Scanlon's parched mouth. Together, the boys hand fed the sorcs, who were slower to revive. Their injured wing muscles had stiffened during the night, and both were weak with loss of blood.

"Are we still alive?" moaned Ironwing.

"Yes, but the Tree is not," Windsong grunted. "Surely the Prophecy's words have come to pass, 'Its life for theirs the Tree will trade.'"

"If Waganupa hadn't told us about dipping those weapons in the river, Felgor would have killed us all," said Scanlon softly.

"Instead, the Tree died, and it was my fault," Rolin wept.

"You mustn't blame yourself," said Windsong. "You had no choice. Besides, you didn't kill Waganupa."

"Then who did?" Rolin retorted. "The gorks?"

"They inflicted some nasty wounds, all right, but they were weeks from reaching the Tree's heartwood. And the sorcerer's crude arts could never have created that lightning bolt. Gaelathane cut short the Tree's sufferings."

"Poor Waganupa," Scanlon murmured.

"Poor us, if we don't find more food and water soon!" grumbled Ironwing.

"We'll make do with what's at hand," said Rolin. Exploring the stump in the dim light, he and Scanlon came upon a small pool on the hollow's east side. Several rabbits were drinking at its edge.

"This must be the spring that feeds the Glymmerin!" Rolin exclaimed.

Ironwing crawled over to the pool, scattering the rabbits. "*Fed*, you mean," he said sourly. "The water's probably unfit to drink."

Rolin sipped from the stagnant spring. "It's still good," he told the others. Warily, then eagerly, his friends drank their fill of the sweet water. Next, the boys rummaged through the bags they had salvaged from the fire, discovering four more sacks of amenthil fruits, and—

"Dubaya!" Rolin announced, sheepishly holding up a sorry-looking lump of the brownish bread. "The yegs ate everything else." The others groaned.

"So it's fruit or dubaya," Scanlon summed up.

"Ugh," said Rolin, who was having visions of oatcakes hot off the griddle. "I think I'll fill a honey bag with some water, before the pool dries up." Grabbing a sack, he set off toward the spring, cutting across the cavern floor. He was halfway there when he nearly stepped into a gaping gash in the ground. "Over here! Hurry!" he called to the others.

Scanlon and the sorcs rushed to his side. "So this is the source of our fresh air!" said Windsong. The boys lay with their heads hanging over the crack, gulping in the cold, pure air flowing from it. Curious to know the chasm's depth, Rolin dropped a small stone into it. When there was no sound of the pebble's hitting bottom, he and Scanlon tossed in larger rocks, which the crevasse also silently swallowed up.

"Do you suppose it goes all the way to Gundul?" they asked.

"Shush! Don't even think of such a thing!" said Windsong. "Gundul's gates are closer than you might imagine."

The next morning, Rolin and Scanlon pulled several scorched seaweed bags out of the stump split and peered outside. A steady rain was falling, dousing some still-smoldering blazes and cooling the ashes. When a few squirrels and raccoons scampered through the crack and disappeared into the rain, the boys pushed out the rest of the bags and followed them.

Rolin gasped. Gone were the trees, the hemmonsils and all the grass, leaving a stark landscape of bleak grays and blacks. Only a mournful wind moaned through some leafless snags. The air reeked of death. Rolin shivered, though not from the cold.

Crick! A sharp, snapping sound shattered the awful stillness.

"What was that?" exclaimed Rolin, scanning the ground and sky. Had the batwolves returned to finish off the fire's survivors?

Crack! came the noise again, this time from some charred limbs.

"Maybe it's just the rocks cooling," Scanlon suggested. Then a *Pow! Pow! Pow!* split the air, like popcorn kernels exploding on a hot stove.

"That's not rocks," declared Rolin. He ran to the debris pile, finding hundreds of greenish brown eggs lying on a bed of soggy cinders. As he looked on, one egg after another burst open with a *bang*, scattering purple pellets that pattered like hail on the ground.

"What are those?" Scanlon asked.

"I don't know—" Rolin began. Then it struck him. "Cones! The cones are opening!" He rushed back to the stump and returned with an armful of empty honey sacks. "I'd forgotten all about them," he breathlessly explained.

"About what—the sacks?" asked Scanlon.

"No, no. The cones. They open only after a fire, remember? We've got to hurry." He dropped to his hands and knees.

"Hurry to do what?"

"To collect the seeds, of course, as the Tree told us to." Rolin tossed Scanlon a sack, then scooped some of the small, shiny seeds into his own bag. Muttering under his breath, Scanlon did the same. Meanwhile, the griffins had ambled over to watch, their broken wings dragging awkwardly on the ground.

"What are the seeds for?" asked Windsong.

"To plant," replied Rolin, scraping more of the purple pellets into a pile.

"But where?"

"Here on Luralin, in Liriassa, around Beechtown—everywhere!"

"And how do you plan to get off this island?"

"I don't know, but I will," Rolin said. "Gaelathane told me I must serve Him not only here but in other torsil worlds, too."

"If wishes were wings, we'd all be griffins," sneered Ironwing. "Thanks to Felgor, you'll rot here with the rest of us!"

"Poor old Ironwing," clucked Windsong, watching his friend plod off. "He once could fly longer, faster and farther than any other sorc. Now neither of us will ever fly again."

"I'm sorry," said Rolin. "If I'd known you two would come to harm on this journey, I never would have left the Willowahs in the first place." He looked Windsong in the eye. "But since we're still alive, we must obey the Tree by planting these seeds in every torsil world we can."

Windsong clicked his beak softly. "You are not the same two-legs—er—*boy* you were before. You've gained a faith and courage you didn't have before we came here. Maybe that's what the Tree meant by being 'remade and renewed.' It's something that starts on the inside and works its way to the outside."

With Windsong's help, Rolin and Scanlon gathered seeds all that day, stacking their full bags against the trunk. Ironwing sulked next to the pool, glowering at anyone who came inside the stump for a drink of water.

At dusk, Scanlon heaved the last seed sack onto the stack and collapsed beside it. "When I shut my eyes, all I see are purple specks," he groaned.

"Me, too," Rolin said. As he leaned against the Tree, something tickled his cheek. Scratching the spot, he felt a sharp pain, and a strip of skin came away in his hand.

"Rolin—your face!" Scanlon gasped.

Rolin felt around his forehead and nose, finding more peeling skin. His arms were also painfully blistered, while his fingers were cracked and bleeding from beating out embers on the griffins' backs and picking up seeds.

"Ugh—what's this?" Scanlon held up his palm, which was coated with a reddish, sticky substance.

"I've got it on my hand, too," said Rolin. "Look—here's a puddle of the stuff. It must be tree sap that's dripped off the stump!"

"I can't get it off," Scanlon complained, rubbing his hand.

"Say, I think my burns feel better," Rolin said. Dipping his other hand in the syrupy sap, he smeared some on his face and arms.

"You look like a raccoon!" laughed Scanlon.

Rolin wiped his hands on Scanlon's face. "Now you do, too!" he said with a grin. Then he and Scanlon scooped some of the sticky sap onto slabs of bark before scouting around the Tree for more of the burn ointment. They soon discovered a fire-hardened glob of the pitch.

"This might be useful," said Rolin, pocketing the lump.

Back inside the Tree, the boys daubed sap on the worst of their mounts' wounds. The griffins feebly protested that it matted their fur together, until they felt the salve's soothing power.

That night, Rolin slept fitfully, dreaming of yegs that spat fire and dragons that could carry off entire islands. Once, awakened by Scanlon's snoring, he saw the sorcs thrashing about in their sleep, snapping at phantom enemies.

When Rolin awoke, his head was throbbing, his clothes were drenched with a fever sweat, and his mouth was drier than punkwood. The bright sun hurt his eyes. The sun? How could he see the sun? The stump must have caved in!

He staggered to his feet and stared upward. The cavern ceiling was still intact, lit with a brilliant glow from below that banished the shadows from every crack and cranny.

"What's happening?" Scanlon cried out. "Where's that light coming from?"

"Down there!" Rolin exclaimed, pointing to the fissure.

"The fires of Gundul!" screeched Ironwing. "We'll all be consumed!"

The earth quivered and quaked. With a roar, the rift split wide open, and a dazzling splendor exploded into the hollow stump. As a fluted crystal column rose from the chasm, a voice proclaimed, "Do not be afraid; I am He Who was dead, and am alive forevermore!" On reaching the cavern ceiling, the growing pillar split the stump down both sides with a deafening *boom*. The two halves fell outward, leaving the stunned companions in the open air, prostrate beside the Tree's shining trunk.

The island shuddered as Waganupa grew larger, its top piercing the clouds. Then, with a rumbling roar, a fountain gushed from beneath the Tree.

"The Glymmerin!" cried Scanlon. Now a rich rose-red, the reborn river overflowed its banks, sweeping all ash and debris before it. Then it split into four forks, each flowing toward a point of the compass. Vibrant with life, the voice spoke again:

"When you return home, take My waters with you. They are for the healing of your land and its people. I shall go before you to prepare your way. No weapon the enemy brings against you shall prosper, for I shall be with you, even until the end of the age. After you have planted Me in all My worlds, I shall come again to receive you to Myself. I am the Torsil of torsils!"

With that, the Tree rose from Luralin, leaving behind a bubbling pool that fed the Glymmerin's four streams. Rolin and his friends gazed skyward until the Tree vanished into the clouds. Then they heard the voice say, "I am the resurrection and the life; he who believes in Me shall live, even if he dies; and everyone who lives and believes in Me shall never die."

CHAPTER 19

BEAUTY FOR ASHES

The four companions gaped as Luralin changed before their eyes. When the water had subsided into the Glymmerin's four channels, a green sheen shimmered across the barren landscape as long-stemmed grasses sprouted and grew into broad meadows filled with nodding, white hemmonsils. Trees and bushes sprang up to form lush, deep forests. Birds and furry creatures appeared on the scene, flying, creeping and climbing amongst the tall trees. Amenthils flourished along the rivers, their flowers perfuming the air.

Then, like the quickening of streams in a spring thaw, the voices of Luralin's new creation joined in singing:

> Praise Him Who fell, to fall no more,
> And lives in light on high;
> His kingdom stands from shore to shore,
> That men no more may die!
>
> He made Himself an offering,
> His blood will break all chains;
> The Tree of trees and King of kings,
> In majesty He reigns!

For all the former things have passed,
Behold, His world made new;
All evil's power put down at last—
The sorcerer is through!

Let all that lives and all that breathes,
With gratitude proclaim,
Upon the earth, beneath the seas,
His glory, grace and fame!

"Luralin is made new!" Rolin marveled. Reminded of Gaelessa, he gingerly picked a shriveled little ball out of his pocket, all that remained of the flower of death and life. He was about to toss it aside when a tiny voice peeped, "Water!"

Rolin ran to the Glymmerin and dipped the dried flower in its waters. In the blink of an eye, the blossom unfurled; the withered stem straightened; and the whole plant glowed a rich, deep purple. When the others asked where he had found the flower, he told them of his visit to Gaelathane's kingdom.

"Imagine that!" Windsong exclaimed. "The very light of Gaelessa, brought down to our world in this wisp of a flower."

"Plant me here!" said the flower.

Rolin poked a hole in the earth beside the stream, then inserted the stem. After he had filled in the hole, the flower sweetly sang its Gaelessa song:

High praise to Him Who made the Tree,
And all that lives and breathes;
Who was and is and is to come;
His blood has made men free!

"Of whose blood do you sing, little flower?" Ironwing asked.

"I sing of Gaelathane, Who shed His blood for all of us."

"We know that the Tree has died and lives again," said Windsong patiently, "but surely Gaelathane cannot suffer the pangs of death."

"Out of love, He suffered with the Tree, for they are one," the purple flower replied. "Does not the Prophecy speak of it?

But three days hence new life will grow,
In place of water, blood will flow,
To cleanse the land from shore to shore,
And what was lost, with love restore.

"The Tree has revived on the third day, just as foretold," Windsong said. "But does this mean the Glymmerin really flows with Gaelathane's blood?"

"Not with the same red sap that nourishes your body," said the flower. "It is His life, poured forth freely and abundantly for the renewing of all worlds."

Rolin looked down at the wine-red water, then at his friends. "Let's go!" he yelled, plunging into the river. Scanlon and the sorcs followed, splashing about like playful otters. The water washed away Rolin's weariness, filling him with the same peace and contentment he'd found in the Tree's presence.

An hour later, he and his companions lay refreshed on the riverbank, drying themselves in the sun. A doe and its fawn eyed them curiously, while butterflies danced in the air.

"That was marvelous," murmured Windsong, lazily dabbling a wing tip in the water. "I feel so . . . so . . ."

"New?" asked Rolin. "I feel it, too. It's as though the old me went away and a new one took his place."

"Praise be to Gaelathane, I do believe I could take on a whole pack of yegs!" yowled Ironwing, rolling in the grass.

"Rolin—look at yourself!" Scanlon cried. Glancing down at his hands, Rolin saw the blistering burns were gone. The skin on his face felt fresh and whole.

"I'm healed!" he cried.

"So am I!" laughed Scanlon. Then they stared at the sorcs. Could it be? Windsong twisted his neck back to examine his wings, then cautiously tested them. With a screech he shot into the sky, Ironwing close behind. On the ground, Rolin and Scanlon cheered as the griffins looped, dove and rolled.

"Take us with you!" the boys shouted up to them. Soon, the sorcs returned to earth, kneeling to allow their riders to climb on.

Scanlon and Rolin whooped and screamed as they frolicked on griffinback above the island.

"I feel like a griffling again, finding my wings for the first time," Windsong told Rolin happily. "We're healed, just as Gaelathane promised in His Prophecy. The Tree had to die, so we could live!"

Hovering nearby on Ironwing, Scanlon shouted, "Say, if we stayed here, maybe we'd live forever!"

"We can't stay here," Ironwing chided him. "The Tree said, '*When* you return home,' not *if*. That means we must go back."

"Without Waganupa, the island's not the same now, anyway," Rolin told his friends. "So, while we're waiting for the Tree's return, we'd best be about the Tree's business!" The sorcs flew back to the split-open stump, where the boys filled their remaining honey sacks with spring water. Rolin also stuffed his pockets with amenthil fruits to chew on during the return trip.

"Ow!" he cried, tripping over a small stack of smooth, shining rods. He knelt to touch one. Though solid, it was as crystal clear as the risen Tree. A soft light shone from within.

"They're staffs!" Scanlon exclaimed. "The Tree left some for us after all." He brandished one of the wands like a sword. "Do you suppose this could turn yegs to stone, like Grandfather Bembor's?"

"I hope we don't have to find out," replied Rolin with a shiver.

After loading their gear on the griffins, the boys hopped on their mounts, who wheeled above the island, then turned toward the rising sun. "May Gaelathane watch over you, Isle of Light!" murmured Rolin. "And may your trees never taste fire again."

Seeing the Glymmerin's eastern branch cascading in clouds of crimson spray over a high cliff, he recited, "'The Glymmerin will flow in peace, her waters nevermore to cease.'" Then, recalling Bembor's *Ballad of Luralin,* he sang:

Luralin, O Luralin,
The home of trees that never die,
Across the sea, beyond the sky,
In dreams, I'll walk your woods again.

CHAPTER 20

AMENTHIL WINE

The sorcs flew strongly all that afternoon and into the evening, despite the heavy sacks they were carrying. Rolin's stomach began to churn. What would they find at the griffins' lair? Was Whitewing waiting for them, or had Felgor already made good his promise to slaughter the sorca? Worse yet, might Windsong and Ironwing lose their way in the dark?

All at once, he saw a bright light blaze up in the sky some distance ahead, as if someone had lit a giant torch. Was the dragon flying out to meet them?

"Look at that star!" Scanlon called out.

"That's no star," said Windsong. "It's too large. Besides, the clouds are covering the stars tonight; I can't imagine how we'll navigate without them."

"Maybe Golgunthor is erupting," Ironwing suggested. "The last time it—"

"No, no. Don't you remember what the Tree said?" interrupted Windsong. "'When you return . . . I shall go before you to prepare your way.' This is none other than Waganupa guiding us home."

Gazing upon the Tree's splendor, Rolin felt the warmth and joy of Luralin welling up again in his heart. Wherever his path might lead, he knew Waganupa would light his way more clearly than the brightest moonwood.

Dawn was reddening the eastern skies when the sorcs came within sight of Lucambra's shores. "We'll be in our dens within the hour," Windsong promised as he and Ironwing passed over the Elmarin's pristine beaches. The griffins panted with exertion, their wings weary from the long flight across the sea. Now they flew into a high pass leading through the coastal range.

Screeeech! A harsh cry came from above, and a dark shape hurtled past Rolin. Yegs were diving on them from all directions.

"Hang on!" cried Windsong. Rolin grabbed the griffin's fur with both hands as his mount twisted and turned in the air. Raking a huge, hairy yeg with claws and beak, Windsong sent the creature plummeting to the ground.

"Hooray!" Rolin yelled, shaking his fist at the yegs. Then something slammed into his back, knocking him off Windsong. "Help!" he screamed, flinging out his arms to catch himself. He found only air. Spinning earthward, he had fleeting thoughts of home and Marlis before darkness overtook him.

When Rolin groggily awoke, he vaguely remembered the yeg ambush but not how he'd survived his fall—or how he had ended up lying on a cold stone floor. He tried to stand but fell back with a groan, his aching body protesting. A thick, sulfurous stench stung his nose and throat.

Rolin saw he was in a small, windowless room containing stacks of empty boxes. Opposite him stood a stout-looking door, gray light leaking around it.

Raising himself on one elbow, he croaked, "Hey! Ho! Is anybody there?" The door flew open, and an armored gorkin guard flung something at him.

"Here's your day's ration, tree maggot!" growled the guard. "You're lucky to be alive. If you hadn't fallen on that yeg, you'da' been dragon meat by now. It's too bad the dungeons are already full, or you'd be joining your friends!" With that the guard slammed the door.

Dazed, Rolin sank back to the floor. Evidently, a yeg had broken his fall, then brought him here—wherever *here* was. From the sound of it, Scanlon and the sorcs were also locked up in this place. At least there was some chance that they, too, were still alive. Noticing a small door near the back of the cell, he tried the handle but found it locked.

His stomach growling, he sniffed at the morsel the guard had tossed him. Hard and black, it resembled a dried-up chunk of meat. He pitched it against the wall. In spite of his hunger, he couldn't bring himself to eat it. Seized with a lonely despair, he laid his head on an empty cask and slept.

Without sun or moon to mark the days and nights, Rolin lost all track of time. Waking, he nibbled on the amenthil fruits he had brought in his pockets. Sleeping, he dreamt of nasty, crawly things pinching and poking him. Awake or asleep, he constantly shivered from the damp chill in his stone prison.

Every so often, the door would open partway and a hunk of rancid meat or moldy bread would sail through, or a clawed foot would slide a rusty cup of brackish water into the cell. Otherwise, there were no visitors.

Then one day the door creaked open and someone stepped inside. Rolin shrank back from the shadowy figure, until he realized it was a brown-haired young girl, looking no more than ten years old.

"Wh-who are you?" he cried out.

The stranger put a pale finger to her lips. "Shhhh—I can't stay . . . long, or they'll . . . come looking for me." She spoke haltingly, as if unaccustomed to talking. "I brought you some food. They won't miss it today. There's a . . . celebration planned." The girl took a loaf of bread from a pocket in her frock and handed it to him. Rolin's mouth watered. He couldn't remember the last time he'd tasted fresh bread.

"Thank you!" he mumbled, biting off a piece and ravenously chewing it. "What's your name?"

"I'm called Emma." The girl blushed and bit her lip, then dropped a key into Rolin's lap. "This opens the side door, to a room with a window."

"That I could escape through?" Rolin's spirits rose.

The girl gave him a horrified look. "No! You can't get outside that way."

"Then can you tell me where I am?"

Emma stared at him with lost, hopeless eyes. "You are *inside*."

"Are my friends here—?" But she was gone.

After finishing the bread, Rolin tried the key in the door. Turning it in the lock, he heard a satisfying *click*, and the door swung open. He blinked his eyes. Bright daylight streamed through a deep-set hole in one wall, falling on fifty or sixty squat wooden barrels standing in neat rows. When Rolin jostled one, it made a sloshing sound.

He stood on tiptoe to see out the window. Below, there was a thousand-foot drop ending in jagged rocks. Beyond that, a desolate wasteland of gray cinders and black ashtags stretched for miles. So that's what Emma had meant by "inside." He was a captive in the dragon's mountain, and there was no way out. If only he had the wings of a griffin!

Late that night, Rolin awoke to the slip-slapping of gorkin feet hurrying through the hall outside. Guttural voices bellowed orders, while others grunted in surly reply. The whole fortress rang with shouts, laughter and raucous singing. Closer to dawn, the tantalizing aromas of roasting meat and baking bread wafted into Rolin's cell.

Tormented by the cooking odors, he crawled over to the box holding his last few amenthil fruits. He was removing one when a dazzling light lit up the cell. A blindingly bright Person appeared beside him. Rolin fell to the floor, shaking with fear. Then a gentle hand touched his shoulder.

"It is I, Rolin; do not be afraid."

Rolin looked up into Gaelathane's kindly features and gasped. Purple scars snaked across His face, neck, arms and hands. Someone or something had horribly disfigured the King of the Trees.

"What happened to You?" Rolin asked.

"I bear the wounds of the Tree of Life. Having died, I am never to die again. I hold the keys of Death and of Gundul."

"Then it was I who did this to You!" Rolin covered his face and wept bitterly. "If I had not told Felgor—"

"It had to be so, that all the words written of Me in the Prophecy should be fulfilled," Gaelathane said tenderly. "My agony restored My people to Me. I was pierced for your pardon; every bite of the ax and every drop of My blood was for your healing."

"Then why am I here? I want out of this horrible place!"

"As I led you to Luralin, so I have brought you to the gates of Gundul."

"But why?" Rolin pleaded.

"You cannot understand now but you shall in the days to come. Will you trust Me, Rolin son of Gannon?"

Wordlessly, Rolin nodded.

"Then this is what you must do." Gaelathane spoke briefly and quietly. ". . . and when you are finished, you must tell the warbler what you have done. Do not forget. Many lives depend upon your obedience." Rolin nodded again.

"Below you, My people await deliverance. Let them taste of Me and know that I am good, for I offer My water of life freely. Then all must take Me as their life tree."

"What if they won't accept me?" said Rolin. "I'm only a boy, after all."

"If they mistrust you, show them your sap ball." Then the King vanished.

As soon as Gaelathane's light had faded from the cell, Rolin carried his box of amenthil fruits into the next room and set it on one of the casks. Then he pried the stoppers out of all the barrels, using a rusty spike he'd found on the floor. His eyes watered at the pungent odor of wine.

Following Gaelathane's directions, he squeezed a trickle of amenthil juice into the open bunghole of each barrel and replaced the plug. When he was through, all that remained of the fruits was a pile of seedy pulp.

"'Squeeze the sweet and save the sour,'" he grumbled, repeating the King's words to himself. "I can't imagine why He wanted me to keep this stuff. I certainly can't eat it. And what's a 'warbler,' anyway?" Wrapping the pulp in an old rag, he crammed the bundle back into his box. He was leaving the room when he heard a twittering sound. A small, black-and-yellow bird was perched in the window, shivering in the cool, early morning air.

"Well?" it chirped, cocking its head with an inquisitive look.

Rolin stared at the little ball of fluff. He hadn't talked with a bird since leaving Thalmos, and the funny thing fascinated him.

"Catbird got your tongue, has it?"

"Who—I mean, why—or rather, what do you want?" Rolin stammered.

"I'm the warbler, you ninny! I'm told you have a message for me."

"Message?" Then Rolin remembered what he was supposed to tell the bird.

The warbler fluttered onto his nose. "Hurry up, will you? The bat things are still on the prowl, and they eat snoops."

172

Rolin took a deep breath, then let it out again. Could he trust the brash bird? "I've . . . put amenthil juice in these wine casks," he blurted out.

"And had some wine while you were at it, I shouldn't wonder," muttered the warbler, flying off. Rolin watched it disappear into the distance, then left the room and closed the door. Satisfied he had carried out Gaelathane's instructions to the letter, he settled down to await the outcome.

Minutes later, he heard the wine room's outer door opening and the sound of gorkin voices. He pressed his ear against the side door.

"Well, Three-Eyes, today's the day," grunted one gork, speaking loudly above the thumping and bumping of casks being moved.

"It's about time," growled another. "We haven't had a feast like this since the old skinflint's two-hundredth birthday, or I'm not a gork." Muted laughter. "So what's the occasion, Munca? A fresh batch of slaves?"

"Haven't you heard? Felgor torched the Staff Tree and the island with it. As a reward, he's taking his pet town-baiting. I can't wait. One look at Gor and them small-eyed rats will all jump in the river."

"No more Tree, no more staffs, eh?" said Three-Eyes. "That suits me. Say, where'd we get this lot, anyway? It smells well aged."

"The cook says he's never tasted finer. It's from the same place we're visiting today. Can't tell you its name—orders are orders, y'know, and I don't want me tongue cut out for blabbin' about some little backwater world."

"I'd have a drink now, if I thought I could get away with it," Three-Eyes said, lowering his voice. "How about it, Munca? Care to join me?"

"I wouldn't if I were you. The last steward lost his head for thievin' from a barrel of poorer stuff than this. Say, you're sure you haven't sampled some already? This one's wet around the plug."

"Naw. They're all like that. Pressure inside makes 'em leak. When everyone's too drunk to know the wine casks from the water drums, I'll add this beauty to my private stash." Three-Eyes rapped on one of the barrels.

"Just be careful," Munca warned. "You could lose all three of your eyes if the wine runs out before Felgor gets some. You know how he likes a glass or two after his conquests—and not of the dregs, either."

"Don't worry. I'll make sure he gets his sip of the strong and the sweet. We wouldn't want the old prune to dry up completely, would we?" Three-Eyes brayed like a donkey. "So when do you leave?"

"This afternoon, and we won't be long. I expect Gor will make short work of the rabble. They won't know what hit them."

"Then I'll propose a toast to the scum this evening," Three-Eyes chuckled. "'To the dragon bait; may their wine always fill our cellars!'" There was more laughter and bantering, growing fainter as the two gorks rolled their casks down the corridor and out of earshot.

Rolin fidgeted while Three-Eyes and Munca closed and locked the wine room's outer door. Then he unlocked the side entry and stepped inside. All the barrels were gone. "I hope they choke on their wine," he muttered. "It's a shame amenthil fruits aren't poisonous!"

Some time later, he saw a lone yeg flitter past the window, bearing on its back the figure of a man whose long, gray hair streamed in the wind. Immediately behind them, a cloud of yammering batwolves darkened the sky. Gorgorunth followed hard on their tails, like a gigantic bat chasing a swarm of moths. Felgor sat astride the black serpent's neck, waving a staff.

"Gaelathane, have mercy on that world, whatever it may be," Rolin whispered, then turned away from the window.

CHAPTER 21

THROUGH GUNDUL'S GATES

Rolin was dreaming that a yeg was dragging him across the floor by his hair when he snapped awake. Something *was* pulling on him! He rolled over to find the warbler beside his head with a beakful of chestnut hairs—his hairs.

"How did you get in here?" he demanded. Then he noticed the wine room door was ajar. He must have fallen asleep before closing it.

"Get up! Get up! They're here!" twittered the bird.

"Who? Who's here?" Had Three-Eyes and Munca returned?

"Hurry—to the window!" The warbler flew up to grab more strands of Rolin's hair, tugging him toward the door.

"Oh, very well," Rolin grumbled, rubbing his head. Were all warblers so cheeky? Just as he opened the door, he heard voices.

"There he is! Rolin! We're out here!" Windsong and Ironwing were hovering outside the window. Emmer and Scanlon sat astride Windsong.

"How did you know where I was?" gasped Rolin.

"Can't explain now. Just climb on my back!" ordered Ironwing.

But even after squeezing into the window, Rolin was a good six feet from the sorc, who couldn't fly much closer without catching a wing tip on the rocks. Rolin glanced down at the dizzying drop and clutched his reeling head.

"Well, do something!" the warbler chirped, fluttering back to the griffins, who looked at one another as if to say, "This wasn't my idea!"

"Does anyone have a length of rope?" asked Emmer.

"Rope—of course!" Windsong cried. "There's some in my saddlebags."

Emmer found the rope and tied one end to the griffin's middle, then tossed the other end to Rolin. "Wrap it around yourself and hang on," Emmer told him. Rolin coiled the rope under his arms and around his chest. As Windsong took up the slack, the rope tightened. Shutting his eyes, Rolin slid into space.

"Erk!" he gurgled, swinging beneath Windsong's belly. "Let me down!"

Windsong quickly dropped to earth, followed by Ironwing. As his feet touched solid ground, Rolin saw Opio, Gemmio and Bembor waiting with Keeneye and Spearwind. Scanlon and the scouts welcomed him with hearty backslaps, while Bembor beamed.

"Thank you all!" Rolin said. "I was afraid I'd never get out of that dreadful place." He hugged Windsong's neck. "How did you find me, you old griffin? I thought you and Ironwing were locked up with Scanlon in Felgor's dungeons."

Windsong clicked his beak. "Not at all! To begin with, after chasing off the yegs, we couldn't find you anywhere. When we returned to our lair, Whitewing was most displeased to learn we'd lost Lucambra's future king."

"He threatened to strip me of my neck feathers and put me to work in the scullery," Ironwing put in. "Imagine that: me—in the scullery!" The sorc's back rippled and twitched like a miffed cat's.

"We were ready to mount a full-scale search for you," Windsong went on, "when Spearwind came in to report that Felgor had put the People of the Tree under some sort of spell and that they were all trooping into Mt. Golgunthor."

"Not all of them," Keeneye corrected him.

"Oh, yes—a stray yeg we waylayed told us a few of the captives were still being held in Liriassa. We decided to see for ourselves."

Scanlon picked up the narrative. "When we got to the valley, Keeneye spotted some tracks outside the council chamber. We broke inside and found Father, Grandfather, Opio and Gemmio tied up. They all had the sickness but Grandfather was the worst."

"*Had* the sickness?" Rolin interrupted. He glanced at Bembor and the scouts. Each looked as fit and strong as a young oak.

Scanlon grinned. "After drinking our Glymmerin water, they got well!"

"More than well, my boy," said Bembor with a smile. "We're renewed! I've never felt better."

"But why were you in the council chamber in the first place?" Rolin asked.

"The morning after you left for Luralin, the rest of us returned to Liriassa," Bembor began. "Since the valley was a smoking ash pit, we decided to set up camp in the council cave. Grimmon was inside. He's gone over to the enemy."

"The traitor's even taken an ashtag sythan-ar!" Emmer spat out the words as if detesting their very taste.

"And now his eyes are blacker than Felgor's," said Opio with a shiver. "After he seized Bembor's staff, his men tied us up and locked us in the cave."

"Grimmon not only told Felgor about Liriassa," Gemmio added, "but he also gave away the location of every staff-bearer's sythan-ar, so the dragon would be sure to destroy them. As chief councilor, Grimmon stood to inherit all six Rowonah rods, which he intended to hand over to Felgor."

"I'd have given my blowpipe to see the knave's face when Grimmon gave him those staffs," Opio grunted.

"What do you mean?" asked Rolin.

"They must have withered when the Tree died," Bembor said. "About four days before Scanlon and the sorcs found us, Grimmon came storming back into the council chamber. 'You'll pay for ruining my staffs!' he screamed at us and shook a bunch of dead sticks in our faces. I thought he was going to kill us right then and there. Instead, he decided to let the sickness take its course."

"You still haven't explained how you managed to find me," said Rolin.

"We were flying south for the Willowahs when the warbler brought us the news that you were still alive and had spiked Felgor's wine!" Bembor said.

The bird hopped onto Ironwing's head and puffed out its chest. Ironwing waggled his head but the strutting warbler stayed put. The boys sniggered.

"We nearly ran into a whole yeg battalion on our way here," Emmer said, "not to mention Felgor and the dragon."

"I saw them, too," said Rolin grimly. Then he told the others what he'd learned from Three-Eyes and Munca, ending with a description of the gray-haired yeg rider leading the sorcerer's winged army out of the mountain.

"That was Grimmon," said Bembor with a disgusted look. "Felgor no doubt promised him a torsil world of his very own as the reward for his treachery."

"Pity that world," Emmer said, shaking his head.

"This is a bad business," muttered Opio. "There's no telling when Felgor and his war party will be back."

"In the meantime, we'll have a little party of our own," Bembor announced.

The scouts stared at him. "What sort of party?" they asked.

"A rescue party, of course! Our people are somewhere in this mountain, and I aim to find them."

"What about the gorks?" asked Gemmio. "We didn't see many with the yegs. This place is probably crawling with them."

"And what if Felgor returns while we're still inside?" Opio added.

"That's right," said Spearwind, ruffling his wings nervously. "Rescuing Rolin is one thing, but playing right into the serpent's jaws is another matter."

"This may be our only chance to free those prisoners," Bembor argued.

"Perhaps, but you'll have to do it without us," retorted Keeneye. "We sorcs are going home. Our only job was to find you and the other Servants of the Tree. You may join us or remain behind as you wish." He and Spearwind spread their wings, but Windsong and Ironwing refused to move.

"We're not going anywhere without Rolin and Scanlon," said Windsong defiantly. "We promised King Whitewing we'd look after them."

"Then take them with you," Spearwind snapped.

"We mustn't go yet," Rolin said. "I met a girl inside. We can't just leave her there. Besides, Gaelathane wants us to save all the Lucambrians."

"You've seen Gaelathane again?" his companions asked in astonishment.

"Yes, but He's different. He's—"

"Can we get to your friend from here?" Emmer broke in.

"I doubt it. The doors are bolted. They're very strong and heavy, too."

"Then we'll have to use the front entrance," declared Bembor. "You heard Gaelathane's orders. We've no choice but to obey. Hop on, my boy!" Rolin scrambled onto Windsong's back, sitting behind Bembor. Scanlon and Emmer climbed on Ironwing, leaving Keeneye and Spearwind to carry Opio and Gemmio. "To the gates of Gundul!" cried the Father of the Oak Clan.

With a flurry of wings, the four sorcs sped around the mountain, skimming above the tops of the ashtags. Then they dropped down before a pair of tall iron gates. No yegs or gorks stormed out of the dark, forbidding entry to challenge them. They heard only the echoing of boisterous laughter and singing.

"They must be enjoying themselves," muttered Emmer.

"Let's hope they're too busy banqueting to notice we're here!" said Opio, stringing his bow.

"What if they do see us?" Keeneye quavered, his neck feathers bristling.

"We'll be in and out before anyone gets wind of us," Windsong assured him.

"But how do we open the gates?" asked Gemmio. Standing flush against the mountainside, the gates were secured with a heavy padlock and chain.

"We won't have to!" Scanlon said, slipping between the bars. "See? What are you waiting for, Rolin? Come on!"

Rolin hesitated. Should he risk losing his freedom a second time by going back inside? Then, remembering Emma's despairing look as she left his cell, he squeezed through the gate's heavy rungs. After promising Bembor not to do anything rash, he and Scanlon stepped into the tunnel's black mouth.

"What are we looking for?" whispered Scanlon.

"I don't know," Rolin replied. "Maybe there's a stairway leading to the upper levels. We should find Emma there." The boys felt their way through the passage, choking from the smoke and acrid fumes.

"*Phew!*" Scanlon gasped. "If it smells this bad when the dragon's gone, it must be awful when he's here!"

With the tunnel's every twist and turn, the sounds of merry-making grew louder. When the boys came to a half-open door, Rolin risked a quick peek inside and saw a large banquet hall where a riotous feast was in full swing. Harried slaves hurried among greasy tables, bearing platters of meat and pitchers of wine for drunken, demanding gorks. One of the servants slipped and fell, breaking her pitcher and spilling wine all over the revelers nearby.

"You clumsy little fool!" bellowed a hulking, three-eyed gork. "Go fill up another and be quick about it or I'll have your ears!" Recognizing the voice as the wine steward's, Rolin wished he had his sword. The cowering girl hastily scraped up her broken pitcher and headed for the door. It was Emma!

Rolin flattened himself against the wall, his heart pounding. When Emma rounded the corner, he pulled her close beside him, covering her mouth. She struggled, her eyes wild with fear.

"Don't be afraid!" he whispered. "It's me, Rolin. I've come to save you! This way—we've got to hurry."

The girl pulled away, protesting, "Get back to work, or they'll punish us all!"

"Shhh!" Scanlon hissed, but it was too late. At Emma's outcry, a gork poked its bug-eyed head out the door and raised the alarm. Tables crashed, platters clattered and iron rang as the carousers jumped up and drew their swords.

"Run!" cried Rolin. He, Scanlon and Emma raced toward the entrance, gorkin feet drumming down the corridor close behind them. Arrows whined overhead, ricocheting off the rock walls.

"Hurry—they're gaining on us!" Scanlon panted. Rolin glanced back at the long-legged creatures loping after them and lengthened his own stride. The three shot out of the tunnel scant yards ahead of the gorks. The boys slipped through the gates, but Emma stuck fast, her frock caught on a sliver of iron.

"Help me!" she screamed, stretching her hands through the bars. "Don't let them take me back there!" Just as Rolin grasped the girl's hand, a bowlegged gork lurched up and seized her. The two played tug-of-war with Emma until Ironwing gave a terrible roar and the gork fell writhing to the ground, its arm severed at the shoulder.

"That's for what you filth did to my wings on Luralin," Ironwing grunted, drawing back his paw. In a flash, Rolin and Emmer pulled the girl through the gates, tearing her smock. Emmer held Emma's bony, shivering body, wiping away the dirt and tears that streaked her haggard face. Then he froze.

"That mole," he croaked, pointing to a brown spot on Emma's left cheek. "Just like Nelda's. It's you, my daughter Mycena! I've found you at last!"

Recognition flickered in Emma's vacant eyes. "Father, oh, Father!" she cried, throwing her arms around him. Weeping softly, Bembor made the hug a threesome.

Meanwhile, hundreds of raving gorks had crowded behind the gates, hurling spears and shooting arrows through the bars. "Open them!" they howled, rattling the rungs. As the Servants of the Tree retreated before the deadly hail, two hunchbacked gorks tore off the padlock and chains and pushed. The gates groaned and the gap between them slowly widened.

"Stop!" Bembor faced the gawking gorks. "If you open these gates, you shall all perish. 'The gates of Gundul shall not stand!'"

"It is you who will die," the gorks jeered. "You have no staffs, since our master has seized them all. When Gor returns, he'll tear you to pieces, if we don't kill you first!" They banged on the gates and hooted, "Faster! Open them faster!" Some had already squeezed partway through.

"Follow me on foot!" cried Bembor. He and Rolin leapt astride Windsong, who dashed toward the ashtags with his fellow sorcs and their riders. Once they were well within the wood, Bembor raised his hand and the sorcs halted.

"Hear this, trees of Gundul," he cried. "The One Tree lives! Your master failed to destroy it. Now you will perish with him!"

The ashtags gnashed their branches, sputtering and cursing. "To the Pit with you!" they screeched. "You shall all burn and your Tree with you!" Just then, Rolin heard their pursuers crashing through the forest behind them.

"Now, griffins, fly for your lives!" Bembor commanded. The sorcs promptly beat their great wings, bearing their riders high above the raging black trees.

Once they were safely out of arrow range, Rolin leaned forward to speak into Bembor's ear. "Why did you do that?" he asked.

"I wanted to provoke them. Just wait, and you'll see why."

Far below, the gates had swung wide open, disgorging a ghastly flood of gangling gorks, all clamoring for the heads of their enemies. Yowling and yelling in drunken fury, they poured into the ashtag forest. Then those in front stopped and stared around with befuddled looks. Some covered their ears, while others swatted at the air, as if driving off stinging gnats.

"I thought so!" Bembor chortled. "Your amenthil-laced wine is giving them their first taste of ashtag speech, and it's driving them insane!"

"With some help from the trees' stinging seeds," observed Windsong.

"They're escaping!" Scanlon shouted, as the half-crazed gorks bolted back toward the mountain. Suddenly, with a blinding burst of light, the resurrected Tree appeared at the gates. Terrified shrieks rose from ten thousand tormented throats. Blocked from entering the citadel and hemmed in on the other three sides by hopping-mad ashtags, the roaring sea of panicked foot soldiers surged left, then right, forward and backward.

Then the sky darkened and the air *thrummed* as wave upon wave of winged shapes streamed over Golgunthor's peak. "The sorca have come! The sorca have come!" Rolin cried.

Seeing the griffins, the gorks completely lost their senses, and in a frenzy of sword and spear, hacked one another to pieces. Those that escaped the slaughter found the sorca waiting with their ferocious claws and beaks. Blood ran in rivers among the ashtags. In minutes, not a single gork remained alive.

"They're all dead!" the Lucambrians rejoiced. "Praise be to Gaelathane!"

"The Prophecy's words have come to pass at last," cried Bembor:

The gates of Gundul shall not stand,
When He shall come to cleanse the land;
They'll face a foe they cannot fend;
In drunkenness shall doom descend.

"There's no time to celebrate now," he added. "Quick—to the Tree!" The griffins landed beside Waganupa, where Bembor met with Whitewing.

"We thank you, O King of the Sorca," he said, bowing low. "You have come to our rescue a second time! Today you have truly proven your loyalty to Elgathel's heir. You and your race are free of any further fealty to him or to our people. I ask you only to grant us the continued assistance of these four staunch sorcs until we have captured or killed the sorcerer and his serpent."

"We are honored to have taken part in the defeat of our mutual enemy," replied Whitewing courteously. "Though we are no longer bound by our former oath, our allegiance to the People of the Tree remains firm. As a token of our esteem, I gladly release these my humble subjects into your service. We have quite enough help in the scullery for the present," he added, winking at Ironwing. Then the griffin king unfurled his wings and majestically rose to rejoin the ranks of his proud army, which swiftly disappeared southward.

Rolin and his companions surveyed the grisly battlefield scene before them. Slain gorku lay everywhere, many still clutching their weapons. Then, taking in the Tree's glory, the eleven cried as one, "The Tree lives! Long live the Tree and Gaelathane, King of the Trees!" The earth shook as Waganupa thundered, "You must deliver those who still lie in the bonds of darkness."

Rolin touched the Tree, and his hand slid into the trunk like a hot knife through beeswax. He stepped forward, light surrounding and filling him. Again, Gaelessa's wondrous joy welled up within, like the Glymmerin's ever-flowing spring. Looking back, he saw his friends following him. Together, they swam through the living light to the Tree's farther side and stumbled out onto the blood-stained courtyard. The gates had disappeared.

"Ugh," sniffed Opio. "What a horrid place! I wish we'd stayed in the Tree."

"We have lives to save," Bembor reminded him. "Mycena, can you take us to the dungeons?" Everyone followed the Lucambrian girl through the main tunnel and down a long flight of winding stairs. The boys lit the way with their new staffs.

At last they came to a stone door with a pitted iron ring in it. Emmer, Opio and Gemmio pulled on the ring, and the door scraped open. A dank, musty smell oozed out. Hundreds of frightened eyes reflected back the light of Rolin's rod as he and the others entered, leaving the griffins on guard outside.

Starving, hollow-eyed and hopeless, men, women and children sat chained to the walls and floor. Recalling Gaelathane's words, "Let them taste of Me . . . for I offer My water of life freely," Rolin enlisted Scanlon's help in pouring Glymmerin water down parched throats. Eyes brightened and cracked lips mumbled thanks as the boys moved down the long lines of prisoners.

"Bembor!" someone called out. "Bembor son of Brenthor, are you here?"

"Who asks for me?" Bembor responded, making his way toward the sound of the voice. Rolin and Scanlon tagged along.

"It is I, Marlon!" Weeping, the brothers embraced, each remarking how gaunt the other had become during his captivity. "You arrived just in time," said Marlon. "Last night, Felgor came to make us an offer, as he put it."

"What kind of offer?" asked Rolin, helping Marlon to a sip of water from his honey bag.

"He knew most of us had lost our sythan-ars in the raid on Liriassa, so as a 'good-will gesture,' he was prepared to give us new ones—as a condition of our release."

"New sythan-ars?" snorted Bembor. "All he's got here are—oh, no. Not *those*."

"That's right," Marlon replied. "Ashtags. His Trees of Life and Liberty."

"An ashtag sythan-ar can prolong one's life," Bembor explained to Rolin, "but only in such an agony of soul that we call it the *living death*."

"I'd rather die!" said Scanlon fiercely.

"So would the rest of us," Marlon said, coughing in the dungeon's chill air. "We were all expecting to perish here anyway. I never thought I'd see you to return this in person." He drew a soros from beneath his ragged tunic.

"Keep it for now, Brother," said Bembor graciously. "You're still chief of the oak clan, at least until I've seen Rolin crowned king. Now, let's have those chains off." The two brothers wrestled with Marlon's heavy irons, but they held fast. Next, Gemmio and Opio tried to break them.

"This is no good!" Opio panted. "What we need is a hammer and chisel."

"Luralin sang us a song about this," said Rolin. What were the words? "'His blood will break all chains.' I think that's how it went."

"That must mean the Glymmerin water!" Bembor exclaimed.

"How could mere water break iron shackles?" scoffed Opio.

"This is no ordinary water," Gemmio reminded him, deliberately pouring a few drops on Marlon's chains.

Snap! The links broke apart. In a trice, every able-bodied scout had a honey sack in hand and was shattering shackles left and right. The captives filled the cavern with cries of gladness and relief. Someone even began playing a flute.

"Father! Rolin!" a familiar voice rose above the hubbub. Emmer and Rolin ran to a pathetic figure huddled in the corner.

"Father, dear Father, where were you?" Marlis sobbed, as Emmer swept her into his arms. "I was terribly lonely without you and Scanlon."

"I missed you, too, my child," replied Emmer, tenderly releasing his eldest from the chain chafing her ankle. Then he folded her into his arms again.

After taking a sip from Rolin's water bag, Marlis revived like the flower of death and life, the color returning to her cheeks. "We spent days and days in those dreadful caves," she began. "I could never stay warm. Just when we were going to leave, an avalanche buried all the escape holes."

"Hush, little one," Emmer said, stroking her hair. "It's over now."

"Then there was a loud sound and the snow and ice started melting. We thought you and Grandfather had built a fire to free us, but it was the dragon! When he'd made a big enough opening, he stuck his ugly old snout inside." Marlis began weeping again. "We thought he was going to burn us up, but instead of fire, some awful-smelling green smoke came out of his mouth."

"What happened then?" asked Rolin.

"I don't remember much, except that we all crawled out and followed the dragon down the mountain. Then we walked here."

"More of Felgor's sorceries," muttered Emmer. His face brightened. "But now you're safe with us, my dear, and if you'll come along with me, there's someone I'd like you to meet."

After Emmer led Marlis away, Rolin returned to breaking off shackles, then joined Scanlon and the scouts in encouraging the newly freed prisoners to move about. Many were still too weak to walk or even stand.

"They need food and fresh air," Bembor sighed, "but there is neither here."

"And outside, they'd be fair game for the dragon," said Gemmio.

"Is there any water left?" Emmer interrupted. With Marlis at his side, he stood cradling Mycena's limp form in his arms.

"She took one look at me and fainted," Marlis tearfully explained. "I do hope she'll be all right."

"Great snakes and salamanders!" cried Bembor. "I'd forgotten about Mycena!" With Scanlon's help, he trickled Glymmerin water into her mouth. She coughed, swallowed and opened her eyes, cringing before the tall Green-cloaks surrounding her. Then the fear drained from her face, and she slept.

"It's a wonder she survived all this time, cut off from her life tree," Bembor remarked. "Rolin, why don't you and Scanlon search the upper passages for others like her in distress? Bring along your water bags, just in case. And be careful; stray gorks may still be lurking about!"

After the long climb back up the stairway, the boys soon came upon knots of slaves cowering in corners or huddling in the hallways. Many were even younger than Mycena. Some fled in terror from the intruders. Others stared blankly with the glassy, black eyes of the living dead. A number appeared to be from other worlds. For all who would drink, Rolin and Scanlon poured out draughts of the crimson, life-giving liquid.

"They've lived in the dark so long that our staff light frightens them," Rolin said as he and Scanlon approached another group of wary slaves. "If only they'd go outside and have a look at the Tree, they'd know they were free!"

"Maybe they're afraid we're going to punish them for slacking off," said Scanlon. "How can we make them understand their taskmasters are dead?"

"Except for Felgor," Rolin remarked, holding out his honey bag to the emaciated slaves. None took it.

"They simply won't trust us," said Scanlon sadly. "I can't blame them; they must think we're offering them poisoned wine!"

That reminded Rolin of Gaelathane's parting words to him in the wine room. He fished around in his pocket for the reddish brown lump he'd found beside the Tree and held it out for Scanlon to see. "Gaelathane told me this would convince anyone who wouldn't believe."

"It must be a spasel," Scanlon said, touching the glassy surface. "Do you think it would show us Luralin?"

"I've never looked into it, but—" Rolin gasped as the already warm ball glowed white with scenes of wondrous beauty. "It's Gaelessa!" After the suspicious slaves had gazed into the spasel and heard how the Tree led to the spasel land, they all gladly drank of the Glymmerin water.

Next, the boys explored the higher levels, where Rolin showed the sap ball to all the slaves he and Scanlon met, telling them of the King's love and of His country's marvels. Most of Felgor's former captives readily took the water.

Then they came to a set of tall wooden doors embellished with carvings of yegs and other hideous beasts. Rolin listened at the doors, then squinted through the crack between them, seeing an empty, cavernous hall with a black throne at the far end. Motioning for Scanlon to follow, he eased inside.

"That must be Felgor's!" said Scanlon, staring at the throne. "Do you suppose there's anything magic in here?"

"Let's find out!" Rolin replied. He and Scanlon tiptoed through the room, poking and prying into cupboards and cubbyholes. To their disappointment, they found only a few dusty relics from Felgor's subject worlds. Then they came upon a long glass case. Inside, spasla of every shape and color nestled in a bed of velvet. Each bore a metal tag inscribed with neat letters.

"Look at all of them," Scanlon exclaimed. "There must be hundreds! I've never seen so many spasla."

Rolin squinted through the glass at a flattened spasel. "Parthos," he read. "What a funny world that must be!"

Scanlon pointed to another. "This one says 'Thalmos.'" Rolin felt a pang of homesickness—and fear. Had his father and aunt despaired of finding him? He wished he could send them word that all was well.

"Here's one that doesn't have a tag," Scanlon said, gesturing at a round, shiny black spasel in the center of the case. "I wonder . . ."

The boys slid the lid off the case and lifted out the large black ball, placing it on the floor between them. It felt warm to Rolin's touch and grew still hotter as he gazed at it, smoke coiling off its polished surface. Lurid flames spurted up within, while shadows flitted in and out of the flickering light. The flames divided into twin fiery eyes burning with an all-consuming malice. Unable to look away, Rolin felt himself falling into a black, bottomless well.

"Don't tamper with that!" called a distant voice. More words echoed faintly from above. Then the well collapsed and Bembor's face rushed at him.

". . . who is king of all torsil worlds?" Bembor was shouting, shaking him by the shoulders.

"Gaelathane, of course," Rolin replied, feeling as though he were awakening from a nightmare. Scanlon sat beside him, rubbing his eyes.

"It's fortunate I found you when I did," Bembor sighed. "You could have come to grief looking into Gundul like that. Never touch a sorcerer's spasla!"

"If the Gundul spasel is dangerous, shouldn't we destroy it?" asked Rolin.

Bembor hesitated, then picked up the still-smoking ball and hurled it against the wall. It struck with a thud, then fell to the floor unmarred.

"I thought as much," he said with a bleak look. "Since this spasel is made of ashtag sap, it's harder than the black trees themselves. I know of nothing that can unmake it."

The three stood staring at the spasel, scratching their heads. Then Rolin had an idea. From the rear of the room he retrieved his light staff, which he touched to the ball. There was a sizzling sound.

"Get back!" cried Bembor. With a flash and a bang, the black ball burst into a million tiny shards, knocking Rolin to the floor.

Bembor helped him up and brushed him off. "Felgor won't be happy to find his prize spasel in pieces," he said. "Are you all right?"

Rolin nodded. "But why was the ball so important to him?"

"He must have drawn his strength from it," replied Bembor. "I suspect he also received messages the same way."

"Messages?"

"Yes. Though Felgor styles himself 'lord of Gundul,' he likely bows to the will of another greater than he." Rolin shuddered, recalling the glowing eyes.

"What's this?" Scanlon broke in. Rolin and Bembor found him studying a snarl of green growths beneath Felgor's throne.

"Why, these are the six staffs Grimmon stole!" Bembor exclaimed, picking up some sticks attached to the foliage. "When the Tree came back to life, they must have sprouted. This one here is mine. I never hoped to see it again."

"And that is mine," said Rolin, pointing to the floor. Underneath the sprouted staffs lay Elgathel's sword.

"Take it, by all means," Bembor said, reverently handing him the sheathed weapon. "No living Lucambrian has as much claim to it as you do!"

"There's one more thing," said Rolin, buckling on the sword. He went to the glass case, where he removed the sap ball labeled "Thalmos" and polished it with his sleeve.

"Leave that here!" Bembor ordered. But Rolin was already warming the spasel in his hands, calling forth a swirl of colors that abruptly came into terrifying focus. He cried out, nearly dropping the ball.

"What's the matter?" asked Bembor and Scanlon, staring at him.

"They're burning Beechtown!" he wailed.

CHAPTER 22

THE BATTLE OF BEECHTOWN

G reat toads and tadpoles!" exclaimed Bembor. "Are you certain?"

"I'd know our town square anywhere," Rolin choked out. Tears splashed onto the spasel resting in his trembling hands. He dared not look into it again, for fear of seeing his father or aunt among the merchants and housewives fleeing from swooping yegs or trapped by burning docks and buildings. He'd never dreamed Munca's "little backwater world" was Thalmos.

"So that's where Felgor's army went," Bembor muttered. "I should have known, after your run-in with those yegs last summer. I wish I knew what torsil he's used to get into Thalmos!" There it was: Felgor had gotten into Thalmos and was making good his promise to wreak havoc on the "river rats."

"I'm going back there to fight Felgor," declared Rolin, drawing his sword. "I'll make him rue the day he ever heard of my world!"

Bembor nodded approvingly. "It's time we prepared him a proper Thalmosian welcome—one he won't soon forget!"

The three returned to the dungeon, where Bembor told the others of Felgor's invasion. The griffins clucked their tongues sympathetically.

"We're very sorry, Rolin," said Keeneye. "If only we weren't so few . . ."

"Few are many, when Gaelathane is with them," Bembor reminded him.

"And we can't let Felgor pluck Thalmos like a ripe plum!" said Windsong.

"Keeneye is right," growled Gemmio. "'The strongest arm and sharpest sword may fall before the greater horde.' Not only do we lack the strength of numbers but also suitable weapons, and Rolin's sword is untested in combat."

"What about these?" Rolin said, handing out the shining Rowonah rods from Luralin. Their light blazed like a bonfire in the dungeon.

"What good are moonwood sticks in a pitched battle?" argued Opio.

Bembor glowered at the scout. "One of these 'moonwood sticks' blasted Felgor's Gundul spasel to smithereens!"

"Even so, we don't know what they'll do to a yeg—or Gorgorunth," Gemmio said.

Then Emmer spoke up. "With these new staffs Gaelathane has given us and the element of surprise on our side, we'll trounce the beggars, hair and hide."

Bembor nodded. "Well said, my kinsman. Four scouts, four staffs, four sorcs—to battle we go!"

Four scouts? Rolin's ears perked up. Were he and Scanlon to be left behind? He glanced at his friend, who shrugged and rolled his eyes. Meanwhile, the sorcs were apparently having second thoughts. Keeneye objected to fighting a dragon while carrying a full-grown two-legs, especially if the two-legs was Opio. Then the scouts and griffins fell to squabbling again.

By the time they decide who will ride whom, there won't be anything left of Beechtown! thought Rolin in disgust. As he quietly backed out of the dungeon, Scanlon gave him a wink and a grin. Marlis also caught his eye, raising her eyebrows questioningly. Rolin waved at her and slipped through the door, suspecting she knew just what he was thinking.

Once outside the mountain, he sat on a rock to clear his head. He didn't want to stay in Lucambra while Bembor and the scouts flew off to do battle with the sorcerer. After all, it was his fault that Felgor had learned about Thalmos and was even now turning Beechtown upside-down.

"I thought I might find you here!"

Rolin spun around to see Windsong's large, round eyes twinkling at him. "Aren't you supposed to be with the others?" he asked.

Windsong stretched his wings and yawned. "They're still snapping at one another down there. Perfectly boring. We'll never save Thalmos that way."

"Then what do you suggest?"

The sorc sidled over to rub catlike against Rolin's leg. "Why don't the two of us see about spoiling Felgor's party?" he purred.

"I left my staff in the dungeon, and I can't fight without it!"

"Did I say we were going to fight?" asked Windsong innocently. "That would be foolish, wouldn't it—we two against Felgor's yeg legions. Let's just make it a scouting expedition, until the others arrive."

"A scouting expedition, you say?" Rolin replied, pursing his lips. It sounded reasonable enough. Still, he would like to petrify a yeg or two.

"On the other hand, if we do run into trouble, we might need these," said Windsong with a slow, sly, griffin wink, turning his side toward Rolin. In the sorc's saddlebags were several shining staffs and some bags of Glymmerin water.

"What a clever griffin!" laughed Rolin, ruffling Windsong's neck feathers.

"Clever enough to know what's on my master's mind," retorted the sorc. "Now are we leaving, or would you rather wait for a personal invitation from the sorcerer himself? It's getting dark, you know, when the enemy will have the advantage."

"But it will be lighter in Thalmos," Rolin reminded him, hopping on. Just as the griffin flexed his wings, a bird lit on his head.

"Where are you going?" the warbler asked.

"To Thalmos," Rolin sighed. There wasn't time for palavering. He needed to reach Lightleaf before Felgor seized the high ground around Beechtown.

"Do you know the way?"

"Of course—why do you ask?" snapped Rolin.

"Tut, tut! No need to be rude!" the warbler huffed. "I know of a shortcut, if you're interested."

"In that case, my wings are yours, warbler!" said Windsong, lofting into the air. Rolin was relieved at this turn of events. Since Lightleaf lay many miles away and might be dead by now, the bird could save them valuable time.

A few minutes later, the warbler alit in an ancient torsil. The tree looked as though a tornado had struck it, stripping off leaves and battering branches.

"Mossbark is my name," wheezed the torsil. "You're not going to tear off my leaves and limbs, too, are you?"

"We won't so much as break a twig," Rolin replied. "Who—or what—did this to you?"

"The bat things and the fire monster," said the warbler. "I followed them here." So that was how the bird knew where to find a Thalmos torsil! Then Rolin recognized Mossbark as the tree he had first climbed into Lucambra.

Windsong flew into the torsil's tattered top, taking them to Thalmos, where a sultry summer sun still hung on the horizon. Thick with smoke, the hazy air lay heavy on the high, wooded ridge where Rolin's adventures had first begun that fateful spring morning.

"What's the highest point in town?" asked Windsong. "We'll need a lookout post where we can see without being seen."

"The bell tower, I suppose," Rolin replied. That landmark was visible from the top of the tallest fir tree in his father's bee yard.

"To the tower, then!" cried Windsong, launching himself out of the torsil. As the sorc glided into the valley of the Foamwater, Rolin saw batwolves swarming like flies above the burning town. There was no sign of Gorgorunth.

"There's the tower!" he called out, pointing to the white steeple rising above Beechtown's tiled roofs. But why was it still standing, when the dragon had already smashed so many other buildings to smoking rubble? Windsong swooped into the belfry and landed heavily on the wooden floor.

"What was that?" a voice cried through the bell's rope well.

"Just a yeg looking for a roosting place," growled another. "Shoo, yeg! Fly off and find yourself a fat, cornfed shopkeeper. You can sleep tomorrow."

After sliding off Windsong, Rolin peered through a crack in the floor and saw Felgor glaring up from the room below. His tongue stuck to the roof of his mouth. Speechless, he flapped his arms at Windsong, startling the sorc into tripping over his own four feet and falling backwards with a *thump*.

"I told you to get back outside, yeg!" roared Felgor.

Rolin flapped his arms more vigorously, until Windsong took the hint and noisily beat his wings, raising a dust cloud. Rolin stifled a sneeze.

"There, it's gone," grunted the sorcerer. "Now, where were we?"

"I was asking if the resistance is always so feeble," whined the other voice. Pressing his eye to a knothole in the floor, Rolin looked down on Grimmon's gray-haired head. The tower had been spared because the sorcerer and his apprentice had been using it as their own observation post!

Felgor snorted. "Given a taste of dragon fire, most rebels lose their nerve. By morning, these filthy potato grubbers will be groveling at our feet."

"If there are any left by then," muttered Grimmon, wincing at the piercing screams of terrified townspeople.

"What—turning squeamish now, are we?" Felgor mocked. "Didn't you do away with your rivals by cutting down their life trees? Your methods may be cleaner, but mine are quicker. Let's have no more of this spineless talk, or I'll make someone else viceroy of Thalmos!"

"Yes, Lord Felgor." Sweat glistened among Grimmon's gray hairs, and he mopped his brow.

"After Beechtown has fallen, we'll make an example of three or four other villages," murmured Felgor, staring out the window through a starglass. "Magnificent! Raftsmen throwing themselves off a burning barge. If only I'd stocked this river with eelomars, we'd see some real sport!"

"Eelomars?" repeated Grimmon.

"Rolin—your staff!" Windsong hissed. Rolin glanced up to see a yeg's snarling snout poking into the belfry. Just then, bowstrings twanged. With a cry, the yeg flung back its head and disappeared.

"Remind me to thank Beechtown's bowmen if I ever have the chance," Rolin whispered to Windsong. Returning to the knothole, he caught Grimmon sticking his head out the window. Felgor jerked him back inside.

"You fool—do you want to be shot, too? I thought you said these people were defenseless!"

"They are—that is, they were—I mean, they looked as harmless as mice!"

"As I recall, your 'mice' nearly wiped out my first yeg patrol."

"It was a fluke! Most of these bumpkins wouldn't know a bow from a bale of hay, even if it hit them. Anyway, they've given us no trouble since then."

"Until today," Felgor dryly reminded him. "Now, where's that dratted dragon? Chasing cattle or sheep, no doubt. He's never around when I need him. He'll make short work of those blasted bowmen!"

At that very moment, something punched through the belfry roof, narrowly missing Rolin as it plunged through the floor and landed next to the sorcerer.

"What in the name of Gundul is that?" Felgor cried, leaping out of the way.

"The front half of a yeg, from the look of it," observed Grimmon.

"No!" screamed the sorcerer, beating his fists on the yeg statue. "It can't be! The Tree is dead! I hewed it to splinters and burned it with fire!"

Windsong nudged Rolin. "I'd say our friends have arrived. Time for some fun!" Rolin leapt onto his mount, and together they soared out of the steeple.

Once in the air, they spotted a yeg swarm high above them. "For Gaelathane!" cried Rolin as Windsong charged into the fray. Flailing about with his staff, Rolin caught eight yegs off guard, sending their petrified bodies plummeting to earth. The rest scattered with frightened yelps, leaving Rolin, Bembor, Emmer and Scanlon alone on their griffins in the dusky sky.

"Well done!" cried Bembor from Keeneye's back. "But why didn't you wait for us? If the warbler hadn't tipped us off, we'd still be searching for you!"

Then Rolin explained how he and Windsong had been keeping an eye on Felgor and Grimmon in the bell tower, while Gorgorunth was elsewhere.

"That's just like Gor," growled Emmer. "He roars in and sets things afire, then flies off to hunt his dinner, leaving the yegs to mop up after him."

"While the serpent's away, the sorcs will play," said Scanlon with a grin. He pointed out several roving bands of batwolves. "Let's have a game of tag!"

"All right, but stay together, and try not to lose your staffs!" Bembor warned the boys. "If these stiff-necked sorcs hadn't refused to carry Opio and Gemmio, I'd have left you both behind."

Flying wing tip to wing tip, the griffins dove on a yeg swarm. "From stone you came, and to stone you shall return!" Emmer roared, tapping the first batwolf to flash by. The beast froze in midflight, then tumbled out of the sky. As Windsong tore into the milling yegs, Rolin lunged out with his rod at a large, slow-flying batwolf. "You're it!" he yelled, but the yeg swerved aside, only to petrify in a solid stream of light lancing from the staff.

After collecting his wits, Rolin tried to alert the others. "You don't need to hit them, just point your staffs!" he called.

"What?" they shouted back.

"Just point them!" Realizing his friends hadn't understood, Rolin told Windsong to prepare for a second pass. Below, more batwolves gathered into a compact cluster, then rapidly rose to meet them.

"We can't possibly take on so many at once!" Windsong protested, nervously clicking his beak.

"Just hold steady!" said Rolin. When the lead yeg's glaring red eyes came into view, he pointed his rod at its ugly snout, crying, "The Tree lives!"

The wand spat a bright beam that caught the creature full in the face. Turning to stone, the yeg spun out of formation. The next few minutes were a blur. With screeching batwolves attacking from every quarter, Rolin barely had time to fire a light burst at one before another took its place. Hundreds of staff-smitten yegs plunged earthward. Finally, the sky was clear.

"Where did they all go?" exclaimed Ironwing. He and the other sorcs had arrived just as another huge yeg ball boiled up from below, engulfing them.

"Do as I do!" Rolin yelled. A light staff in each hand, he brought down two yegs at once. Following his example, Bembor, Emmer and Scanlon began petrifying every batwolf in sight. The survivors fled in a panic.

"To the streets!" cried Rolin. He and Windsong led the others on a hair-raising chase among Beechtown's shops and houses, sending yeg statues cartwheeling across the cobbles or crashing through tile roofs. Then they dealt with any pillaging gorks foolhardy enough to put up a fight.

After routing or petrifying all the batwolves and gorks they could find, Rolin and his friends landed in the deserted town square. Rolin noticed a few daring souls peeking through their window blinds at the four fell strangers and their ferocious-looking mounts.

Yowr! roared the sorcs. "We've won!" As their savage cries echoed through the ravaged town, shutters and blinds banged shut again.

"Not if Felgor escapes, we haven't," Bembor retorted. "To the bell tower!"

They had scarcely taken to the air when a batlike shape sailed across the face of the rising moon. "There he goes!" Scanlon cried.

"After them!" Bembor ordered. In a flash, the griffins took up the chase. Soon, Rolin and Windsong were close enough to hear Felgor cursing the slack-winged serpent for devouring so many fat cows. Then the dragon abruptly dove into the forest and disappeared, leaving a trail of smoke in his wake.

"He's escaping through Mossbark!" cried Bembor. "Follow him!" Rolin's stomach turned over as Windsong hurtled downward, then veered off to avoid a ball of red flame engulfing the torsil. Within moments, nothing remained of the tree but a smoldering heap of ashes.

"Felgor just closed his back gate," Bembor said grimly. "The serpent burned Mossbark to keep us from pursuing him into Lucambra. We may never catch him now."

"Then we're trapped in this wretched world!" wailed Keeneye.

"What about Lightleaf?" Rolin asked, hovering on Windsong.

"An excellent idea!" Bembor exclaimed. "If conditions are favorable tonight, your torsil will turn silver in Lucambra's moonlight, making him easy to pick out."

"I knew I shouldn't have joined this expedition," Spearwind muttered. "How does he expect us to find a single tree after dark in these hills?"

Overhearing Spearwind's remark, Rolin panicked. What if the griffin was right? At night, all the familiar landmarks looked different. And if Lucambra's moon were waning or covered by clouds, the "silver tree" wouldn't be silver at all. Worse yet, Mulgul and his friends might have smothered the old torsil.

Then Rolin spotted a glow below him. He tapped Windsong's neck and the sorc spiraled downward. Since Lightleaf had never shone so strongly, was this a different torsil leading to a world with a larger moon than Lucambra's? Or was it a stray fire, kindled from the flying embers of Beechtown's burning?

Crashing through a thick canopy of fir branches, Rolin and his mount found themselves in a pool of intense light. Then someone addressed them.

"Hail, strangers! Come ye as friends of the Tree or as foes?"

"As friends," replied Rolin, shading his eyes from the powerful glare. "We seek the tree of passage known as Lightleaf."

"I am he. Welcome, Rolin son of Gannon! It has been many a day since last I heard your voice."

"But why do you shine so brightly? Is there a full moon in Lucambra?"

"It is the Tree's light that illumines me. Bless Gaelathane, I feel a hundred years younger already! Now then, how may I assist the king?" Briefly, Rolin explained the purpose of his visit.

"Old Felgor and his fire beast, fleeing for their worthless lives?" cackled Lightleaf. "That is news indeed! The snake trees on the other side have turned up their roots, too. They can't abide all this light. But I am delaying you with my chatter. You must make haste to catch our enemies!"

After Windsong had summoned the other sorcs, Bembor told Lightleaf that the griffins would fly with their riders into his top, rather than climbing.

"It is a privilege to grant passage to four of that favored race," the torsil replied. "The queen often spoke highly of the sorca. Since you are all about the king's business, my limbs are yours. You may pass, with my blessing."

Once in Lucambra, the eight friends found the sullen snake trees had shriveled and shrunken in the Tree's blazing light like clumps of kelp wilting on a beach. Even the Hallowfast seemed cheerier, despite the ashtag tendrils still clinging to it. "To the dragon's mountain!" cried Bembor. With rapid wing beats, the sorcs soared into the air.

CHAPTER 23

INTO THE PIT

"There they are—beside the Tree!" Keeneye raised the alarm when Rolin and company were still miles from the mountain. Rolin made out a dark shape belching orange tongues of fire at Waganupa, which only shone more fiercely.

"Old Felgor must be fit to be tied," chuckled Bembor. "He's lost his entire army, with nothing to show for it. Worse still, the tree he left for dead on Luralin is very much alive and more formidable than ever!"

"Now what's the dragon doing?" called Scanlon. Gorgorunth had stopped spitting fire and was skirting the Tree, first on one side, then on the other.

"He's trying to get into his lair, but Waganupa's blocked the entrance!" Emmer shouted. All at once, the serpent blazed up the side of the mountain and disappeared behind a small peak.

Flying as swiftly as their wings could carry them, the griffins shot toward the Tree-lit peak. As the sorcs swooped over cliffs and crags, Rolin and his friends saw no signs of Gorgorunth or his master. It seemed the enemy had gotten away after all.

"They've escaped inside," groaned Emmer.

"Perhaps—but how?" Bembor said. "It's too cold for ashtags up here, much less real torsils."

Scanlon blew on his hands. "It's too cold for me, too."

"Maybe there's a side entrance," suggested Spearwind.

"But how could we have missed a hole big enough for Gor?" said Keeneye.

"What if it weren't big enough," Rolin answered, "and he's still out here somewhere?"

"Of course!" Bembor cried. "Split up and watch for anything out of place." The griffins fanned out, combing snowbound valleys, cracks and crevasses.

Suddenly, Windsong doubled back over some hillocks in the snow. "See that steam vent down there?" he said to Rolin. "It looks unusually large. Still, it's probably nothing."

Following Windsong's head tilt, Rolin saw a white plume rising lazily from under a rocklike object. "That's no steam vent!" he declared. "We'd better call Bembor." Windsong chirruped, and Keeneye appeared, bearing Bembor. The old scout took one look at the vapor cloud and gave a low whistle.

"It's the serpent, all right. He's pulled in his head, legs and tail to imitate a boulder. The fire in his belly gave him away." Bembor brought the griffins down behind a large snowdrift, where he took aside Rolin, Scanlon and Emmer. "We'll approach the canny beast on foot, without the sorcs," he explained. "If anything happened to them, we'd never get down from this mountain."

After scaling the drift, the four trudged single file up a steep, snowy slope toward the billowing cloud. Cresting the rise first, Rolin and Bembor came face to face with the dragon, who was crouching in a steaming pool of melted snow. The serpent snorted and pulled his head out from under one wing. Startled, Bembor staggered back into Emmer. The two men tumbled down the hill, taking Scanlon with them. A rumbling laugh rattled in the dragon's throat as he uncoiled his tail.

"So it's you again," he growled, fixing Rolin with his burning gaze. "I thought you and your sniveling friends had fried on Luralin. I should have eaten you then. No matter. I'm always in the mood for roast boy."

Rolin reached for his staff, but it wasn't in his belt. He tried to shout, but nothing came out. Gorgorunth opened his powerful jaws, then clapped them shut again. Muscles rippled under his scaly green hide as he lumbered closer, then demanded, "What's that you've got there?" Rolin's knees turned to jelly when he realized he was still wearing Elgathel's sword.

"It's *his* sword, isn't it! How dare you bring that thrice-cursed thing into my presence! My master took it from you on the island—how did you get it back? How?" Rolin quailed as smoke spurted from the beast's flaring nostrils. Where were his friends and their light staffs?

"See here?" The serpent raised one leg. "That stinking tree toad did this to me, before I boiled him in his own juices!" Gagging, Rolin looked upon the dragon's mangled foot. "You impudent, two-legged river scum!" Gorgorunth roared. "Did you think you could finish what he started? You shall suffer the same fate for your audacity!"

Just then, Rolin felt the brush of fur and looked up to find Windsong beside him. "You must overcome them with the blood of Gaelathane!" said a deep voice. Yanking a sack of Glymmerin water from one of the sorc's saddlebags, Rolin hurled it into the serpent's open maw. Gorgorunth shuddered and his eyes bulged. Then he swelled up and burst into flames. In seconds, the blaze had consumed the beast down to the very bones.

Rolin and Windsong were still gawking at the pile of smoking cinders when the others scrambled up to join them. Emmer had found Rolin's staff. "What happened?" gasped Scanlon, his eyes as big as the dragon's.

"Gorgorunth choked on Rolin's water bag, and burned himself up from the inside out," Windsong declared.

Bembor shook his head. "Dragons are invulnerable to fire, whether their own or another dragon's. Only Gundul's inferno can destroy them. It was Gaelathane's blood that saved us. Praise be to the Tree; the dragon is dead!"

"The dragon is dead! Long live Gaelathane, King of the Trees!" they all cried. Rolin buried his face in Windsong's soft fur.

"Thank you for coming to my rescue, dear friend!" he murmured. "You risked your life to save mine."

"No need to thank me," the griffin clucked, nuzzling against Rolin's head. "It was all Gaelathane's doing. He picked me up and carried me here, saddlebags and all."

"Then if it weren't for Gaelathane, I'd be——"

"There's no time to worry about what might have been," Bembor interrupted. "We've got to find the sorcerer's secret passage."

"It must be somewhere nearby," said Emmer. "Felgor probably left his pet outside to guard the entrance." Moments later, Scanlon found the opening, which was partially concealed by overhanging rocks and snow.

"You were right, Rolin," Bembor said, peering inside. "The dragon couldn't have squeezed his head in here, let alone the rest of his body."

"I think he'll fit now," quipped Rolin, giving the others a good laugh. Then he ducked into the tunnel after his friends. Jogging down the passage with their staffs to light the way, the boys made up a lighthearted ditty about their fallen enemies. It went like this:

Drink-a-drop, drank-a-drop,
Make a gork giddy!
Drunken sot, drooling sot,
Slain without pity!

Tap-a-yeg, tag-a-yeg,
Turn him to stone!
See him stall, see him fall,
Look out below!

Fling-a-bag, flung-a-bag,
Down the dragon's throat!
Let him gag, let him sag,
Till his belly bloats!

Break-a-beast, bake-a-beast,
How the fiend fried!
Make-a-feast, bake-a-feast,
Now the dragon's died!

"Hush," Bembor told them. "Underground, the slightest sound echoes far. We wouldn't want to find a welcoming committee at the other end!"

Soon, Rolin noticed a light glimmering ahead. After a sharp turn, the tunnel opened onto a much wider passage. Bembor peered down the hall. "It's all clear!" he whispered, stepping out and motioning for the others to follow.

Gripping their light staffs, the four riders accompanied their mounts down the corridor until they came to a pair of wooden doors. Muffled voices rose and fell from within.

"It's the sorcerer's throne room!" whispered Scanlon. "Let's go inside and give them a big surprise!"

"On the count of three," Bembor said softly. "One—two—three!" Then they all burst in. Startled, Felgor and Grimmon looked up from the spasel case.

"Bembor son of Brenthor," Felgor sneered. "I might have known you and your bird-lions were behind my troubles!"

"You have only yourself to blame for your misfortunes, Felgor," replied Bembor. "Surrender to us, or much worse may befall you! Even Gorgorunth cannot help you now."

"Surrender? How absurd! You may have gotten past my pet, but I'm not finished yet." Whipping out a long, black stave, he hurled it at his enemies.

The stick struck Emmer. "Father!" cried Scanlon. Rolin gasped, expecting the scout to fall dead. Instead, Emmer touched his light rod to the black staff, which broke into flames. Rolin then recalled Waganupa's words, "No weapon the enemy brings against you shall prosper." But did Felgor have other tricks up his sleeve?

The sorcerer quickly recovered. "You can't stop me for long. I'll find a way to destroy your Tree, just as I did the other one. Then your pretty new toys won't work. Now, what have you done with the black spasel? It's mine and I want it back."

Bembor pointed at the floor. "That's what is left of your spasel, though I'm afraid it's beyond saving."

With a cry, Felgor tried to piece together the shattered ball. "Look what you've done," he wailed, spasel dust sifting through his fingers. "It's ruined! Ruined! But if you're thinking of stealing my worlds, I alone know where their torsil gates grow, and without these you'll never find them!"

Quicker than a striking snake, the sorcerer snatched up a double handful of spasla from the glass case, flinging them at his pursuers. "Here are your kingdoms—catch them if you can!"

Taking his cue, Grimmon also pelted them with sap balls. As Rolin and his friends retreated before the barrage, Felgor darted behind his throne, which sank into the floor with a grinding sound. Like a nimble, black weasel, he slithered into the hole.

"Don't let Grimmon get away, too!" Bembor warned, as the sorcerer's apprentice lunged for the escape hatch. Bounding forward, Spearwind pounced on the terrified Lucambrian, knocking him down and sending his spasla flying.

"Please don't let it hurt me!" he pleaded.

"Stop your blubbering," growled Spearwind, pinning Grimmon firmly to the floor with one paw. "I won't harm you, though I'd like to tear your miserable head from your body!" Grimmon moaned, the whites of his eyes showing. Never having met Rosewand or any other amenthil, the former councilor evidently hadn't understood a word Spearwind had said.

"Keep him there until we return," Bembor called over his shoulder. Then he looked down at the sunken throne. "Time to explore another stairwell!" Rolin and Scanlon groaned.

Descending the spiraling stone stairway with his companions, Rolin heard only the magnified sounds of his breathing and the scraping of feet on stone. The air burned hot and foul in his lungs, and he felt the mountain's massive weight bearing down on him. At last, when Rolin's aching legs couldn't wobble another step, the stairs ended at an iron door. Emmer pushed it open.

Following his friends, Rolin stepped through the doorway into an immense cavern lit with the ghastly, blue-white light of a monstrous ashtag. The tree's thick, contorted limbs snaked across the ceiling, growing right into the solid rock. Pools of its venom hissed on the floor, giving off a vile, acrid smoke.

"That must be Hrothmog, first of all the black trees," whispered Bembor. "Like other ashtags, it feeds on stone by dissolving it with a potent acid."

Clutching something like a smooth, white stone, Felgor leapt into the ashtag, climbing into its topmost branches as nimbly as a tree lizard. "Behold my sythan-ar, the Tree of Death," he cackled. "It is the very gateway to Gundul. Would any of you care to visit the Land of the Dead, perchance?"

"Do not answer him," Bembor cautioned.

"I thought not," said Felgor, his lip curling. "You'll each have your turn later, I daresay—like it or not."

"Come down from there, Felgor," ordered Bembor, pointing his staff at him. "Gundul's armies are no more and your prisoners are freed. Your feeble sorceries are no match for the might of Gaelathane and His Tree."

"A pox on your Tree!" Felgor snarled.

"Come down, or we'll demolish Hrothmog with you in it."

"Don't be a fool! Destroy this tree and the whole mountain will collapse on us. Hrothmog alone holds this fortress together and all worlds above and beneath. If my tree dies, it will be the downfall of Lucambra and Thalmos."

"Gaelathane is the Sustainer of Life, and all things hold to-gether in Him!" Bembor replied. "Come down, or you and Hrothmog will both perish."

"Never!" The sorcerer released his grip on the ashtag and fell. The Lucambrians gasped as his body dropped faster and faster—then disappeared.

"He's escaping into Gundul!" cried Bembor. "Use your staffs!" Four light beams struck the Tree of Death, which exploded with an ear-splitting roar.

"To the stairs!" Emmer shouted. He herded Rolin and Scanlon through the door just as Hrothmog's shattered limbs and trunk crashed to the floor. The ground rumbled and shook, opening great cracks in the stairwell. Then the shaking stopped and a soft light shone through the broken door.

Peering inside, Rolin saw the Tree towering in the midst of Hrothmog's ruin, its top piercing the crumbling cavern ceiling and anchoring it in place. After reentering the cave with the others, he tripped over a wooden tube lying in the wreckage. "Look what I found!" he cried, holding it up. "A starglass!"

"It seems Felgor left you a parting gift," remarked Bembor. "Now you'll be able to see farther than Keeneye."

"What's this, Grandfather?" Scanlon called from beside a wide, polished basin in the stone floor, its rim thickly encrusted with yellow sulfur. At the bottom lay a cluster of oblong, white objects. Bembor, Emmer and Rolin hurried over.

"It's the dragon's nest!" exclaimed Bembor. "See where the creature's scaly hide wore the rock smooth? And those are its eggs. The gray patches at the ends are where the babies are picking away at the shells with their sharp egg teeth. They must be nearly ready to hatch. We arrived just in time."

"It looks like one is missing," Rolin said, pointing to a gap in the cluster.

"Didn't I see Felgor taking such an egg with him?" Keeneye remarked, nodding toward Hrothmog's stump.

Bembor scowled. "I believe you're right. We can only hope the sorcerer and his egg perished in Hrothmog's destruction."

"What about the others?" asked Rolin. "Will they still hatch?"

"Probably not, but even one hatchling could cause untold havoc. We cannot take that risk." Bembor trained his staff on the egg cluster. There was a flash of light, a puff of smoke and the eggs were gone. Rolin shuddered.

Just then, Windsong chittered excitedly. The other Servants of the Tree ran to his side, finding a huge stone vat filled to the brim with gold, diamonds, rubies and other priceless jewels and objects of value. The pile sparkled enticingly.

"Felgor's loot, mined or stolen from his torsil worlds," Bembor murmured, admiring a gold crown.

"We're rich!" Scanlon whooped.

"We sorcs can't possibly cart all of this back," protested Ironwing, standing on his hind legs to look into the vat.

"Nor shall we ask you to," Bembor assured him. "Still, it seems a shame to leave so much wealth here, when it could be put to good use. We two-legs shall fill our packs and pockets with whatever plunder we can carry."

The return trip was long and difficult, with frequent stops to clear the stairs of rubble dislodged by the earthquake. When Rolin and his friends reached Felgor's throne room, Spearwind was still standing over a very subdued Grimmon.

"Whew!" Rolin gasped, flopping down on the floor. "I never want to climb another set of stairs again." Removing their moccasins to massage aching feet, Scanlon and Emmer heartily agreed.

"We can't stay here," said Bembor. "Though the mountain won't collapse with the Tree propping it up, this room could still cave in at any time."

"What about me?" Grimmon cried. "You're not leaving me to die here, are you?"

"No, you're coming with us," said Emmer, tying his hands behind him. "Now march!" Rolin paused at the glass case to pocket several of the sorcerer's remaining spasla, then hurried out the door after his companions.

"Felgor is gone, and you are free!" the Servants of the Tree told all the slaves they met. "Follow us, and we'll take you *outside*." At every turn they saw the Tree, whose thick, shining trunk still stood in the midst of the mountain. Joining the company of recovered Liriassans swarming up from the dungeons, the jubilant throng swept Rolin and his friends through the main tunnel and into the warmth of a bright July morning.

CHAPTER 24

THE HEALING OF LUCAMBRA

"People of the Tree, hear me!" cried Bembor, raising his glowing staff high. "Felgor and his serpent are no more. His armies lie rotting before you or turned to stone. Gaelathane has saved you, as He promised in His Prophecy!"

"Glory and honor to the King of the Trees! Praise to His Tree of Life!" roared the crowd. The sounds of laughing, shouting, crying and singing mingled in a gladsome drone that drowned out the ashtags' caustic insults.

Standing beside Bembor and Emmer, Rolin cast shy, sidelong glances at Marlis, who flushed and looked the other way. Bembor sighed contentedly. "To think I've lived to see the Prophecy's fulfillment. It's almost more than this old heart can bear!"

"I don't wish to trouble you with other matters," Emmer said, "but how will we feed all these people? What little we have on hand isn't nearly enough for so many, and we can't expect them to forage for food on this killing field."

"Maybe I can help," Mycena piped up. "There's plenty of food left over from Felgor's feast, and the kitchens aren't far from where Rolin was."

Bembor lifted Mycena into the air. "What a splendid idea!" he laughed. "That's just what we need." A half-hour later, the four sorcs had flown Mycena, Rolin and Scanlon to the wine room window, where they discovered that the earthquake had jarred open most of the doors on the upper floors.

Using ropes, the boys passed bags of cheese, bacon, and roasted mutton to the griffins hovering outside, who flew them back to the hungry multitude. Thanks to this flying food brigade, everyone had enough to eat. Afterwards, as the oak clan listened to Rolin describe how he'd first found Rosewand, Marlon asked, "Where are Sigarth and Skoglund?"

Bembor blanched. "Weren't they with you in the dungeon?"

"No, don't you remember? You left them in Thalmos to guard the amenthil."

"Great snakes and scorpions! How could I have forgotten? Here we are feasting and making merry while those poor fellows are probably starving to death." Bembor hastily summoned Windsong and Ironwing to retrieve the two scouts.

"They've never seen a sorc before," he warned the griffins, "so don't let them mistake you for yegs. Tell them I've sent you and they'll come."

"What if we can't find your friends?" yawned Windsong.

"Come back immediately. I don't want you flying about and frightening the locals. They've had enough excitement lately."

"So have I," Ironwing grumbled. "After this, I'm going to curl up in a nice, quiet corner somewhere and sleep for a week."

Later that day, the griffins returned with Sigarth and Skoglund, who appeared to be far from starving. Ironwing was indignant after nearly being shot on sight by Sigarth and asked anyone who could understand him, "I don't look like a yeg, do I?"

While the brothers dined on the sorcerer's bounty, Bembor recounted the adventures of the Servants of the Tree. The scouts shook their heads in wonder.

"So you two rode these sorcs all the way to Luralin and back?" Skoglund asked Rolin and Scanlon. The boys nodded and grinned.

"And here's a spasel to prove it!" Rolin said, showing him the sap ball.

Sigarth rubbed his stubbly face. "When Felgor and his friends came into town, we thought the game was up."

"It almost was," said Emmer, pouring out the tale of Grimmon's treachery.

"I'd like to skewer that rat," growled Sigarth, glaring at Grimmon, who sat nearby under Spearwind's watchful eye.

"'Revenge is sweet to the tongue but bitter to the stomach,'" Bembor said. "It's what made the sorcerer what he is—or was."

"Whatever happened to Felgor, anyway?" asked Skoglund.

"We've all been wondering the same thing," Bembor said, describing Felgor's last stand. "We'll hear no more from him, I'm sure. If he isn't trapped in the netherland between our worlds, he's stranded in Gundul—or dead. Whatever his fate, he can't get back into Lucambra without Hrothmog."

"Aren't all ashtags Gundul torsils?" Rolin asked. An uneasy silence followed as the oak clanners threw wary glances at the brooding black trees.

"He wouldn't dare return now!" said Bembor fiercely, and that was that. Upon learning that Rosewand was well, he rewarded Sigarth and Skoglund with draughts of Glymmerin water.

Drinking deeply of the water, the brothers' eyes brightened. Sigarth forgave Grimmon his treachery, and apologized to Rolin for accusing him of stealing the seventh soros. The men were still talking when there was a commotion on the outskirts of the camp, and a couple of Lucambrians with a bellowing bull of a scout between them stumbled into the staff light.

"Young Delwyn!" exclaimed Bembor, who had been showing Marlon Elgathel's sword. "Whatever is the matter?"

"Tell these two birchers to unhand me or I'll—" Delwyn muttered something unintelligible.

"We were searching Felgor's fortress for a boy named Arvin when we found this fellow poking around in a storeroom," explained one of the scouts. "He had this with him." The Lucambrian held up a heavy-looking brown bottle.

"That's *mogwuar*!" Mycena burst out. "It's made of ashtag drippings and other awful stuff."

"Delwyn, you're drunk!" Bembor sternly said. Rolin knew the signs, too—the swaying gait, slurred speech and unfocused eyes— from seeing bargemen stagger back to their boats after a night spent in Beechtown's taverns.

"What if I am?" retorted Delwyn. "Drunk 'r sober, I can shtill tell you a thing 'r two. Me 'n my fir men ain't takin' orders from you er any yer oakers."

"Rolin," said Bembor evenly, "offer our guest a sip of Glymmerin water, won't you?" Rolin brought a honey sack to Delwyn, who swatted it out of his hands and knocked him to the ground. Rolin's ears rang and his head spun.

"You an' yer filthy water can go to Gundul, potato eater!" Delwyn roared. "Ain't nuthin' wrong wi' me that a new sythan-ar won' mend. An' don' tell me yer Tree beat Felgor. Them gorks got drunk like me, 'n killed eash other."

Marlis ran to Rolin's side and helped him up. "Are you all right?" she asked anxiously. Rolin weakly nodded, still seeing stars.

A deathly silence seized the onlookers as Bembor drew the sword of Elgathel and deliberately leveled its point against Delwyn's chest. "If you weren't drunk and unarmed," he said through clenched teeth, "I'd run you through here and now for striking the king." Delwyn's eyes goggled.

"Take him away, and tie him up," Bembor told the birch clansmen. "We'll decide his fate tomorrow. And don't let anyone else near that mountain!"

After the three had left, Bembor returned the sword to its new owner on bended knee, over Rolin's objections. "Forgive me for taking up your sword in anger, sire," he said. An astonished murmur rippled through the assembled clan.

The next morning, the Servants of the Tree convened a new council composed of representatives from every surviving tree clan. As Bembor rose to speak, one of Delwyn's escorts from the night before approached and whispered in his ear.

"Delwyn son of Erwyn has just died," Bembor announced. "How many more of our people must perish needlessly? Isn't Gundul full enough already? Why do some still refuse to drink of the Glymmerin's waters?"

"You're hoarding it all for your own clan, that's why!" someone shouted.

"That's not true!" retorted Opio hotly.

Rolin stood. "Gaelathane bade me share His water of life with all who wish it," he said. "There will be plenty for everyone."

"What is this half-breed doing here?" cried another scout. "The Tree is for Lucambrians, and Lucambrians for the Tree!"

"Waganupa's sacrifice wasn't just meant for us but for the peoples of other torsil worlds as well," Gemmio shot back.

"Peoples *and* griffins," Ironwing interjected.

"'Peoples and griffins,'" sighed Gemmio.

"But not for the likes of me, eh?" rasped Grimmon from the edge of the crowd. Rolin hurried to the Lucambrian's side.

"Come to gloat over your defeated adversary?" he grunted.

"Not at all," replied Rolin. "I only want to help you."

"Help me! How?" Suspicion pinched Grimmon's sallow face.

"By giving you some of my Glymmerin water, of course."

"How noble—and useless." Grimmon spat and turned his back.

"No water for the traitor!" a bystander burst out.

Others took up the cry. "No water for the traitor or for anyone else who took an ashtag sythan-ar! There won't be enough left for the rest of us."

"You see?" said Grimmon bitterly. "You're wasting your time, potato eater. Now go away and leave me alone."

"You don't understand," said Rolin. "All of us have betrayed Gaelathane in our own way. That's why the Tree had to die: to purchase Gaelathane's pardon for our rebellion and unbelief."

"Fine words, I'm sure," Grimmon sneered, "though they'll not change my fate. Since my sythan-ar was a shoot from Felgor's own death tree, it must have withered with Hrothmog's destruction. If I don't die soon of the sickness, Bembor will have me hanged."

"No, he won't," said Bembor, coming up beside Rolin. "This is not a day of vengeance but of forgiveness and reconciliation,

Grimmon. We've nothing to gain from punishing you. You've already received the reward for your deeds in full."

"Yes—death and Gundul's everlasting fires."

"Gundul!" Rolin exclaimed. "Why do you speak of it? Gaelathane has already broken Gundul's gates. No one need go there anymore."

"Look at my eyes," said Grimmon. "Are they not as black as the pit? I can already smell the stench of that dreadful place."

"Gaelathane can deliver you from Gundul's torment," Bembor said earnestly. "All you must do is accept His forgiveness and drink of the Glymmerin water, which is His blood."

"Would it not burn me like fire?"

"He died to deliver you, not to destroy you," Rolin pleaded. "The water will cleanse, not consume." He flipped open one of Windsong's saddlebags, where he found his last water sack. Though it felt empty, there was a slight splashing sound when he shook it.

"There's just enough in here for you," he smiled, offering the sack to the former councilor.

Grimmon took the bag, hope and despair wrestling in his features. "It's too late," he groaned. "Gundul is calling me!"

"Drink from it," Bembor urged him. Hesitantly, Grimmon lifted the sack, pouring its contents into his mouth. Long he held it to his lips, until Rolin thought the bag was surely dry. When at last Grimmon lowered the sack, peace shone in his face.

"It's gone," he wept. "The shame, the hatred, the fear—it's all gone! How great is His love, how boundless His mercy!" A new light gleamed in Grimmon's now green eyes, then faded as he slumped into Bembor's arms.

"Today, Gaelathane has welcomed a new son into Gaelessa," murmured the old Lucambrian, tears streaming down his own face.

"What about us slaves?" cried a gaunt mother with child, reaching for Rolin's bag. "We want a drink of that water, too!"

"You'll all get your turn," said Bembor. Scanlon passed out three more full water sacks among the people.

"Take Me higher!" Rolin looked this way and that. Who had spoken? "Take Me higher!" Rolin gaped. Had Gaelathane actually spoken through his water bag? Oddly, it felt full again. Realizing what the King was asking, he went to Windsong's side and lightly stroked the sorc's neck.

Windsong opened one eye. "What is it?"

"I need you to carry me one more time—higher."

"My wings are yours," said the griffin, kneeling down.

"Where are you going with that bag?" some council members called to him.

"He's stealing the rest of the water!" others cried. "Stop him!"

But Windsong had already left the ground, soaring above a sea of upturned faces. As the sorc spiraled higher, Rolin could see the Hallowfast poking through the knobbly ashtags. Then the Willowahs came into view, their rugged, snow-clad peaks glistening in the sun. With sharp, rasping breaths, Windsong climbed into the regions of the sky where even eagles dared not fly. Rolin, too, panted in the thin, frigid air.

"Still higher." A million tiny needles stabbed Rolin's lungs and his vision blurred. Dizzy, he gripped Windsong more tightly.

"Now." Opening the water sack, Rolin flung it into space.

Bursting from the bag, the liquid hung in the air like a big, red bubble before exploding into a sparkling spray that fanned across the sky. As Windsong followed the ruby mist earthward, Rolin watched the shimmering, rose-colored curtain settle over mountains, rivers, lakes and woods like a gentle spring rain. The land flushed crimson, as if caressed by the dawn.

Then a wondrous transformation occurred. The ashtag forests dissolved into an inky fluid that soaked into the ground. Fresh green grass sprang up in their place, spreading rapidly to soften the raw scars left by dragon fire and Felgor's wanton mining.

When Windsong landed, Rolin found laughing children romping in the fragrant new meadows, while their parents stared about in bewilderment. Then Bembor addressed the people: "Friends, Gaelathane's last gift crowns His first. He has restored to us everything we've lost, as the Prophecy foretold, and more besides. Now that the ashtags' dread voices are stilled, let us share in the blessing of the amenthil." Then the Servants of the Tree rolled out the remaining barrels of amenthil wine.

Drinking of the wine, the people fell on their faces as they heard all creation worshiping the King of the Trees. Waganupa grew in glory until it outshone the sun, then vanished, leaving Mt. Golgunthor unsupported. The earth trembled violently. Rocks groaned and splintered. With a deafening roar, the mountain caved in, hurling a cloud of snow, ice and crushed stone into the sky. Dust and debris boiled out of the collapsing main tunnel. The mountain's death agonies rumbled across the hills, then died away. In the ensuing silence, the people stirred in song:

> How great is He Who cleansed the earth,
> And gave to all a second birth;
> Who vanquishes our every foe,
> And every mountain has made low.
>
> How marvelous His perfect plan,
> That wrought redemption for each man;
> When we were lost, His blood availed
> To buy us back from death's travails.
>
> His Tree has shone into our hearts,
> Reaching to the lowest parts
> Of Gundul's grimmest dungeons dim,
> For nothing can be hid from Him!
>
> Let all who hear our worship song,
> Believe that we who sing belong
> Again to Gaelathane the Wise,
> Who made the worlds and never dies!

ROLIN, KING OF LUCAMBRA

Three years later, Rolin sat fidgeting across from Bembor in the Hallowfast's drafty throne room. A weak wintry sun shone through the high, narrow window, now hung with curtains. Bembor had set the people to work tidying up the royal residence, removing the centuries of accumulated filth and covering the walls and floors with bright, new tapestries.

"You wanted to see me?" said Rolin, puzzled at Bembor's urgent summons.

Bembor stroked his beard and smiled. "It's arrived."

"What's arrived?"

"The crimson tide. People are bathing in it; and the sick, the lame and the blind are being healed, just as in your dream. You know what that means."

Rolin clutched the arms of his chair. Weeks earlier, he'd dreamt that when the Glymmerin's eastern branch had flowed across the sea "to heal all hurts from shore to shore," Gaelathane would soon crown him king. Evidently, that time had come.

"But I am not yet ready to be king!" he protested.

Bembor gazed affectionately back at him. "When you first visited Lucambra, you were not," he agreed. "However, your hardships have seasoned and prepared you for the throne. Now you are one of the finest marksmen in all the land with bow or blowpipe and look every inch a Lucambrian scout."

Rolin stared at the floor. He was not anxious to lay aside the carefree days of youth for the heavy mantle of leadership. Still, Lucambra had become his home, and he would do anything to protect and restore the land and its people.

"Why don't you take the crown?" he suggested. "After all, you're Elgathel's relative, too."

Bembor's bushy eyebrows shot up. "Who told you that?"

Rolin grinned impishly. "A certain sorcerer."

"I should have known. Lucambrian genealogies always intrigued Felgor. He was sure his eyes were greener and lineage truer than anyone else's."

"Then you are?"

"Related to Elgathel? Yes indeed, though not as closely as you. Even as a pure-blooded Lucambrian, my claim to the throne is no stronger than yours. Besides," he sighed, "I am an old man, even as we Lucambrians measure the years. Governing the affairs of others is a job for the young. It is the place of the aged to give counsel when necessary and to keep silent when it is not."

"But will the people accept me, a Thalmosian half-breed?"

"I believe they will, my boy. After all, they owe their lives to you! They've seen you and Marlis traipsing the length and breadth of Lucambra, planting Waganupa's seeds for them to use as sythanars. Some day, our old tree clans will be no more, and we'll all belong to the clan of the One Tree."

Rolin shrugged. "Waganupa told us to gather and sow as many seeds as we could, and that's what I've been doing."

"Not only in this world, from what I've heard."

"That's true." Rolin blushed. "Since our sacks never seem to run out of seeds, I've planted quite a few in Thalmos. That reminds me: I'm worried about Lightleaf. He's getting old—"

"And if our dear friend were to blow over in a winter storm, we'd lose our torsil gate into Thalmos. So you've been planting the torsil's nuts, too."

Rolin nearly fell over backwards in his chair. "How did you know?"

Bembor winked. "The warbler, of course."

"I'd like to exile that pesky bird somewhere," Rolin muttered.

"Oh, but your idea is a good one. If even half of Lightleaf's nuts grow up to be Thalmos torsils, we'll have a much easier time getting in and out of that world. Speaking of Lightleaf, how is our plucky tree of passage? You took so long getting back, I thought we'd lost him—and you, too."

"It nearly turned out that way!" Wishing to visit Thalmos again before leaf fall, Rolin had gone to Beechtown with Bembor for a look at the half-burned hamlet. Their arrival on Windsong and Ironwing created quite a stir, until Bembor persuaded the local militia of their peaceable intentions. As a token of the Green-cloaks' goodwill, Bembor even gave the portly, perspiring mayor a sizable share of the dragon's hoard to help him in rebuilding the town, and a torsil horn, should any "wolf bats" return.

The mayor then showed the visitors his new bridge, built on the backs of the batwolves petrified during the Battle of Beechtown. (Most of those yeg statues had conveniently fallen in the Foamwater, creating a rough stone causeway from one bank to the other.)

Afterwards, Rolin had stopped at his mother's and grandmother's graves to pay his respects, then chatted briefly with Rosewand before going on with Bembor and the sorcs to the cabin, which he had not seen in months. When no one came to the door, Rolin thought Gannon had at last bowed to his sister's badgering and moved to town. How else could the place have become so run down? Then the door had creaked open and a grizzled head cautiously poked out.

Gannon was overjoyed to see his son again, although the griffins shook him up a bit. He made Rolin retell his latest adventures at least twice, from amenthil to yeg. Then he prepared his guests a steaming batch of oatcakes, all the while repeating to himself, "So he's really part *Larcassian*."

After the long-suffering sorcs had lunched on fresh creek fish, they allowed Rolin to load them up with bee gear, then flew him and Gannon to the bee tree, where Rolin's weather-worn rope still hung. Several trips and a few stings later, the honeycomb was snugly stored in Gannon's cellar. Just when Rolin, his father and Bembor were sitting down to more honey-slathered oatcakes, the door banged open and Aunt Glenna flounced in.

With a joyful chirp, she rushed over to Rolin and smothered him with kisses and embraces. Then, catching sight of Windsong, she collapsed in a dead faint. When Bembor and the griffins had fled the scene, Gannon brought Glenna around, easing his hysterical sister out the door with assurances that the next time Rolin visited Janna's relations, he wouldn't bring back any more of "those scabby, bird-headed lions." Before Glenna left, she also made Rolin promise he'd settle down with an eligible young maiden from among Janna's kin.

During the following weeks, while Rolin helped his father trim the wild honeycomb for market, Marlis was often on his mind. How could he explain to her the tingly way he felt when they chanced to plunge their hands into a seed sack together? Would she laugh if he confessed how flustered he felt in her presence? If only girls were as predictable as trees!

Caught up in dreams of Emmer's daughter, Rolin lost count of the blustery autumn days. One morning, he awoke to discover winter was marching down the mountain passes, dusting the firs with snow and bringing the tree sleep that could lock him out of Lucambra until spring. Gathering up a few belongings and bidding his father a tearful farewell, Rolin set off in search of Lightleaf. He found the torsil's snow-crusted branches nearly bare.

"Lightleaf! Lightleaf!" he cried, but there was no answer. Had he arrived too late? Only by tapping on the tree's trunk and warming its limbs with cold-numbed hands did he succeed in rousing the sleeping torsil—and just in time. After making passage into Lucambra, he looked up to see the tree's last remaining leaves tremble, then flutter to the ground.

". . . so, is that all you've been up to?" Bembor was saying.

Rolin blinked and stammered, "Well . . . um, no. You remember the seedy pulp I saved from squeezing amenthil juice into the gorks' wine?"

"How could I forget?" Bembor chuckled. "You planted some of those seeds around the Hallowfast. The warbler is guarding them from other hungry birds—when he's not keeping track of you. He's very proud of his post."

"Well, I also sowed some near Rosewand, so she'll have company."

"Ah, yes. That's the other reason I called you here."

"Rosewand?"

"Not exactly. You see, if you're to gain the people's complete confidence, you must take a Lucambrian life tree."

"But you've said yourself that Lucambrians take only one life tree!"

"You're no ordinary Lucambrian. Being Thalmosian and Lucambrian, you belong to both worlds. It's only fitting that you should take a sythan-ar from each. 'Of field and forest, fairest fruit,' remember? Planting a sythan-ar here won't weaken your ties with Thalmos but will win your subjects' loyalty."

"And if I cannot find a life tree in the Land of Light?"

Bembor smiled. "With the pick of Lucambra's best, I'm sure you will. Just remember, 'Though one may seek beyond the sky, one's heart's desire may be nigh.' Something tells me that in searching for your heart's desire, you'll gain more than a sythan-ar!"

Rolin had ample time to find a life tree. His coronation would not take place until the torsils were in full leaf, allowing Lucambrians living in Thalmos and other lands to attend. Still, he spent many long, dreary days combing remote valleys and lonely mountaintops for a tree to make his own.

One snowy December afternoon, he was tramping through the endless groves of head-high Tree seedlings. Like Waganupa, they softly shone at their branch tips. Hardy hemmonsils bravely blossomed among them, having sprouted from seeds carried from Luralin on Windsong and Ironwing's fur.

Fine looking though the saplings were, none compared with Rosewand's quiet beauty. Discouraged, Rolin turned aside onto a narrow path leading into a steep-sided, stony dell. A small stream gurgled beside the trail, reminding him of Cottonwood Creek. At the valley's head, he came upon a stunted Tree seedling that had somehow sprouted apart from its brothers and sisters. Rolin had never seen a more scraggly sapling. As he sadly retraced his steps, a delicate tree voice fell upon his ears.

"Don't leave."

Rolin looked back. What tree had spoken: the spindly evergreen, or one of the big firs behind it?

"It is I, Spirelight," said the runt, its top as straight and well formed as the Beechtown bell steeple. "You are Rolin, king of Lucambra, are you not?"

"How did you know my name?" Touching the tree, Rolin felt a tugging at his heart. Was this the one?

"She who claimed me often speaks of you."

Rolin's heart sank. Someone else had already chosen Spirelight as her sythan-ar. But who could possibly want such a straggly life tree?

Then out of the shadows stepped a young woman with flowing, golden hair. Under her shawl she wore a gown as green as Queen Winona's.

Rolin's heart raced. "Marlis! What are you doing here?"

"Visiting my sythan-ar," she replied with a winsome smile. "Soon, I will be moving Spirelight to her new home. She may be plain looking, but her heart is purest silver. Are you still seeking a life tree of your own?"

"Yes, but I haven't found one yet." He glanced down at the homely little evergreen. "Since Spirelight is yours, I will continue searching."

"But you've already found what you are looking for," said Marlis softly.

"No, I cannot take your sythan-ar. There are plenty of other trees in Lucambra. It's only a matter of finding the right one."

Marlis took Rolin's hand in hers. "'Though one may seek beyond the sky, one's heart's desire may be nigh,'" she said, tenderly looking up into his face with eyes the color of the sea. "Did Grandfather ever tell you how two may share the same sythan-ar?" Rolin shook his head.

"Then I'll explain . . ." Afterwards, sitting in the snow with Marlis as she admired the myriad twinkling lights of the Forest of the Tree, Rolin sang:

If I were a tree, I know what I'd be:
A servant of Him Who created me;
Whether oak or ash or cottonwood,
On hill, in meadow or wherever I stood.

But I'd be content, whatever the view,
Knowing I'm meant to share it with you;
Soaking up sunshine, growing together,
Singing and laughing in all sorts of weather.

If I were a fir, then I could be sure,
That you'd have the same sweet needles of myrrh;
Or if sycamore leaves were our lot to share,
No tree could compare with "Marlis, the fair!"

I'd only aspire with you to grow higher,
To glorify Gaelathane in all He requires;
To bear fruit for Him, with root, leaf and limb,
Until that fair day, when we'll hear Him say,
"Well done, faithful ones, you may now enter in!"

Six months later, Rolin stood beside Bembor, Scanlon and Whitewing on a platform outside the Hallowfast, dressed in royal robes of green. Surrounding the dais were thousands of expectant faces, including a host of long-lost Lucambrians from other worlds.

Among the spectators were Rolin's father and aunt, whom he had flown to the Hallowfast by griffin. Presuming that Rolin's new-found kin lived only a day's hill journey on foot from Beechtown, Glenna had fainted again at the sight of the sorcs and had to be tied to Ironwing. From the platform, Rolin could make out his aunt's flaming red hair, glassy-eyed stare and open mouth.

"We are gathered this day to witness the coronation of Rolin son of Gannon, grandson of Elgathel," Bembor's solemn voice echoed across the crowd. As Bembor related the saga of Rolin, Servant of the Tree (beginning with the death of Elgathel and Queen Winona's escape into Thalmos), Rolin's eyes strayed toward two white-clad figures on the far side of the assembly.

At last, Bembor turned to him. "Do you, Rolin son of Gannon, swear to uphold, keep and honor the Tree's truths, as long as you shall live?"

"I do."

"Will you rule these people fairly and faithfully, according to the wisdom Gaelathane has granted you?"

Rolin swallowed, his mouth suddenly dry. "I will."

Bembor then addressed the spectators. "Do you, the People of the Tree, promise to honor and obey your king?"

"We do!" they roared enthusiastically.

"Kneel, my son." Bembor touched Rolin's head and shoulders with the sword of Elgathel. "According to the laws and traditions of this land, I dub thee Rolin, King of Lucambra, Lord of the Hallowfast, Sovereign of all torsils, griffin-friend, dragonslayer and staff-bearer. Rise, King Rolin."

Bembor buckled the sword about Rolin's waist. Then Scanlon handed his grandfather two cloth-covered objects taken from Whitewing's emerald-encrusted saddle (a gift from Rolin). Removing the cloths, Bembor held aloft a stunning gold crown and scepter for all to see. Then he placed the crown on Rolin's head, the scepter in his right hand and a light staff in his left.

"Behold, People of the Tree, your king! Long live King Rolin— may his sythan-ar ever flourish!"

"Long live King Rolin—may his sythan-ar ever flourish!" thundered the throng, cheering and waving banners that bore Rolin's coat-of-arms, a design similar to the one on his box.

"Long live King Rolin!" echoed the hills and trees.

"Long live King Rolin!" chorused a medley of growls. Rolin looked up to see a grand assortment of griffins lining the sorcathel's battlements. He smiled and waved to an ovation of *clicks* and *clacks*. Then, while the king's bell pealed, man and beast, bird and tree joined in singing Luralin's praise song:

Praise Him Who fell, to fall no more,
And lives in light on high;
His kingdom stands from shore to shore,
That men no more may die!

He made Himself an offering,
His blood will break all chains;
The Tree of trees and King of kings,
In majesty He reigns!

For all the former things have passed,
Behold, His world made new;
All evil's power put down at last—
The sorcerer is through!

Let all that lives and all that breathes,
With gratitude proclaim,
Upon the earth, beneath the seas,
His glory, grace and fame!

All at once, Gaelathane appeared on the dais, dressed in dazzling white robes. Bembor, Rolin and Scanlon fell to their knees, while Whitewing bowed his head. Rolin removed his crown and placed it at Gaelathane's feet. "As the true King of Lucambra," he said, "this is Yours to wear, not mine."

"And as your master, I have chosen you to reign over this land," replied Gaelathane. "In that you have humbled yourself before Me, you have shown yourself worthy to wear this crown. Yet you are to be not only a king but also an ambassador, the first of My emissaries to all torsil worlds, proclaiming My freedom to those who have long lain in darkness. As the 'torsil tree of tender years,' you shall build bridges of friendship between Thalmos and Lucambra. Rise now and serve Me." Gaelathane replaced the crown on Rolin's head and disappeared.

Then Bembor motioned for the crowd to part, and the figures in white floated toward the platform to the strains of Opio's flute. First came a beaming Mycena, clad in a simple bridesmaid's dress.

Marlis followed, radiant in a satin gown. Rolin toyed with the gleaming gold band he would soon place on her finger. Then he, Bembor and Scanlon descended to meet the bride and her sister beside a small but sturdy evergreen—Spirelight.

"Dear friends," Bembor began, "this young tree symbolizes Rolin's and Marlis's love for each other. May their mutual sythanar never fail them." He paused to wipe his eyes. "These two precious children of Gaelathane have pledged their lives to serve Him and each other. I now have the greatest privilege and honor of joining them in marriage."

After the wedding rites, Rolin kissed his bride, and the joyous throng shouted, "Long live Queen Marlis!" Then the new king and queen joined in the general feasting and celebration of which the Lucambrians had become so fond. That evening, before retiring to the Hallowfast, the newlyweds bade their families farewell.

"Thank you, Grandfather," said Rolin and Marlis, embracing Bembor in turn. "If it weren't for you, we never would have met each other."

"Your happiness brings me great joy," Bembor replied. "May Gaelathane bless your reign and your new life together as king and queen!"

Emmer handed Rolin a brand new blowpipe. "I am grateful for your saving both my daughters," he said, "and I'm sure you'll make a fine king. I am proud to call you my son-in-law!"

"Thank you, Emmer, and may your sythan-ar ever flourish!" returned Rolin. Then he hugged Gannon. "Goodbye, Father. I shall visit when I can."

"I'll have oatcakes and honey waiting for you and Marlis any time you do," replied Gannon, kissing his daughter-in-law on the cheek. "The cabin won't be the same without you," he added wistfully.

"Please do come again and teach us to tend bees," Emmer said, shaking Gannon's hand in the manner of Thalmos.

"And don't forget to bring some honey with you!" quipped Scanlon with a sly wink.

"That I shall!" said Gannon. Then he hefted a bulging bag. "My wedding gift to the bride and groom—honeycomb!"

"And I have something for you, too," Rolin said, pressing a yellowish fruit into his father's hand. The Lucambrians chuckled at Gannon's startled expression as he bit into it.

"There's nothing silly about my cap," he tartly answered a saucy blue jay. "In fact, a couple of jay feathers might improve its looks!" Everyone laughed, even Aunt Glenna, who for once hadn't a single thing to say.

Adelka. Rolin's grandmother.

amenthil. Tree of Understanding.

ashtag. Gundul torsil; black tree.

Beechtown. Nearest town to Rolin's home.

Bembor son of Brenthor. Father of the oak clan.

Black staff. Felgor's staff, taken from his ashtag life tree.

Cottonwood Creek. Stream near Rolin's home.

dubaya. Griffin bread.

Elgathel. Former king of Lucambra (Rolin's grandfather).

Emmer son of Fandol. Father of Marlis, Scanlon and Mycena.

fallinga mellathel. Message flowers (from amenthil trees).

Felgor. Sorcerer (formerly Finegold).

Foamwater. Beechtown's river.

Gaelathane. King of the Trees.

Gaelessa. Gaelathane's home, reached through the Tree.

gilder. Thalmosian coin.

Glenna. Rolin's aunt (Father's sister).

Glymmerin. Stream flowing from beneath the Tree.

Gorgorunth. Dragon (black serpent).

gork. One of Felgor's foot soldiers (plural—gorks or gorku; adj.— gorkin).

Green Sea. Thalmosian body of water.

Green-cloak. Thalmosian name for Lucambrian scout.

griffanic. Griffin (adjective).

griffling. Young griffin.

Grimmon. Lucambra's chief councilor.

Gundul. Underworld; place of darkness and death.

Hallowfast. Tower of the Tree (near the Sea of El-marin).

Hemmett. Gannon's father.

hemmonsils. White flowers growing around the Tree .

Hrothmog. Sorcerer's personal sythan-ar (Tree of Death).

Ironwing. Griffin character (Scanlon's mount).

Janna. Rolin's mother (deceased).

Larkin. Oak clansman.

Lightleaf. Torsil to Hallowfast (Silver tree).

Liriassa. Lucambrian settlement (Valley of the Tulip Trees).

lisichki. Type of edible wild mushroom.

Lucambra. Land of Light—home of the People of the Tree.

luniceps (moonbonnets). Lucambrian mushrooms that glow in the dark.

Luralin. Lucambrians' original (island) home; Isle of Light.

Marlis. Scanlon's sister.

Marlon. Bembor's brother.

mellathel. Amenthil flowers.

Misty River. Nearest river to Liriassa.

mogwuar. Gorkin beverage made from ashtag drippings.

moonwood. Luminescent wood infected with lunicep mushrooms.

Mossbark. Rolin's torsil (of first entry).

Mountains of the Moon. Easternmost Lucambrian mountain range.

Mt. Golgunthor. Location of Felgor's fortress; dragon's mountain.

Mulgul. Ashtag near the Hallowfast.

Mycena (Emma). Marlis and Scanlon's sister captured by batwolves.

Nelda. Scanlon, Marlis and Mycena's deceased mother, killed by batwolves.

Opio and Gemmio. Lucambrian brothers; oak clansmen.

People of the Tree. Lucambrians.

poganka. Type of poisonous wild mushroom.

Rolin son of Gannon. Main character.

Rosewand. Rolin's amenthil sythan-ar (Thalmos).

Rowonah. Tree's staffs (plural).

Scanlon son of Emmer. Lucambrian boy and Bembor's grandson.

Sea of El-marin. Lucambrian sea; location of Isle of Luralin.

Servants of the Tree. Rolin, Scanlon, Bembor, Emmer, Opio and Gemmio.

Sigarth, Skoglund. Green-cloaks who first chased Rolin.

Sonya. First Lucambrian to plant a sythan-ar.

sorc. Griffin (plural—sorcs or sorca).

sorcasorosa. Lucambrian griffin masters/riders.

sorcathel. Pinnacle of Hallowfast, where griffins gathered.

sorcathon. Griffin council.

soros. Riders' medallion (plural—sorosa).

spasel. Torsil sap ball (plural—spasla).

Spearwind, Snowfeather, Keeneye, Flamefeather, Farsight, Sharpclaw, Longfeather. Other griffins who helped the Servants of the Tree.

Spirelight. Rolin and Marlis's sythan-ar (Lucambra).

Stubblefield, Greyson. Thalmosian farmers attacked by batwolves.

sythan-ar. Lucambrian life tree.

tara-torsils. Torsils of intra-world passage.

Tartellans. Mountains above Beechtown.

Thalmos. Rolin's home world.

Thannor. Bembor's great-grandfather.

Threeclaws. Griffin king whom Elgathel rescued.

torsils. Trees of passage.

vilna. Griffin beverage made from fermented mulberry juice.

Waganupa. Tree of Life (growing on island of Luralin).

Whitewing. King of the griffins.

wilith. Griffins' name for a spasel.

Willowahs. Mountains where sorcs live.

Windsong. Griffin character (Rolin's mount).

Winona. Former queen of Lucambra.

yeg. Batwolf (plural—yegs, yeggoroth; adjective—yeggorin).

To order additional copies* of:

The King of
the Trees

Visit our website:
Greencloaks.com

For check orders, please send $11.99 plus $3.95
shipping and handling to:

Bill Burt
3237 Sunset Drive
Hubbard, OR
97032-9635

*Quantity Discounts Available